A World Possessed

This is not a game.
She was standing on the brink now, able as yet to back away from the void beyond and continue her life as Rebecca Mulligan, artist and illustrator and citizen of Skye, undisturbed – relatively – by the realm of magic and wonder that had touched her.

But the void tugged.

If I allow him to talk, Rebecca thought, *I'll never be the same again.*

But all her questions would be answered, and she would know.

Rebecca said, 'What is not a game?'

And the Knave of Vines told her.

For Barbara,

Joanna O'Neill

January 2012

Also by Joanna O'Neill

A World Invisible

A World Denied

A World Possessed

JOANNA O'NEILL

Wooden Hill Press

For my mother

Published by Wooden Hill Press

First Edition 2011

Copyright © Joanna O'Neill 2011

The author asserts the moral right under the Copyright, Designs and Patent Act 1988 to be identified as the author of this work.

All Rights reserved. No part of this publication may be reproduced, stored In a retrieval system, or transmitted, in any form or by any means without the prior written consent of the author, nor be otherwise circulated in any form of binding or cover other than that in which it is published and without a similar condition being imposed on the subsequent purchaser.

ISBN: 978-0-9564432-2-9

Prologue

The trees were all around her right from the start; she had never seen what lay behind.

They were squat and old at first, the trees, their trunks wider than she could have hugged had she wished to, the bark deeply fissured, branches jutting, twigs crooked, all angles and corners. She would have ducked beneath the low canopy to protect her head and face, but of course she was not really there.

She seemed to be walking, or something like walking. She could not feel the ground but she could see it was treacherous, lumped with roots and pitted where the soil had subsided beneath the blanket of seed cases and decaying leaves.

The smell of old growth was bitter in her throat.

As the ground began to rise, craggy trunks gave way to taller, slimmer columns with smoother bark, sometimes mossy, sometimes with a sheen almost as if polished, marked with horizontal bands. There would have been no need to duck here; the branches sprang from higher up and spread to form a roof above her which would have protected her, had it been raining for instance, or hot under a noon sun.

The silence was profound; her footfalls made no sound and she could not hear herself breathe.

In time the ground became clearer and the air sweeter. The trees around her now were higher and straighter and ever more slender, and their branches soared upwards, arcing only at their tips, until what they resembled most was the audacious grace of English Gothic architecture. Winding tendrils of ivy brought decorative detail to the smooth trunks, like carvings in a cathedral or the artful detail of a Jan Pienkowski silhouette. She passed between columns of misty grey beneath an intricate tracery like fan vaulting, and when the smooth stone wall appeared between the trees it once again took her by surprise, even though she was expecting it.

The flight of steps began shallow and then steepened.

Now she breathed a chill air and understood that the passages through which she passed were cold despite the plaited rushes and tapestries. She knew she would never remember the path she was led along and did not try, and turnings and doorways and steps up and down arrived and passed behind her until, as she knew she would, she came to the long hall with its tiled floor, its rows of triple lancet windows and, at the far end facing her, the hard, pale throne on its dais.

Her breath smoked.

She moved towards the dais as slowly as always, time seeming to shift gear, and already her focus was on the curtain beyond the throne, heavy folds of velvet the colour of storm clouds behind which something moved, stirring the hem.

This time…would she see it this time?

She drew level with the throne, still staring at the curtain, holding her breath now, willing herself to stay, straining to see the movement she knew would come any mom–

And there it was – the twitch of the cloth, the soft bulge as whatever was behind there moved; and as the curtain began to lift aside she knew she had stayed longer this time than ever before, and that this time she would find out what was–

With a jolt, she woke.

Chapter One

Rebecca Mulligan stepped sideways to avoid a unicyclist, and said, 'I had that dream again last night.'

'Oops. Bother. What dream?'

Rebecca waited while her friend stuffed the last two inches of ice cream cone into her mouth and dug about for a tissue to wipe her coat. It had been daft to buy it anyway; the temperature might be mild for New Year's Day but it was too cold for ice cream.

'Never mind,' Steph said cheerfully, tossing the damp tissue into a bin. 'It's washable. What dream?'

'The same one. With the trees.'

Rebecca hadn't made up her mind whether the castle was in a forest or a wood. 'Forest' sounded geographical: acres of standing timber, a natural resource, a habitat; 'wood' was intimate, even claustrophobic, a setting for fairytales and nightmares. The very consonants seemed to agree – *forest,* free-flying, breezy, open to suggestion; *wood,* deep, dark, and final.

Foresters use chainsaws. A woodcutter wields an axe. The two were poles apart.

'Trees?'

Rebecca considered her friend. Steph was brilliant, bright and brainy, a linguist with a doctorate from Oxford and on the threshold of what would no doubt be a dazzling career in Beijing. She was a talented oboist and a mean pianist too. Rebecca knew her to be well read, competent with technology, and abreast of current affairs. Why then did she persist in forgetting about Rebecca's dream?

Curiouser and curiouser, Rebecca thought, even though she had never liked Alice, in Wonderland or out of it.

'I'm in a wood.' (Definitely *wood.*) 'And then there's a castle, and in the castle there's a throne room. Hall. Big.'

'Sounds alright,' Steph said, as if hearing all this for the first time. 'Any people in this dream?'

'No, but there's a curtain behind the dais, and I'm sure there's someone...yes, someone behind it. It moves.'

It was disturbing to confront the idea that the 'someone' might in fact be a 'something', and Rebecca decided not to mention it.

'Why don't you look?'

'I can't. I always wake up.'

She was getting closer each time, though. A month ago the dream ended at the steps to the castle; with each recurrence Rebecca had been taken a little deeper into the maze of corridors and chambers until she had arrived at the throne room. Three nights ago she had noticed the curtain stir. Last night she had really thought that this time...

'The thing is, I'm not honestly sure I want to see what's behind there. I mean, who.'

She felt Steph's attention on her. 'Does it worry you?'

Rebecca thought, *How very perceptive,* but cloaked her irritation. 'A bit. I've never had a recurring dream before.'

This was true. However, she did have previous experience of her subconscious being hi-jacked and was feeling the stirrings of alarm. She didn't like the ivy twined around the trees at the edge of the castle. She suspected it of insinuating itself, or something else, into her mind, even if as yet it hadn't interfered with her work. She wasn't drawing trees and castles.

Correction: she wasn't drawing *only* trees and castles. Trees and castles cropped up in her sketchbooks quite a lot as she was an illustrator and had made her name, such as it was, in the field of fairytales, myths and legends. At various times she had been compared with Arthur Rackham, Pauline Baynes and Jan Pienkowski, all of which pleased her immensely. How could it not?

The irony had not escaped her, and had a commission come her way to produce illustrations for a story about children starting school or an adventure at the seaside she'd have snapped it up, but so far it had all been witches, princes, and the wild, wild woods.

Wild, wild woods.

The unicyclist passed them again, from behind. He was high up, dressed in jogging bottoms and a tee-shirt. Perhaps maintaining his balance generated heat.

'How do they even get up there to start?' Steph mused aloud, proving that once again Rebecca's dream had failed to hold her.

Rebecca sighed.

The street performers were out in force along the wide pavement of the South Bank and there was a holiday atmosphere. They strolled past a pair of living statues in stiff Elizabethan costume sprayed bronze, and a thin boy in a beanie hat near the second-hand book market who was contact juggling, persuading passersby that his crystal sphere was floating.

Steph took photos with her mobile. There were fire-eaters with blackened, smutty arms and faces, and two students playing a flute and a bassoon outside the Queen Elizabeth Hall, a pairing which was fresh and funny and haunting.

Up ahead a movie pirate look-alike was swaying and swaggering in front of a gaggle of open-mouthed children.

'He's good,' Steph said.

Steph had never lived in London, having gone from their school in Suffolk to Oxford and then to China. Rebecca had spent a brief few months at art college and then four more years in the capital before astounding everyone who knew her by moving to the Isle of Skye off the west coast of Scotland. She loved it there, but still considered herself a Londoner in many ways and rather believed anyone who wasn't to be less sophisticated. Arrogant, but a fact.

Steph had a point about the pirate, though. It was a popular character and Rebecca had seen far worse, including one wearing ordinary wellies for boots. This guy could do it properly, and as they passed him Rebecca glanced sideways for a second look.

The face was wrong, of course, but everything else was–

The pirate met her eyes, and somewhere something flashed.

Rebecca staggered, and collided with Steph, who caught her deftly.

'Sorry…I…What was–'

'Are you alright?'

Rebecca pulled herself together. 'Sorry. I tripped.' Although she hadn't. 'Was that a camera flash?'

Steph pulled a face and shrugged.

'No. Sorry. Stupid shoes.' *Change the subject, quick.* 'What about coffee? Or are you too stuffed with ice cream?'

* * *

When they emerged from the café Rebecca scanned the pavement in both directions but the look-alike pirate was nowhere to be seen.

Mild it might be, especially after the sharp freeze before Christmas, but the cloud cover brought dusk early. Already the deep blue lights on the avenue of trees in front of the London Eye were sparkling, and the neon lights above the Hayward Gallery were waking up.

Steph was flying back tomorrow. She had come home to spend Christmas with her parents in Suffolk, and Rebecca, who had business in London in January, had foregone Hogmanay on Skye this year to meet her. Rebecca was staying in her great-aunt's tall Edwardian terraced house in Tooting Bec, and Steph had joined her there for the last two nights.

The previous day they had taken sandwiches and flasks and grabbed a pitch on the Embankment for the countdown to midnight and the beginning of the New Year. The fireworks centred on the great wheel of the London Eye had been without question the largest and longest firework display either had ever seen, from the choreography of the first explosions against the chimes of Big Ben to the final fading of pink and blue smoke over the city skyline.

It had been a late night, and they needed to be up early tomorrow for Steph's flight. They headed towards Waterloo Station.

'Any chance of missing the mince pies?' Steph asked.

Rebecca snorted. Her aunt was the oldest and longest resident in her street. She had never married and took great interest in her neighbours' children, including doling out cash rewards for every exam passed from A-levels to swimming a length of doggy-paddle. She was much loved, and someone had delivered a batch of home-baked mince pies before Christmas.

Auntie Edie didn't eat mince pies but took great pleasure in offering them to guests, dutifully reheating them in the oven over and over. By now they resembled tar. It had taken Rebecca an age to get it off her teeth.

'It was jam tarts the last time I was here,' Rebecca said. 'I wonder if I should have a word with the neighbours.'

She jumped slightly as something brushed against her, and found the movie pirate had overtaken them. Disconcerted, she watched him draw ahead, his arms swinging and his coat skirts flapping. From the back, especially, he really was a very close look-alike.

'I wonder if he's got the tattoo,' Steph said, with admiration, and Rebecca saw suddenly in her mind the spiralling tendrils of vines tattooed on a man's wrist, and thought, *Michael.*

It was chilly on the exposed footbridge and Rebecca put her hands in her pockets.

In the left one there was a piece of paper. She was sure it hadn't been there earlier.

She drew it out as they walked and angled it to catch the light.

'What's that?' Steph asked.

Rebecca stuffed the paper back into her pocket and picked up pace. 'Nothing.'

And her heart thumped within her ribcage as she strode towards the station.

Chapter Two

Rebecca dreamed, but not of the wood and the castle and the curtain. This time, in place of branches laced above her head there was the open sky and stars, and a chill she could feel on her cheeks and lips. Even in the dark she knew she was on a high place, the space wide about her, and the only sound the distant hush of the sea.

She turned, pivoting, unwilling to step forward onto ground unseen, and found she was not alone. There was a person, a man, a black profile silhouetted against navy blue, and as she looked a wind sprang up and blew his hair and his coat. It buffeted Rebecca too, snatching at her, whipping her hair into her eyes, and she shifted her feet to keep her balance.

The man's head moved so that his profile was lost, and it seemed to Rebecca that he turned towards her, not away. He was looking at her, she was sure, and she opened her mouth to speak, but the wind took her voice even before she knew what words she would make. She was leaning against the force of it now, staggering a little despite her efforts, and the howl was all around her, in her eyes and in her head, and as she filled her lungs to shout–

–she woke with a jerk, a spasm, as if she had fallen, and lay without breathing until she believed fully that she was in bed after all.

Her eyes were wide open. After a moment or two she sat up and groped about. The bedside lamp was on an elderly brass stalk and Rebecca had to find the flex and follow it to the plastic switch.

There. The forty-watt bulb that had seemed so dim earlier now flooded the room with brilliance that made Rebecca wince. She shaded her eyes with her hand and waited for her sight to adjust.

The man, the shadow on the hill, who was he? She had not been able to see his features, yet there had been something about him that was…well, not familiar but not utterly strange. Something vaguely like someone…

Rebecca felt tired. Dreaming and then waking in the early hours was happening too often; often enough for her to have learned that it would be at least half an hour before she'd be ready to sleep again. It was inexplicable and annoying, and the fact that she had lived through inexplicable and annoying phenomena in the past didn't really help.

Inexplicable...

An idea formed in Rebecca's mind.

The light was alright now. Moving quietly, conscious of Steph sleeping the other side of the wall, Rebecca crossed the room, grimacing when the floorboards creaked, and retrieved her sketchbook from the chest of drawers. She took care to avert her eyes from the piece of paper lying next to it, folded in half under her watch.

She stuffed the pillows behind her back and reached for her phone.

Calendar first. Yep, as she thought – more than a week between her appointment with the publishers in Loughton Square and her visit to Portree High School; plenty of time to stop off in Oxford.

She opened the sketchbook and turned to the first blank page. The paper lay before her, open to suggestion, inviting her mark.

Do I really want to do this?

Rebecca shivered. The Edwardian house was cold overnight, but there was more to the raising of goose flesh on her arms than mere temperature.

She smoothed the paper with her thumb.

At least I'd know.

Rebecca ran her eyes round the walls as if taking a record of this mundane room, a symbol of reality, before embarking on a voyage, far away. Then she settled the pencil in her hand and began to draw.

Drawing was, in a way, her default status. The hours she had spent with a pencil in her hand must surely amount to months by now, years even, obliterating the margins of newspapers and leaflets, consuming jotter pads and notebooks, filling sheet after sheet of beautiful white cartridge paper. Scribbles defaced even her books; it was just something that happened when there was a pencil in her hand – and there usually was – and she often became aware of it only later.

Now the graphite lines formed on the page, and joined up with one another, and with the aid of a little cross-hatching took on the illusion of three-dimensional forms. Touches of shadow grounded them on unseen surfaces. Finely drawn lines bestowed on them details of hinges and fastenings and handles, and decoration on lids and lock plates. Rebecca drew keys, her steady hand laying down the straight shafts and complex wards. Dimly, she was aware that she was working across the spread of paper, moving ever closer to the lower edge, and even more dimly that time was passing.

When her hand slipped off the bottom corner of the book she laid down her pencil. Her neck felt stiff, which was hardly surprising as drawing in bed was not ideal. She checked her phone: three forty-five; she had been drawing for nearly two hours. She had to leave for the airport at seven thirty.

Rebecca felt uneasy, her eyes tired yet not quite ready to close, her mind unsettled. Sighing, she slipped into her sweater and crept downstairs to make hot chocolate in the hope of encouraging sleep. It was tricky extracting a saucepan from the stack without too much clatter, but at least the kitchen was beneath her own bedroom, not Steph's.

The floor was cold and the cupboard doors sagged. Rebecca lit the gas under the pan and thought affectionately of the house she had built on Skye, nestled at the foot of the Quiraing, within sight – just – of the sea.

Building her house – or at any rate having it built, because she had not handled the bricks herself – had practically taken over her life for a whole year, while she met with solicitors and local government officials and architects, and moved from land purchasing through planning permission to exploring house designs in software packages that enabled her to take a virtual stroll inside her house-to-be.

She had immersed herself in the business from the start, buying glossy magazines about self-building and paying visits to previous clients of the architects she had chosen. The partner assigned to her project had been easy to work with and happy to discuss ways to incorporate her own sketched ideas into the final design.

The result had been a house not particularly large in floor area but idiosyncratic and perfectly tailored to Rebecca's needs. She had given no thought to resale, only to living in it; its value lay not in investment but in the pleasure of occupying the space.

The rooms at the back, facing the hillside, were given over to storage, bathroom and kitchen, and, meanly, a guest bedroom. Rebecca didn't anticipate receiving many guests, and those that did come would have to put up with it. Her own bedroom and the sitting room faced the sea, and one-third of the whole house was given to a studio with a glorious floor-to-ceiling window projecting like the prow of a Viking ship. The light from the north poured into this room even when it was raining, and it had become simply Rebecca's favourite place to be.

It had cost a bit, but thanks to her income from letting Ashendon House to the hotel chain she could manage it. It helped that Michael's share of the income had been split between herself and Connor.

The milk began to shiver in the saucepan. Rebecca turned out the gas and poured hot milk into her mug.

There had been few other options, and it was what the instructions Michael had left directed them to do. But she had felt bad making the arrangements, although much of that was probably caused by simple grief.

She had known him for so little time. He was so much older than her, yet the intensity of their shared experiences had bound them in a way that was stronger, perhaps, than if they had been lovers.

She paused from stirring the chocolate. Did she really think that? That their bond had been stronger than hers with Connor?

Rebecca laid the spoon quietly in the washing up bowl. Connor was different. It had been amazing when he returned as if from the dead, and his experiences ought surely to have made him more detached from reality, not less. Yet he had matured, and settled, and relaxed at last into his life. No doubt Oxford played a large part in his contentment now, and Rebecca chose to believe she had seen where his destiny lay even when they first met, as teenagers.

With herself bewitched by Skye and Connor enmeshed in Oxford, their chance of a life together had foundered almost as soon as it had begun. But in any case they were not suited. Connor was kind, generous and sensitive; it had been his idea to donate Michael's capital to charity. She on the other hand was intolerant, short-tempered and, to be honest, a bit heedless. They really weren't suited at all.

She still fancied him, though.

Rebecca climbed back into bed and burrowed her icy feet under the covers. With one hand wrapped around the warm mug, she pulled the sketchbook onto her lap and reviewed what she had drawn.

It came as no surprise to her that she had filled the double spread, working as if the spiral binding did not exist. Nor was she surprised to find it was covered with boxes.

She had begun consciously by drawing the beautiful box that Michael had given her for Christmas three years ago. It was intended as a jewellery box, with ranks of shallow, velvet-lined trays, but she possessed very little jewellery other than what she always wore – her mother's old wedding ring and the gold vine leaf on its chain that was a gift from Aunty Edie – and it was sadly underused.

After that, she had begun recording from memory other boxes of Michael's, casting her mind's eye back to the shelves in his studio where they sat in rows: ash-grey, conker-brown and charcoal; slim boxes for a single necklace and small chests with multiple compartments; chunky boxes with knot holes and elegant boxes smooth as satin; boxes you could slip in your pocket and boxes that ought really to be considered furniture.

As she moved down the page, the boxes she had drawn drifted away from Michael Seward's style. Locks appeared on the front elevations and carving decorated the lids and sides: Celtic strapwork, medieval quatrefoils, and tall Art Deco lilies. The designs were beautiful and the draughtsmanship skilful, but as the drawings flowed across the paper more had been added to the mix.

A spider's web stretched, trembling, from chest to casket, and another, torn and drooping, hung from a corner. Leaves drifted and formed eddies and swirls with seed cases and acorns and sycamore wings. On a velvet tray inside one open box were three speckled eggs and, with them, a pinion feather from some unknown bird.

Near the bottom of the page a small group appeared, an

arrangement like a still life: a box, cube-shaped, with a heavy lid; a carriage clock with decorated hands set at twenty-five past two; and a candle in a candlestick, its flame blown sideways by an invisible breeze.

The box was heavily carved with vines.

Rebecca swallowed; her mouth felt dry. She ran her eyes again over the page, noting the border of ivy that idly climbed the edge, with its nodding, heart-shaped leaves and delicate spirals.

Then she raised her eyes to the mahogany chest of drawers against the far wall and the folded paper lying beneath her watch.

Chapter Three

Geoffrey Foster passed beneath the Gothic arch into the warm comfort of the Randolph Hotel and almost smiled.

Not quite. Checked it in time. God forbid that he should be caught smiling inanely by himself.

A smile for the receptionist, now that was different – a kindly chink in the reserve, old-world manners coupled with the suggestion of being completely at ease, that was another matter. Foster signed the registration card and slid it across the polished wood with a murmured *Thank you* which, he was confident, bore the suggestion that he might have added "my dear" had he not been a Renaissance man, fully at ease with a woman's equal professional status. That was safe, and often went down very well.

He had taken a room rather than a suite. A suite had been tempting, but the legacy he had inherited three years ago was sufficient to allow him either to retire from business or to enjoy a luxurious lifestyle, but not both. He had elected retirement, and had to keep a certain degree of restraint on his spending.

The room was up to expectations, though, with the minor exception of the missing perforations on the coffee sachet, which was hardly the fault of the management; in any case, he'd opened it easily enough with his pocket knife.

And it was, after all, the Randolph.

He had dined here three times when he was up, treated each year by Graham Collingwood, or rather Graham's father. The atmosphere and service had burned into his memory. It was one of the reasons he had abandoned science after his degree and entered the City. And it was one of the reasons the collapse of his banking job had rankled so badly, even more so since it was through no fault of his own.

Still, here he was now, thanks to Aunt Margaret, or at any rate thanks to Aunt Margaret's unexpected and convenient death, and he intended to enjoy himself. A stroll down to the Oxford Union for a drink first, he thought, and then dinner in the Randolph's five-star restaurant.

His appointment with Marwell wasn't for another two days, but he had decided to come early, make something of his first proper visit to Oxford in twenty years – that brief call to collect the clock a few years ago hardly counted. He wasn't sure why it should have been so long – possibly a bad taste from having sold out to commerce, as it were. Or perhaps from the knowledge that the Collingwoods of his acquaintance had no need to carve out their own careers.

But he was over that now. He'd remind himself of the layout of the city, revisit the old College, see what two decades had done to the Botanic Gardens and the Pitt Rivers, and check out this high-profile redevelopment of the Ashmolean.

If it had been warmer he might even have gone punting.

Rebecca found Connor at the sink and she had to wait while he finished peeling vegetables before they could talk. She wanted his full attention for this.

She prowled the kitchen, which was large enough to walk around, although, like Aunty Edie's, furnished with shabby cupboards and aging Formica worktops. Like her aunt, the three Dons had no interest in refurbishing, although they were far older than Aunty Edie.

Connor had a room in College during term-time, but in the vacations he still lodged with the three decrepit professors who had taken him under their wing. He seemed serenely happy. It would have driven Rebecca demented.

'What are all those potatoes for?'

'We're having a casserole. Do you want to stay? There's plenty.'

That hardly needed to be said. Rebecca had seen the Dons' idea of a light supper. Her own preferred cuisine relied on salads and stir-fry, not slow-cooked stodge.

She watched Connor's hands, his left turning the potato over and around, his right wielding the peeler. Such a mundane task, but she enjoyed seeing the smooth movement of tendons in his wrists and over the backs of his hands.

He had changed since taking up his place as an undergraduate. He had filled out a little more, although he remained lean, and – rather startlingly – his hair was now cropped really short. As short, in fact, as hers had been when they first met, five, six years ago. How odd that while his had been getting shorter, hers had been getting longer; she mostly wore it in a plait now.

'You're looking well,' she said, thinking aloud, and he threw her a smile over his shoulder.

'Thanks. So are you!'

Once upon a time Connor's smiles had been an endangered species, so rare that when one arrived it stopped your heart. They came easy to him these days, and not because of his inherited wealth. Rebecca had been present when the solicitor sorted out payments and accounts, and knew Connor had diverted the major part of his share to his sisters, giving them independence from their shiftless, abusive father.

When they agreed to donate the money from Michael's parents' estate to a charity, he had chosen Save The Children.

She had wondered last year how easy he had found mixing with the other students. Of course, she wasn't so naïve as to think everyone at Oxford had public school and private finance behind them, but she suspected very few had Connor's tough experience of life.

She recalled him mentioning a fellow undergrad whose family drifted between three highly desirable residences. 'They have spy cameras set up all over the place,' he had told her. 'He can log in from his Mac and see what's going on in Sussex or Belgravia or their castle near Edinburgh!'

But Connor had maturity and a quiet strength to anchor him.

Now he rolled the potatoes into a saucepan three times the size of the largest one Rebecca owned and emptied the sink. Then he sat down at the battered pine table opposite Rebecca and said, 'Alright, what is it?'

Rebecca could almost feel the paper in her hip pocket. She clasped her hands together on the table. 'I was at the South Bank on New Year's Day. Steph was over. There was a look-alike, a pirate. He put a note in my coat pocket. At least, I think he did. I didn't feel it, but…well, I'm sure it was him.' She paused.

'And?'

Rebecca turned to check that the door was still closed. Strains of Radio 4 drifted from the parlour – *Woman's Hour*, probably.

Not that it mattered if the Dons overheard her; if it was what she suspected, she might soon be seeking their advice. But for the moment she wanted just Connor to hear.

She drew the paper from her jeans and placed it in front of him. As he unfolded it, she watched his face.

Stephen Marwell had gained a few pounds and lost some hair, but otherwise was much as Geoffrey remembered him: still large, still slightly dishevelled, still reminiscent of a bear in corduroys. His briefcase was a modern Samsonite one though, so sometime in the quarter-century the scuffed leather job Foster recalled must have gone the way of all flesh.

He arrived at the door to the Physics Labs with paw extended and shook hands with a single strong tug before pushing his spectacles up his nose. Another mannerism from the past.

'Geoff! Good to see you! You're looking well!'

'It's good to see you too, Doctor Marwell. Thank you for–'

'No, no, no, it's Steve now. Not your tutor any more! Sorry, can I just...'

Foster waited while Marwell checked his mobile, and then walked with him into the street, wrestling just a little with memories of undergraduate life.

'The Bird?'

The Bird, short for the Bird and Baby. That had been university slang for the pub called the Eagle and Child. Decades flew away.

'So, quantum entanglement in respect of action at a distance,' Marwell said as they walked along Museum Road. 'What line of work did you say you were in?'

Foster hadn't, of course, and now he murmured something vague and trusted his old tutor to be distracted by the business of weaving between bicycles and buses as they crossed the great breadth of St Giles. He suspected the question was born of good manners rather than curiosity and could be left unanswered.

Safely back on the pavement, he said, 'Communication faster than light. So far as I've been able to discover, the concept has been soundly rejected by the theoreticians, but I'd like your opinion as to the possibility of there being any holes here. Any shaky ground, do you think?'

This was the crux of the matter. It was quite plain that the boy, Connor, had aged more than three years' worth between disappearing from the hidden room at Ashendon into another dimension and returning. A difference in velocity between two locations was allowed for, even required, by theories of time dilation based on Einstein.

But dilation as great as in this case required the distance between the two places to be vast – in separate galaxies, pretty much. Therefore either the momentary quantum entanglement indicated by the visibility of the light beams had connected two planets more than a galaxy apart, or the connection was not the result of quantum entanglement at all, and the boy had been transported not to another planet but to an alternate plane of existence.

This was the stuff of science fiction. Before he trod on such insubstantial ground Geoffrey wanted to be certain that other avenues had been definitely closed off. So he said, 'What do you think? Any dissenters, apart from the cranks?'

'And then there's this,' Rebecca said.

She opened her sketchbook and turned it to face Connor. The scrap of paper she drew back towards herself, the three words starkly written in black ink:

Open Michael's box

Rebecca dragged her attention from it and watched Connor as he looked at her drawings.

'When did you do these?'

'The same night. New Year's Day.'

She had taken Steph to the airport on the second of January and seen the publishers on the third. The meeting had gone well. By a serious effort of will she had succeeded in banishing all thoughts of the actual World Invisible to concentrate instead on the publisher's idea of fairyland, at least for the duration of the meeting.

The next day she had said goodbye to Aunty Edie and come to Oxford.

'A pirate?'

'Yes.'

Rebecca watched Connor's eyes move across the open spread and settle at the lower right-hand corner. She gnawed her thumb.

So little needed to be said. They both knew what could influence her. Once upon a time it had been vines rampaging through everything she drew, until she had been unable to work and had been forced to take dramatic steps to free herself from the obsession. Then three years ago they were together when they discovered that she had been accurately sketching real landscapes she had never seen.

'Did you see him? His face?'

'Not really. Just an impression.'

Rebecca thought again of the flash and the jolt to her body, as if she had accidentally touched an electrified fence. She saw the pirate's flaring eyebrow and the way one half of his mouth lifted in a wicked smile.

'He was dark,' she said.

As were they all – she and Connor and Michael. People remarked upon it: *so unusual, hair that black, do you know who you inherited it from?*

Oh yes.

Connor said, 'So which of Michael's boxes do you think it means?'

'Not mine. I've been opening and closing that for three years.'

It had been her first thought, of course, but she had realised quickly that it didn't make sense. Michael had never, so far as she knew, made puzzle boxes or secret compartments, producing instead boxes that were desirable because they were beautiful. In any case, she had chosen her box from stock, responding to its proportions and contours and warm chestnut sheen where it sat on the shelf in Michael's studio. She simply did not believe that he had allowed her to take away a box containing a secret without telling her.

If the note referred to the ordinary opening of any other of

Michael's boxes, they too had all been opened and closed since Michael's departure. She and Connor had made gifts of some – Rebecca had selected a box for Steph, another for the elderly couple who had lived below her London flat, and one for Aunty Edie, of course, and she was aware Connor had sent boxes to people he had cause to thank in the United States. The remainder of the stock was still in Michael's old cottage at Ashendon, deserted now and locked up.

Rebecca leaned forward and touched her fingertip to the group of objects at the foot of the page.

'I think I've seen this.'

She didn't mean the clock, nor the candlestick.

'Yes.'

'So I'm going to call in at Ashendon on the way home.'

Chapter Four

Rebecca pulled into the car park at Ashendon House a little after five, having stopped at the supermarket outside Matlock to buy supplies. It was already dark, and the windows of the hotel glowed enticingly. Rebecca wondered idly how many people chose the first week of January for a holiday in the Peak District.

The cottage was cold and bleak. Rebecca dumped her bags inside the door and made a swift tour switching on lights and turning up the heating. Uriel Passenger, who had built the house and cottage and then bequeathed it, in a roundabout way, to Michael, Connor and herself, had installed a rudimentary central heating system using radiators. Although the water in the pipes didn't freeze, it would be an hour before the place felt warm.

She checked there was nothing gruesome lurking in the fridge, but of course there wasn't. Connor had been up for a week in September, walking, and he was far too competent to leave half a carton of milk to moulder. Then, still in her coat, she crunched across the gravel to the hotel, to let them know she was in residence. They probably weren't interested, but it was understood they would keep an eye on the empty cottage so it was only good manners to explain why the lights were on.

She didn't recognise the young man on reception, narrow-shouldered and concave inside his navy jacket.

'Rebecca Mulligan,' she said. 'Just letting you know that I'll be in the cottage tonight.'

'Oh. Oh, okay.'

She was on her way back to the door when he called her.

'Miss Mulligan?'

Rebecca paused and turned. He was rummaging under the counter.

'There was a message…somewhere…Here.'

He held up an envelope in triumph. Rebecca took it from him cautiously. Why would anyone leave a message for her at Ashendon Manor Hotel?

'From a resident?'

'I don't know, madam. I'm sorry, I've only just come back from–'

'When was it left, do you know?'

'Sorry.' The receptionist smiled weakly.

Rebecca opened the envelope in the cottage kitchen, always the quickest to warm up. Inside was a postcard, a photograph of sheep grazing on moorland at dawn, their shaggy fleeces sparkling with dew. On the reverse someone had written:

Remember Jack's tallixer.

Rebecca laid the postcard down and clasped her hands together. She rested her chin on her knuckles, and stared at the ink strokes.

There was little doubt that it was the same hand as the previous note. The ink was a different colour, dark blue this time instead of black, but the *x* was formed the same way, two curves back to back, and the *s* after the apostrophe was elongated as before, finishing below the line in a little flourish. Idiosyncratic. Not extravagant, but noticeable; *remember me?* it seemed to say.

So the pirate had been at the hotel? She saw him again, swinging ahead of her on the broad pavement between the Festival Hall and the Thames. Then she changed his flapping eighteenth-century pirate's coat for a hill-walker's waterproofs and rucksack, and sent him striding away along the footpath towards Nether Haddon.

What had his face been like? She could only recall his back now.

Remember Jack's tallixer... How could she ever forget?

The cottage held a basketful of resonant memories for her, despite the brevity of her time here. First there had been its discovery, months after Uriel had passed away, and that long afternoon when the three of them had scoured the pages of his diaries, searching for a hint that they were on the right track. And she would never lose the chill of what occurred the next night in the room behind the mirrors.

Then there had been the visits to Michael when he was living here, and her slow realisation of his increasing withdrawal from normal life.

And finally, of course, the mad, out-of-control happiness of the two weeks she and Connor spent here after their first visit to Skye, before Connor returned to Oxford and his interrupted education.

Rebecca's mouth twitched into a smile at the memory, and then the smile faded as her eyes returned to the words on the postcard in front of her.

Jack's tallixer.

The tallixer, huge and carnivorous, had spent some days at Ashendon lodged in the only safe place, the walled garden they had retained for their own use. Rebecca herself had bought the heavy-duty bolts for the gates. But how could anyone beyond the four of them involved – five if you included Jack – know about that?

And *why* did she have to remember?

She cooked, an omelette and salad, easy food, and then prowled the rooms for the carved box. She was sure she had seen it, but couldn't quite think where. On the bookshelves with Uriel Passenger's journals? Next to the sofa? The ridiculous thing was that the cottage was so small, not much more than a bedroom, bathroom, kitchen, and the long parlour with its brick hearth and windows on two walls.

Rebecca moved curtains, opened chests and dragged furniture about, but it was over an hour before she saw it, just as she was on the verge of giving up.

The box sat on the floor in full view in the corner of the small, chilly back parlour where one wall was completely covered by mirrors in frames. She had already opened the door and looked in twice without noticing it. How? Infuriating.

Irritated with herself, Rebecca carried the box back to the living room and set it on the low pine table. The wood felt chill to her hands. It was quite unlike anything Michael had made, but she was certain it hadn't been in the room when they first entered the cottage six years ago. So if it wasn't Uriel's, and not hers or Connor's, it had to be Michael's, surely?

The wood was dark and not so much polished as worn to a smooth finish. The carving was cut deep into the thickness of the walls, the grooves rough at the bottom and gathering dust. It came as no surprise that the design was botanical, nor that vines featured prominently.

The proportions, just as on the drawing Rebecca had made, were those of a cube, and the lid was shallow, the lock plate set high up on the front face of the box.

Rebecca put her face close and breathed in. Along with the oldness and the dust came a faint trace of something warmer: not spices but sharper, maybe…citrus? Citrus mixed with herbs…

Like something glimpsed in her peripheral vision, the scent eluded Rebecca. She sniffed again, but the strains were even fainter.

No good.

The box was locked, of course. Rebecca had expected as much, already anticipating obstacles. Well, twice in the past she had surmounted worse problems, including breaking a code and deciphering some tortuous riddles, so a lost key was not going to stop her for long. People could pick locks, couldn't they?

She called Connor.

'I'm here and I've found the box. Any idea where the key might be?'

She could hear voices from a television programme in the background. The Dons had an unlikely appetite for game shows, especially the kind where the public can vote. The one she thought of as the Tortoise, for reasons that were obvious when you met him, adored talent shows.

'Not really. The bedroom drawers? The dresser?'

'Hmm. I think I might leave it for tomorrow. It took me long enough to find the box.'

'Anything else?'

Rebecca pictured the postcard on the kitchen table.

'No. Nothing else.'

'Okay. Well, have to go, the muffins are nearly done.'

Rebecca snorted. Life at the Ferry House seemed to revolve around cooking. The three ancient Dons existed on a diet lifted from old-fashioned school stories: meat-and-two-veg and solid puddings, with cakes of some kind every day. The Vulture (that was obvious too) was a good cook, and it now seemed Connor was getting stuck in as well.

The bed was wide and chilly. Rebecca hugged the hot water

bottle with her cold feet and hoped not to dream.

Chapter Five

Geoffrey Foster skirted the crowd spilling out from the Taylor Institute with his mind fully occupied.

It was not unlike being back at university.

He had a list of authors and conferences scribbled into his notebook and the promise of more to come.

'These are just off the top of my head. I'll email you the rest.'

And he'd thought he had more or less covered what was published. He'd be reading for another six months.

It had been pleasant talking with Professor Marwell – Steve – nestled into a corner of the Eagle and Child, discussing theories of parallel universes and access thereto via the vagaries of quantum theory as if such things were possible. Ha! Had his old tutor only known what he now knew...

The choice of pub had been appropriate. Geoffrey was aware, of course, of its reputation as the meeting place of the Inklings, the informal society formed in the nineteen-thirties by Tolkien, C S Lewis and others interested in fantasy fiction. The pub did trade on it rather, with photographs from its past framed on the walls and prominent quotations from the best known works, but fair's fair and it was genuine history.

As they talked, Geoffrey found himself relaxing, which was curious as he hadn't been aware that he was anything other than relaxed to begin with. This was conversation completely unlike anything he'd had access to for many years.

There was no edge of competition.

No need for defensiveness either. Steve displayed no interest in the detail of what he had been doing, the whys and wherefores, and did not probe into Geoffrey's career to date. He seemed perfectly content to kick over theories and impart information without questions, and salaries and prospects and benefits and property never came into it.

Somewhere inside, around where his liver sat, Geoffrey felt the stirring of a question of his own. Not so long ago he had been dismissive, even contemptuous, of people who elected not to pursue wealth – people like Michael Seward, content with a meagre income and concerned more with the quality of the boxes he made than how much he could get for them.

Yet he had seemed content. More or less. At least apart from the business of the other world.

And Steve Marwell seemed content, despite the fact that he must have existed for years with very little security before he landed a college fellowship.

They each had a pint of the wonderfully named Betty Stoggs bitter, and the hands on the big old station clock on the wall reached quarter past seven.

Probably still not married, then.

'So,' Geoffrey said, with care, 'if we were to observe a phenomenon involving the instantaneous travel of some physical matter demonstrating a very large time dilation, would looking at quantum entanglement be barking up the wrong tree?'

He was keenly aware of the gaze that fell on him.

'Is this a *thought experiment* we're talking about, or Star Trek?'

Geoffrey said, 'I'd feel better if we can pretend this is a thought experiment.'

'Nothing wrong with sci-fi if that's what you're about.'

Hmm. Perhaps that might have been a better line to take from the start.

But even a bachelor academic needs to go home at some point. As they separated, Marwell said, 'I'll tell you who might be worth speaking to: Perry. Peregrine. Must be coming up to retirement now, I should think, but he's interested in this sort of thing, or used to be. I don't have his email, but contact Cardinal's and they'll find him for you.'

Then he had gone, ambling along the pavement like a bear who knows both where the honey tree is and that it will wait for him, and it was too late to say, 'Ah, yes, I've heard of Professor Peregrine.'

But he had. Although he couldn't recall how.

The mild weather in London had been left behind; there had been a frost overnight at Ashendon and the walled garden was a landscape in muted tones, the twisted network of bare wisteria branches ashen against the mottled grey of the old timbers that supported them and the stone that surrounded them, and all with a powdering as if of icing sugar sifted from above.

Rebecca pulled out her phone and took a few photographs, zooming out to get an impression of the grid-like criss-crossing of branches and struts, zooming in to detail starbursts of lichen and ice crystals.

Despite riddles and treasure hunts and doorways to magic kingdoms, she was, first and foremost, an artist.

She hadn't dreamed, neither of the throne and the curtain nor of the man and the night sky, or at least didn't remember so on waking. The carved box was still awaiting its key, but for the moment the imperative was with the second message and its instruction to remember the alien beast that had stayed here, under the wisteria, before she and Connor found a way to send it home.

Of course she remembered it; how could she ever forget something like that? So the postcard must be steering her to look here, where the tallixer had been. But what for?

The key?

Rebecca's mouth twisted. A small, presumably grey metal key hidden in this grey garden would be a nightmare to find. *Please don't let it be that.*

She walked the shingle path that wound between the trunks, ducking when necessary beneath the ancient wood. She didn't know the age of the wisteria but thought it likely it had been planted soon after Uriel Passenger built the house, which was well over a century ago. The wood writhed and twisted around and over the framework built to support it. Rebecca patted it from time to time, somehow driven to make physical contact with something that had lived for so long, and it was rough and fibrous under her palms.

The scent, she realised, was like that in her dream: bitter and dry, although colder.

A spark of scarlet flashed at the edge of her vision, and she glanced aside to see a robin perched deep in the tangle, returning her gaze with his bead of an eye as if posing for a Christmas card.

Or perhaps auditioning for a role in The Secret Garden, a book Rebecca had not thought much of as a child; everyone had turned nice so quickly. But the early sequences, with Mary discovering the neglected garden, had been good. The walled gardens in the story had been the first image that flew into her mind when she saw the grounds of Ashendon House that hot August day years ago.

None of the walls here were covered in ivy, though, which was ironic when you thought about it.

The robin switched branches, a flutter and a bounce, and looked at her again in the brazen way robins do, as if they have no concept of relative size and are squaring up for a fight.

'Forget it,' Rebecca told it. 'You're not going to see me off your patch.' Then she said, 'Want to show me this key?'

That was what Frances Hodgson Burnett's robin did, after all. That was how Mary Lennox found the key to the hidden door.

There were so many parallels. Rebecca had lived through too much that was disturbing to shake them off easily. She dragged her thoughts away from robins and neglected children and walked round a corner where her gaze fell upon a cloche, the kind gardeners use to protect vulnerable plants from cold. It sat on the gravel walk, where it had no business to be, an escapee from the kitchen gardens…or the product of theft.

There was no plant under it, but there was something.

Rebecca picked up the card.

Connor answered but said, 'Sorry, I'm about to start on the telethon. Can I call you this evening?'

'Telethon?'

'Calling wealthy alumni and asking them to give the College a donation. There's a team of us. This evening?'

Not much help. Once upon a time he had been almost impossible to get hold of, with no phone and a point-blank refusal to share his address. Then he had vanished. For a few sweet weeks after he reappeared he conformed with the rest of the world and used a mobile, throughout most of which they had been in each other's company anyway. And now…

Rebecca sighed. He had a life of his own these days, and it wasn't one she could share. It was ironic. Despite everyone's agreement that Connor was destined eventually to take over stewardship of the doorway concealed at the Ferry House, his concerns now were the humdrum reality of lectures and exams and College social life. Rebecca had heard mention of something called *bops*.

Whereas she, desperate to be rid of the wretched world of Faerie, cursing her knowledge that it was more than mere myth, and infuriated by the interruption to her career as an illustrator, seemed once more to be enmeshed in some stupid game.

It wasn't fair.

Neither was it fair that when she protested against the unfairness she sounded, she knew, like a spoilt child. Like Mary Lennox, in fact.

Rebecca scowled at the postcards lying on the kitchen table: the dew-laden sheep and the new one, with its image of a spreading oak tree silhouetted against a flaming sunset. On the reverse was written:

Use Uriel's knife.

What for? And where was it? Not in the cottage, she was pretty sure, having turned the whole place over in search of the key to the carved box. It had taken her hours and she had stumbled upon objects which churned up a whole load of memories: a half-used candle, an antique wooden spool wound with gold thread, and a slim brass telescope wrapped in faded silk brocade.

She had found the key, at last, poking up from an eggcup in the dresser, not exactly hidden at all. With a degree of trepidation she had unlocked the box and lifted the lid, but nothing had leapt out at her: no vines unfurled their glossy leaves in her direction, no sparkles of pink fairy dust, no smiling frog wearing a little lopsided crown. There was nothing in the box at all, just the trace of lemon and thyme, and a whiff of nostalgia, although for what Rebecca could not say.

It was disappointing, and she didn't know what to do next.

Find Uriel's knife, presumably.

Who was this man?

She had crossed to the hotel and spoken to Bridget Dixon, the manager, but although Bridget confirmed that the card had been left for her by a resident, she would not, of course, tell her anything else. 'Sorry, Rebecca, client confidentiality. I'm sure you understand.'

And of course Rebecca did. But it was frustrating nonetheless.

So she had little to discuss with Connor when he rang after supper, although he had some news for her.

'Guess who wants to meet Peregrine.'

He sounded playful and light-hearted. He really had been reborn.

'Who?'

'Geoffrey Foster.'

Rebecca nearly choked. 'You're kidding me!'

'Nope. Made contact through the College Secretary. I don't think he realises he already has the number for the Ferry House. I'm not sure he realises who Peregrine is at all.'

'Why does he want to see him?' Rebecca asked. 'What for?'

Connor's voice sounded amused. 'Research into Instantaneous Transportation utilising Quantum Entanglement.'

The very thing they all knew was not just a possibility but concrete reality. Connor better than anyone.

'It's you he should talk to,' Rebecca said.

'I think not.'

Rebecca sighed. 'Well, if you get any brilliant ideas about this knife, let me know. Otherwise you can guess where I'm going to be tomorrow.'

'Matlock,' Connor said, with sympathy.

'Matlock,' Rebecca said, with resignation.

Chapter Six

Robert Banks paused, carton in his right hand, pourer in his left, arrested in the act of replenishing the milk by the shock of the unprecedented request.

'Are you sure, sir?'

'Of course - absolutely!'

Robert – he had always used his full name, *Bob Banks* being unpleasantly alliterative and *Rob Banks* unfortunate – broke the habit of a lifetime in service and, before he was even aware of it, argued.

'But, forgive me, sir, is this really *wise?*'

'Yes, yes! I've told you!'

Professor Lloyd, his bald and speckled head wavering, plastic-rimmed spectacles jauntily aslant, beamed at him with childlike enthusiasm, and Robert felt himself adrift on doubt.

It would happen on his watch.

He had been informed of the standing orders on his first day many years ago by the then Senior Steward: *The corner under the clock belongs to the three of them, whether they are in or not; and they must not be disturbed. Leave them to me.*

He had thought he understood. 'Elderly, are they? Set in their ways?'

'Yes.'

'Not likely to be around much longer?'

'I wouldn't say that.'

And when, years later, he himself became Senior Steward, he had initiated under-stewards in his turn.

'...leave them to me.'

'They do look rather elderly.'

'They are.'

'Not much longer to go?'

'I wouldn't say that.'

For twenty-six years he had gently guided new members to other tables in the lounge, tactfully diverted bright young academics anxious to network, intercepted with smooth efficiency the occasional stranded visitor.

It was part of the job. Occasionally Robert thought about it, but it had been explained to him that questions must not be asked. Mostly he wondered how it was that the other members of the Senior Common Room failed to notice how very long it had been since the three Professors had retired from full-time teaching.

Now he gathered his startled thoughts into better array.

'Professor Peregrine–'

'Yes, yes, Perry's on his way, but he'll tell you just the same.'

Professor Lloyd scuttled back to the corner.

Not at all reassured, Robert refilled the milk pourer.

Geoffrey had never set foot in an SCR before. Well, of course not; he had left Oxford after graduating and cut his ties with his fellow undergrads when he entered the City firm. Thought he'd finished with academic postulating and theorising, which was proof of how little one can predict the future.

He was a little uneasy as he waited at the Porter's Lodge of Cardinal's College. Marwell had said Professor Peregrine was elderly, somehow managing also to convey that he might be irrational and hard to keep on track, which didn't sound promising. The College Secretary, when he rang, made no attempt to disguise her surprise.

'You want to contact Professor Peregrine? You are sure you have the right name?'

But when the Professor presented himself at the Lodge two minutes ahead of the agreed time he looked reassuringly normal. He was middling tall, middling plump, middling bald, with spectacles and a bland, forgettable face. He shook hands briefly, spoke mildly, and was altogether unexceptional apart from wearing a gown over his grey suit, and something, some quality, in his gaze that was unexpected.

Geoffrey followed him across the quad, trying to pin it down. It was a kind of intensity, a keenness, with which the man had looked at him that for a moment left Geoffrey feeling wrong-footed, almost rattled. As if he needed to justify his presence.

But then the old professor had turned away, walking briskly so that Geoffrey had to stride out to catch up.

He had probably imagined it.

The Senior Common Room, that sanctuary for Fellows and their occasional guests, had much the same atmosphere as a traditional gentlemen's club, with armchairs and small tables arranged in groups and newspapers laid out on a sideboard. Side lamps in fringed shades were already on, casting a dim yellow glow over the dark wood and upholstery; it felt more like five o'clock than two-thirty.

'In the corner, over there,' Professor Peregrine said, indicating with a vague circular wave of his hand. 'Mr Banks will bring us coffee.'

The room was not busy. A good-looking woman with her back to the fireplace and a pen in her hand was intent on a pile of papers, and a couple of young chaps in jeans and sweaters were in conversation near the door. Two wizened old men, also in gowns, were seated beneath a dingy oil painting of a man in the cap and furs of a Tudor cleric. Geoffrey realised, with a small shock, that they were watching him, the tall one with a glare not unlike that of the American eagle, the short one with the gleeful excitement of a child on Christmas Eve.

Geoffrey approached with misgivings. This was not like meeting Steve Marwell at all.

Later, back in his room at the Randolph, Foster found the supply of coffee sachets had been topped up but there were still no perforations. He hacked into the plastic with his pocket knife and sourly tipped the powder into the filter. If it was the same tomorrow he'd complain.

He might even complain tonight.

The meeting with Peregrine had been disastrous. He wished now he hadn't gone. For some reason he had found it difficult to concentrate, and it hadn't helped that he had begun to feel hot and a touch muzzy while they were talking, as if hatching a headache.

He knew why the name had seemed familiar. When he glanced at his phone after dialling the number given to him by the College office, a name had popped helpfully onto the screen and not one he was expecting: Connor O'Brien.

It had confused him for several moments before he made the

connection. He had called that number in the past, when Rebecca Mulligan and the boy had been struggling to locate another gap between, well, let's say *planes of existence*. And yes, there was a memory, pretty much buried, of the phone belonging to a Professor Peregrine with whom Connor O'Brien was staying at the time.

Naturally he had mentioned it at the meeting.

'Ah yes, Connor!' Professor Peregrine had said, and the shrivelled one, bald head wavering, sniggered. 'We do sometimes take in a lodger. We have the room.'

'Waifs and strays,' said the tall one with the eagle frown.

'Useful for washing up,' added the shrivelled one.

Had they only been aware of what had been under their noses. *I could tell you a story,* Geoffrey thought, *that would turn your gowns whiter than your hair.*

For they had been interested in his line, all three of them, although they were irritatingly vague.

'I once thought there might be a rending of reality, a passageway out of what we call The World, somewhere in Derbyshire,' Peregrine had mused, while the SCR steward poured coffee for them from an engraved silver pot. 'And there was in recent years a disturbance connected with a village called Boars Hill on the western outskirts of Oxford.'

Ah, the mysterious Beast of Boars Hill, as it had been named by the local press. The story had even made the national news one day, and Geoffrey knew exactly what kind of beast it had been. He had fed it.

And all the while Connor O'Brien had been living under their very roof. Clearly the boy had a cunning side to him Geoffrey had not suspected, although it had to be said the three old men would have been easy to befuddle. Not the brightest bulbs in the box.

So altogether a disappointment and a waste of time.

Geoffrey decided he'd give his head a chance to clear and then go down to the bar before dinner. And he would raise the matter of the coffee sachets on the way.

Chapter Seven

Altogether a disappointment and a waste of time, Rebecca thought, prodding the cube of chicken with a wooden spoon. It was still squidgy. She pushed everything around the pan, mushrooms and peppers and diced chicken, while her mouth made saliva and her stomach rumbled.

She had stayed late at Matlock, keen not to waste a third day searching the boxes. Along with the house, they had inherited its contents, an eccentric collection of mostly worthless paraphernalia which somehow none of them felt they could discard. After two days of rummaging through the storage unit they rented, Rebecca was exasperated to the verge of screaming. She wanted to speak to Connor but it was probably better to give her bad mood time to mend; it might be easier to be nice after she'd eaten.

It was gone nine by the time she made the call. The phone rang a few times, which she guessed meant that Connor was leaving the room he was in before picking up; the Dons were watching noisy television, probably.

'Hi.' Connor's voice sounded buoyant, as it usually did these days. 'How did it go? Any luck?'

'Absolutely none. No knife of any kind anywhere. I'm fed up.'

As they talked Rebecca felt her irritation dissipate. Connor often had that effect, and not just on her, she suspected. He had a soothing presence, an aura of calm, and listening to his voice was like being stroked. Not for the first time Rebecca thought he would make both a wonderful nurse and a brilliant peace-negotiator.

'So how did the Geoffrey Foster thing turn out?' she asked, letting go of her troubles.

Connor sounded amused. 'They ran rings round him. Poor bloke. Problem is, I don't think he deserves it.'

'You don't?'

'Well, think about it. He's known about Ashendon for years now and hasn't let anything out. And we probably wouldn't even have found it without him.'

'He swiped the clock–'

'I know,' Connor said, 'but we survived, and he looked after

Jack and the tallixer for us. We'd have been up the creek without that.'

'Yeah, yeah, I suppose.'

Mostly because you magicked him, Rebecca thought sourly. Quite how he had managed it she did not know, but she hadn't forgotten Foster's five-second about-face, one moment trying to shut the door on them, the next inviting them in, Boar's Hill Beast and all. If Connor, with his comparatively slight skill, had managed to influence the man then it was no surprise that the Dons had manipulated him with ease. It was a wonder they hadn't had him floating out of the SCR on fairy wings.

Connor said, 'Did you find anything else?'

'Pardon?'

'Nothing else of interest in Matlock?'

Rebecca shifted. She was sitting with her legs beneath her on the saggy sofa and felt the approach of pins and needles. 'No. Nothing.'

'Alright. Well. If that's all, then…'

Rebecca finished the call and glared at the playing card lying on the tabletop. How did he always know? When would she ever learn?

The Jack of Hearts gazed away from her, his profile straight, his long hair flowing; the leaf in his hand curling gracefully; the halberd behind him a threat.

But a threat to whom?

Rebecca woke with a shock, a sudden jerk of her muscles which jolted the mattress. And she hadn't even reached the throne room this time.

Wide-eyed in the dark, she explored with her mind the sensation of being in bed – the weight of the blankets, for duvets hadn't ventured into Ashendon Cottage, and the scrape of the sheets against her arms; the dipped mattress under her hip, and the faint scent of herbs, as though Michael were still here.

Or Uriel, of course. It seemed to Rebecca that Uriel would have borne that scent too.

Her nerves leapt again at a sound outside the window.

Instantly all her energy was focused on listening. She froze, eyes straining, shoulders tense, breath held, and – *there,* another scrape and then another, like footsteps on the loose shingle beyond the curtained window.

Rebecca swallowed. Not *like* footsteps: definitely footsteps. They were retreating now, but they had begun sharp and loud, close by.

Someone had been standing outside her bedroom. Someone had crossed the car park and trodden the narrow path through the neglected shrub beds to the cottage, ignoring the prominent sign saying *Private – No Admittance.* He must have followed the wall, ducking under the low branches of the bare trees, until he came to the back of the cottage, where the windows of the small rooms were all in a row: the bathroom, the back parlour, and the bedroom.

And he had stopped at the bedroom.

All her life Rebecca had slept upstairs: in her stepfather's farmhouse, in the tiny flat at the top of Aunty Edie's, in the first floor apartment she had taken over from Michael, and now in her beautiful Skye house. Hotels and bed-and-breakfasts and Steph's shared house in Oxford: all upstairs. She had never given serious thought to break-ins, but supposed on an upper floor one would at least have a few moments to act while a burglar was climbing the staircase.

Sleeping on the ground floor gave an immediacy to matters which was deeply alarming. Someone had stood less than five feet from her bed, separated from her only by a single pane of very old glass and a fold of curtain.

There was silence now. Moving smoothly and carefully, Rebecca swung her legs over the side and stood up. She travelled light and had no robe, but her coat was on the stand in the passage and she put that on.

She listened intently at the door to the parlour, her ear against the cold wood, her eyes downcast while she concentrated. But there was nothing, and she was certain she would know if he had broken in. She would have heard if glass had shattered.

Rebecca opened the door softly, and then hesitated. Turn right towards the kitchen or left towards the hearth?

Left. It might be a cliché, but Rebecca could imagine herself taking a good swing with an iron poker; jabbing a carving knife into living flesh, even flesh that was invading her territory, seemed much less possible.

Armed with the poker, she retreated to the passageway that ran the length of the cottage and stood, poised and intent, ready to attack in any direction should she hear sounds of entry.

In the shadows of the orchard, a man who could see by starlight and could walk when he chose as silently as a lynx, looked back the way he had come. There was no light in the cottage, but he sensed with sureness the fear of the woman inside, in the dark, waiting.

He smiled.

Then he turned and took the footpath past the orchards towards the village.

Rebecca woke late, a slice of daylight probing its way between the curtains.

Eight fifteen. Bother. She preferred to rise much earlier; lying in was such a waste of time.

The poker was on top of the covers. She had gone back to bed, jittery and shivering and with feet like ice, after fifteen minutes of silence convinced her that the prowler had left; but she had taken the poker with her, just in case.

She would talk to Bridget Dixon about this.

After a hurried breakfast, Rebecca slipped into her coat, opened the door, and stopped dead.

On the path, six feet from the step – perhaps to give her a chance to avoid tripping over it – was the cloche. It was frosted over and its contents, if any, were invisible.

Of course it had contents.

Slowly, Rebecca stepped forward and reached down. She grasped the handle and lifted the dome. Underneath, on the damp shingle, lay a postcard with the picture of a dry stone wall taken in close-up, the frame filled with shades of charcoal, blue-grey and white. Curling delicately on top of it lay a tendril of ivy with glossy, heart-shaped leaves.

Chapter Eight

'*Very* easy to befuddle,' Peregrine said with satisfaction.

'*Not* the sharpest pencil in the tin,' added the Vulture.

Professor Lloyd, the Tortoise, hummed pleasantly at the ceiling, swinging his foot.

Connor sighed. The estate agent – ex-estate agent now, apparently – was an irritating man. He was given to smirking, and seemed to think it a good idea to deploy oily charm on anyone from whom he wanted something, when it really wasn't. Connor read him as self-centred and carrying a substantial chip on his shoulder.

But he wasn't evil. It was undeniable that he had helped them locate the gap at Ashendon and, later, had steered them towards the one on Skye. Michael had trusted him enough to leave him caretaking the cottage in his absence. He really wasn't all bad.

He was an Oxford man, too; he'd been at Gloucester College, where Rebecca's friend Steph had been studying back when he and Rebecca had first come together to follow the unlikely trail. He had been so green then, so ignorant, utterly in awe of the golden college buildings and the laughing, fearless undergraduates, and had fallen instantly, helplessly, under Oxford's spell. It had all seemed like a glorious, tantalising dream.

It was still glorious but Oxford had not been a dream for a year and a half; it was real, now.

He hardly ever left the city, even during the long summer vac. Walking to the station now, Connor realised that it was probably the least familiar stretch of road in the whole of Oxford.

Well…she had said please, which was always hard for her; easier than a few years ago, but still hard. It seemed curious to Connor that Rebecca could use all the right words when handling business and yet struggled, even in her mid-twenties, to deal with her friends the same way. It was an aspect of her that intrigued him. Was she afraid of seeming plaintive? Of revealing that she cared? Was she alarmed by the threat of being in moral debt – receiving favours but unwilling to perform any in return?

She wasn't the most gracious of women, in truth – beautiful, oh always beautiful, but prickly. He would never forget what she had said that December, at dawn, at the foot of the Quiraing. He had never guessed it was coming, not for an instant.

So here he was, leaving Oxford to spend a day in London searching, as they both had searched years ago, the collection at the Victoria and Albert Museum.

The great arched opening to the new Medieval and Renaissance Galleries beckoned him when he entered the V&A from Exhibition Road, and he promised himself a swift look before he left, whether he found what Rebecca wanted or not. Then he climbed the marble staircase to the clean black-and-white of the Ironwork Gallery where it had all begun, and turned right.

Rebecca drove, her mind teeming – probably not a safe condition to be in. Around Stockport she turned the radio on and tried to get involved in a discussion about the migration patterns of geese, but it was a struggle.

The pirate was Spanish.

Bridget Dixon had relented in view of the circumstances, not wishing the hotel to seem to be harbouring stalkers. His name was Guillermo Garcia – Bridget pronounced it the Spanish way: *Wiyermo Garthia*, with the 'y' almost turning into a 'j'.

'But he spoke English?' Rebecca said.

'Oh yes. He had an accent, of course…or did he? I can't quite recall.'

'Did he *look* Spanish?'

'I'm not sure. I think he had dark hair.'

As a witness, Bridget Dixon was a disaster. Rebecca reined in her impatience. 'Age? Build? What did he dress like?'

'Oh, middling, I suppose.'

'Middling *what?* Weight? Age? You're not being much help!'

The manager shook her head. 'No. Sorry. I just can't bring him to mind. Dark hair, that's all. And dark clothes. I think.'

As Rebecca was about to leave, she added, 'There is something. Hard to describe, but he was, well, *watchful*.'

'Watchful? How?'

'Perhaps not watchful. Attentive? No.'

Rebecca waited while the manager struggled.

'It was as if he were paying attention all the time. Noticing. Only not in a noticeable way.'

'You noticed it,' Rebecca said.

'Well, yes.' The manager's gaze wandered in thought. 'I wonder if I was meant to...'

Meant to? The whole business looked bad. And then Bridget had snapped back into her usual efficiency: 'Will you report it to the police?' and Rebecca, caught stupidly off-guard, found herself saying, 'Perhaps. I...I think I'll leave it for now. After all, I'm off up to Scotland today, and you said he's on foot.'

'Arrived and departed on foot. He checked out after dinner. It did seem unusual, to set off walking after dark. He must have hung about in the grounds if he was around your cottage after midnight. How horrible. Poor you.'

Yes, poor me, Rebecca thought. She was annoyed that Bridget had not told her the note-leaver was still in residence when she first asked. For some reason Rebecca had assumed the man had left the note for her and gone.

The pirate.

The prowler. The Spanish prowler.

Her stalker.

Should she call the police? And say what? That someone had walked round her cottage one night and possibly – she couldn't prove it, after all – given her some postcards?

It was true the cottage was private property, but it was set in the grounds of a country hotel. It had been dark and the Private sign could have been missed. Perhaps he had been out for a midnight stroll and lost his way.

Like heck.

But she suspected there was little there to interest the police. The notes, while imperative, were hardly obscene.

Open Michael's box.

Remember Jack's tallixer.

Use Uriel's knife.

And now, *Wear Emily's necklace.*

But Emily had been dead for nearly a century, so where would her necklace be?

* * *

Connor moved slowly along the displays of precious and semi-precious stones and silver and gold without much optimism but giving it his best shot because that was what he had promised.

The Jewellery Gallery was dark, with black walls and floor, the objects displayed in lit cabinets as if on stage. Not just precious metals and diamonds, of course. There were pieces from the ancient world, Egypt and Alexandria and China, coral and turquoise and opals, and cowry shells from the Pacific Islands, and porcupine quills from North America. There were cameo brooches of exquisite detail, and lockets holding miniature portraits painted on ivory, and snuffboxes, pocket watches, signet rings and Victorian jet.

Was Emily's necklace made of jet?

Their best bet, only bet in fact, had been Emily Seward, the shadowy figure at the head of their family tree where all the lines came together – his, Rebecca's, and Michael's: Emily Seward, the sole female member of the society called Mundus Caecus, World Invisible, which had been formed in 1850 to make sure the way to Faerie would not be opened for a hundred years.

They had been more successful than they had dreamed.

Connor drifted, pausing at each display to relax the focus of his eyes and reach out with his mind in a way he did not understand and yet which had served them so well years ago. If an object had been planted here, on view to the public, in order to transmit an image to him over a century later, then he would – should – be able to receive it.

But there was nothing.

Rebecca would be on her way north by now. He sent her a text message: *Sorry, no good. Arrange to see stored collection?*

Then, duty done, he headed for the Medieval Court.

Chapter Nine

Rebecca broke her journey at her favourite bed-and-breakfast in Balloch at the tip of Loch Lomond, and slept brilliantly: no prowlers, no dreams, and no postcards.

She hiccupped slightly the next morning on catching sight of a scrap of white paper trapped beneath her windscreen wiper, but it was only a flyer advertising a ceilidh.

The day's drive to Skye was as contradictory as always. On the one hand, the scenery was so beautiful it twisted her heart; on the other, four hours of sharp bends and steep inclines was a strain. The distance from the top of Britain to the bottom was the only serious drawback about living on Skye.

Although that was contradictory too, for it was the island's remoteness that made it the community it was. With every mile north her spirits rose, and as she crossed the Skye Bridge from the Kyle of Lochalsh, Rebecca began to smile.

An hour and a half later she was home.

A slither of envelopes swept across the polished floorboards as she opened the door. She scooped them up to be dealt with later, and then, as at Ashendon Cottage, toured the house, switching on lights and turning up the heating. Unlike the cottage, here everything worked smoothly: water ran without gurgling, doors closed with a quiet *snick*, the blinds, when she chose to lower them, would run down softly.

But not yet; it was barely dusk. Rebecca stood in the prow of her studio, where the angled panes allowed her to look north and south as well as east, and drank in the landscape she loved – the row of hawthorn bordering her land, the tussocky moorland dropping to the lane a quarter of a mile distant, and beyond, the ceaseless, tireless sea.

I've found my place, Rebecca thought, *and I will never leave.*

But there was unpacking to be done.

Most of her clothes could be tipped straight into the laundry basket. Her sketchbooks and papers went into the studio. The carved box, Michael's box, she put in the studio too, but then picked it up again. It was unfinished business, and she feared the sight of it would distract her from working.

She tried it in her bedroom, but decided that would be tempting fate.

Finally she moved some books to make space for it on a shelf in the sitting room, where it looked ancient and uncomfortable beside her small television.

'Tough,' she said aloud. 'I didn't ask for you, and I don't know what I'm supposed to do with you now that I've opened you.'

Opened and put the Jack of Hearts inside – twice. The card she had inexplicably taken away from Matlock had been similar to the one from the modern Waddingtons deck at Ashendon which she had brought out to compare. It was the same design, just older and a little softer, less geometric, more elegant. She had found it in a box containing penny whistles and a tambourine, and had slipped it into her hip pocket without knowing why.

Now both cards, the old and the new, lay in the citrus-scented box in the dark, and Rebecca went to make supper.

Geoffrey Foster left the onions softening in butter on the hob and fetched the bottle of Volnay; he'd have a glass while he was preparing the steak.

He was making boeuf bourguignon. A week of dining at the Randolph had refreshed his enthusiasm for cooking. He'd cook enough to freeze some.

The radio on the windowsill was tuned to the cricket – a summary of the day's play in The Ashes and England was performing well. Cheltenham was blue-skied and crisply cold, the skip had finally gone from in front of the house two doors up, and the Blu-Ray disks he had ordered had arrived in his absence. It was good to be back.

He opened his knife and sliced around the foil on the bottle, aware as he did so that his reflex had been to take this knife out of his pocket rather than use a kitchen knife from the drawer. Since when had that happened?

The knife handle felt comfortable to his hand, and he no longer thought of it as an antique, a piece of evidence, but as something personal to him.

My knife. That was how Uriel Passenger had referred to it in his journal, which was what had set Geoffrey on the trail to begin with.

Technically one might quibble over his possession of it. He hadn't asked permission to remove it from the storage unit. On the other hand, without his input they would never have located Ashendon House, and therefore not have inherited the estate, and had any reward come his way for that? Rebecca had, yes, given him one of Michael Seward's boxes after the man departed, but it had been done grudgingly, he suspected.

And it was only one old knife.

It was individual, quirky, quite unlike the Victorinox knife he used to carry, and he thought it would give him an air of style should anyone notice it.

The handle was deeply carved with curling vine stems, the cuts worn smooth with long use and the wood silvery except for the clean edge where he had had the sliver cut off. The blade, broad and deep, was engraved with the same pattern, interrupted where the two notches had been cut presumably some time later. He hadn't yet come up with a reason for those notches, rectangles a little deeper than they were wide, and it nagged at him from time to time.

But the edge was sharp, the hinge worked smoothly, and he enjoyed being in possession of an artefact from a world more strange and more distant than any archaeological site known to man.

Geoffrey poured himself a glass of the burgundy, then drew the chef's knife from the beech block and began to slice steak.

Rebecca spent most of her second day back working with a group of A-level art students at the High School in Portree. It seemed to have become an annual commitment, and it was one she enjoyed.

When she returned home she opened the front door to find an enormous cardboard box leaning against the wall with a note taped to it at eye level.

Rebecca read the note, then buttoned up her coat and walked

down the lane to her neighbour's white house. It took her six minutes. Neighbours in that part of Skye were not next-door in the sense that they were in London or Oxford.

Maggie opened the door before Rebecca reached it. Her kitchen window overlooked the drive and she must have seen Rebecca approach.

'Come in! Do you have time for a coffee?'

The Davenports were not native islanders but in-comers like herself; there were a lot of those on Skye. They had moved to the island from East Anglia when Colin's business designing websites took off and, also like Rebecca, built a house for working in as well as living in.

They were good neighbours, probably too much older than Rebecca to become close friends, but comfortable and reliable. She knew they'd always help if she needed it, and was happy to swap house keys with them in case of domestic emergencies or accidental lockouts.

The houses were not visible from one another, and in all honesty a flood or collapsed chimney was unlikely to be noticed, but still, it felt more secure.

Rebecca perched on the high stool in Maggie's contemporary, black-and-white kitchen, and said, 'I'm sorry about the delivery.'

'That's no trouble. I took the dogs for a walk.'

A footpath ran past Rebecca's house and on towards the Quiraing.

'Well, thanks anyway. I didn't know it was coming today.'

Rebecca didn't know it was coming at all, but that was not something to share. She accepted the mug of coffee from her neighbour. 'Which delivery company was it?'

Maggie shrugged. 'Don't know. It was an unmarked van. Grey.'

Avoiding Maggie's eyes, Rebecca mustered all her acting talents and asked, casually she hoped, 'What was the driver like?' She put down the hot mug and folded her arms to disguise the trembling.

'Oh, he was alright. I expect it happens a lot.'

'I don't mean his attitude. I just wondered, um, what he looked like.'

This was ridiculous. *Why* on earth would she wonder such a thing? Surely Maggie would smell a rat?

But maybe not. 'Oh, well…I don't know…youngish, I suppose.' Maggie leaned back against the counter. 'He had a black coat, I think.'

'Black hair?'

'Maybe. I think so, yes.'

'Spanish accent?'

'Good grief, no! Scots, of course. Why?'

'Oh, no reason. I just…nothing.' Rebecca looked up and said brightly, 'How was Hogmanay?'

So the driver was not her stalker because he had a Scottish accent and not a Spanish one. Although he had left a similar impression with Maggie as with Bridget: maybe youngish, middling-everything, probably dark. Hardly helpful.

'I can't remember,' both women had said.

There had been nothing at all *not* noticeable about the pirate. Rebecca's heart clunked as the memory of the jolt leapt into her mind and she saw again his wild face, his eyes daring her as he met her gaze. He had been so *live*, in the way that electric current is live. It couldn't be the same man, surely?

He is, though.

He was, and she knew it. She would have laid money on it, and she was not a gambler in any way.

A pirate, a hiker, a delivery man; Scottish, Spanish, and it had seemed to her a very accurate copy of an actor's rendition of English.

So he could be anything.

Rebecca stared at the parcel. It was huge – taller than herself and over a metre wide. The cardboard was marked 'Medici Glass', and the tape sticking the delivery note to the front had printed on it the name of an Edinburgh department store.

It was pointless to put it off. Rebecca fetched her Stanley knife and sliced through the cardboard.

Chapter Ten

The Medieval Galleries were beautiful. The V&A had opened up a vast section of floor to accommodate objects as diverse as stained glass windows and staircases. Connor wandered the cool, echoing spaces between icons and statues and gold candlesticks so elaborate they were sculptures in their own right. There were gargoyles and chalices and even the entire front of a three-storey timber town house. Astonishing.

The V&A had been one of his haunts as a boy. It was peaceful, sumptuous, and free. He had met Michael here, and later had trawled the passages and halls with Rebecca, searching.

Had he not discovered this place his life would have been utterly other.

Connor paused to look closely at a twelfth-century casket of copper and enamel the blue of lapis lazuli, displayed in a cabinet in the open floor so that you could see all the way round.

Not inside, though. Was it lined with velvet or silk? Divided into compartments? Probably it was bare wood and deemed dull, but it would have been nice to know.

Connor moved on. There were several boxes and chests, including one of carved ivory decorated with a pattern of ivy, and another of heavy, worn wood.

All closed.

Connor thought about the box he had chosen for himself from Michael's studio, caramel-coloured maple with a pattern of grain like water flowing. In common with most of Michael's boxes, it contained two trays of small compartments for jewellery. Connor didn't imagine himself ever having a use for these, but he kept his passport and a few precious papers in the shallow space beneath. If anyone were to lift the lid they might assume the box to be empty.

An empty box with something inside…

Connor stood still, and although his eyes remained on the exhibits, his thoughts were suddenly far away.

A pirate, a hiker, and a delivery driver…except that he almost certainly wasn't a delivery driver.

Rebecca had rung the department store and given the reference on the delivery note. The only name on their records was her own as the recipient; the mirror had been bought with cash.

'Not by me,' Rebecca said.

'What a lovely gift!' the despatch clerk replied.

Huh.

After a bout of her very best wheedling, she succeeded in talking to someone in the depot who managed the drivers, and even persuaded him to check the register for her. 'Aye, here it is,' he said, more Glasgow than Edinburgh to Rebecca's ear. 'Liam. Your driver was Liam.'

'Liam what?'

'Ahm…' Rebecca listened to the doubt begin to edge its way in, as she knew it would. 'I'm not sure…He was a temp, you know? Just came in that day…'

'And you hired him without getting his full name?'

'No! Well…aye…ahm…'

Rebecca said, 'Do you remember what he looked like?'

A little swagger of confidence. 'Of course! He was, oh, well, maybe middle-ish tall, about average I suppose, and…let me see …couldn't rightly say how old…'

'Hair?'

'Not quite sure…Was he maybe wearing a cap, now…'

Useless.

Rebecca glowered down the hall at the mirror leaning against the wall, tatters of cardboard and bubblewrap about its base. It was huge and too heavy for her to move alone; she'd have to ask Colin to help shift it.

She had to admit it was rather lovely. The glass was six foot by four and held in a simple, undecorated frame of polished wood, maple according to the delivery note. It was freestanding, with a pair of sturdy feet, so at least it wouldn't need mounting.

Rebecca had an uneasy relationship with mirrors, and at first she had felt trepidation every time she passed it, but so far it had done nothing a mirror shouldn't and she was gaining confidence. She had even looked properly into it, and suspected it flattered her a little.

Her hair was really very long these days.

Connor had drawn a blank at the V&A, which was disappointing, but she had known it was a long shot. It was generous of him to have gone, but that was how Connor was.

He had returned with some ideas, though. First, the necklace.

'If there was a picture of Emily Seward it might include the necklace. Portraits were a big thing back then – you dressed up for them.'

Rebecca grunted. She had already thought of that and before leaving Ashendon had turned the cottage upside down – for the third time – in search of that very thing, including opening every single book on the shelves and fluttering the pages upside down, hoping each time for something to tumble out. A few things had, including a Victorian Christmas card edged with lace, a ticket for Wimbledon dated 1952, and a faded supermarket receipt with the handwritten note *Try Colgate?*, but the only photograph was of a steam locomotive emerging from under a bridge.

She had then called Aunty Edie, who watched over the official repository of family paraphernalia. *There were some Seward cousins,* her great-aunt had said, '*but I don't recall an Emily.*' Still, she promised to look through the drawers of photographs, those in albums and all the loose ones, and send on anything promising.

That would probably take a month.

'It would help if we knew what the wretched thing looked like, or even what it was made from,' Rebecca moaned, stating the obvious because she knew Connor wouldn't and she felt a need to dwell on the unfairness of everything.

After failing to find the necklace, Connor had treated himself to the Medieval Galleries and been struck with inspiration about the box business.

'Might it have a secret compartment?'

'There's no room,' Rebecca said. She had thought of that too, and had peered and tapped and measured, but the box was a simple cube made from wood half an inch thick. There was simply no margin for a hidden section.

'It might be very shallow though,' Connor said. 'Even a millimetre would be enough to take a sheet of paper, for instance.'

Rebecca thought about it.

Maybe.

'There isn't any mechanism though,' she said. 'Believe me, I have looked!'

'Yes. Well. That is a point.'

Rebecca sighed. 'I'll look again. No ideas about Uriel's knife, I suppose?'

'Sorry.'

'Hmm.'

She wasn't doing well so far, with only one object found out of three and even that one not accessed. Out there someone was keeping score, and she didn't know why.

'Connor?'

'Yes?'

'Nobody seems able to describe this guy, or even remember him clearly. Is this something you recognise?'

She waited. Connor had lived in the World Invisible and had experience of things she could only guess about. She knew he did not like to dwell on the past, but surely, given the position she was in, she could ask?

'Yes.' His voice sounded flat. 'My guess is that he's using Skill. Confusing people. Melting into the background.'

Melting into the background was hardly the way she remembered him on New Year's Day. His presence had practically leapt out and clubbed her.

'But that's you,' Connor said, cryptically, and refused to say more.

Colin Davenport turned up late in the afternoon and together they lifted the giant mirror up the stairs and into Rebecca's bedroom. Rebecca wrapped it in a quilt first and the feat was managed without chipping the frame or the walls.

There was only one feasible position for it, and now reflections rebounded to and fro between it and the small mirror over the chest of drawers. Rooms led into rooms which led into more rooms, and sometimes all of Rebecca could be seen and sometimes only part of her, often from the side or behind. It was dizzying. Rebecca decided she'd give herself a day or two and then, if she couldn't acclimatise, would neutralise the new mirror by draping a blanket over it.

It was disconcerting to see herself, naked, repeated in the tunnel of reflections as she prepared for bed.

She dropped her small items of jewellery into Michael's box – the one he had made, that was – and thought again about Connor's suggestion. She too kept a few papers beneath the trays: a photograph of her mother, long dead; her passport; and the haunting playing card of the Queen of Clubs – or rather, the Queen of Clover – that had come from another land. It was hand-painted in colours of the earth and the sea, and once, distressingly, it had seemed to Rebecca to move and speak to her.

Not for a few years, though. Thank goodness.

Rebecca's thoughts jumped sideways to the Victorian Jack of Hearts lying in the carved box in the sitting room.

She wasn't putting the two cards together, that was for sure.

Who knew what they might get up to.

Chapter Eleven

Rebecca dreamed that night, of the wood and the castle and the cold, labyrinthine passages. When she reached the throne room the curtain against the far wall was bulging and the hem shivered as the something, the someone, behind it stirred.

This time, Rebecca thought, willing herself forward, determined not to wake, *this time I will pull it aside...*

The hall was chill; her breath smoked. There came a sound, a mutter, the hush of surfaces scraping together. The curtain inched aside and a long vertical slit revealed darkness and a shadow of something even darker...

And then, all of a sudden, she felt herself being pulled away, which had never happened before, and she shouted resistance–

–but woke, fighting, in her own bed.

She was sitting up, and panting. She took a deep breath. Not nice.

And then she heard it, the sound that had caused her to wake: the crunch of gravel.

Under feet.

New, pale grey gravel was laid all around her house; the architect had recommended it: attractive, easy to maintain, and a deterrent to burglars. Not that there were many of those on Skye, where the crime rate was practically non-existent. Nevertheless it was impossible to move on gravel of any depth without making a noise. Rebecca always heard the post van arrive no matter which room she was in.

So even he couldn't silence the stones.

Fear rattled in her. She had lived alone for years and had never been a scaredy girl, and suddenly she was incensed by his working this effect on her, draining her confidence and turning her into some kind of idiot, afraid in her own home. How *dare* he?

Rebecca got out of bed. Her breathing was too fast and her hands shook, but she ignored that.

I will not stand for this. I will not.

She groped for her clothes and pulled them on, fumbling, and went downstairs, gripping the banister for safety, aware she was trembling.

Boots and coat on. Torch from the kitchen.
I will not. I will not.
Poker from the sitting room. She knew what to do this time, and she'd be damned if it involved waiting.

Heart thumping, she paused, listening, her ear against the panel of the front door. The gravel was still. Was he there too, motionless and watching? Or had he gone?

There was no way she could turn the latch silently; go for speed then.

Rebecca flexed her fingers around the poker and took a deep breath. Then she jerked open the door and charged.

High on the hillside, a man who could become little more than a shadow if he wished widened his eyes and laughed, once, short, like the bark of a fox. Then he fell silent.

He hadn't expected it. And he loved to be surprised.

He watched, eyes narrowed, focused and intent.

Rebecca ran right round the house once and then turned and ran round again the other way, poker raised, torch beam swooping.

There was no-one, nothing. He had gone.
Too slow getting dressed.
But it was hard to attack in pyjamas.

Exertion and noise had made her confident. She toured the outside once more, walking this time, swinging the poker and clearing her throat. It was her property, her territory, and she would make as much sound as she liked.

The third time she reached the door she knew the decision that lay, heavy and unyielding, before her, but was not quite ready to make it.

She stared towards the sea, weighing the matter in her mind.

Above the house, the man rose swiftly to his feet.

He had watched her think, first gazing east, tapping the fire iron against her leg, and then with head bent, her eyes covered by her hand. And then he had watched her act, and his pulse quickened.

In the moonlight he saw her leave the shelter of her house and venture along the track he had recently trodden, between the gorse and the hawthorn, until she reached the pile of stones and rafters that once had made something like a hut; something like a small cow byre, but not for cows. She went right up to the remaining walls, and then stepped carefully over the heaped rubble at one end, torchlight guiding her feet, to lay her hands flat against the monolith planted on the earth floor.

Thorns, he knew, grew around the rock. It had not moved for years.

He watched, rapt, as she circled the monolith, and then picked her way out of the ruins and looked up the hillside towards him. He almost held his breath.

But then she made her way back, her torch directed away now, and in due course a light came on behind one of the windows. She would make herself something to drink. She would be wide-awake now and far from sleep.

He smiled with one side of his face only.

Chapter Twelve

Rebecca had a handy little app on her phone which gave her the times of sunrise and sunset. She had downloaded it for fun because she rarely needed it, but it was useful now.

Sunrise would be just before nine; it would begin to turn light perhaps an hour earlier.

By half past seven Rebecca was at the hut, doing her best not to remember how she had waited there once before, hoping for the impossible as night merged into day.

Nothing to hope for this time. This time she was just checking.

Cold, though. Rebecca stamped her feet and flapped her arms, and then put her hands back in her pockets. Her gloved fingers felt the crisp edge of the postcard.

It was one of her own, printed up for promotional purposes. It showed one of her embroidered silk panels, a detail highlighting the texture of the stitches. Her website and phone number were printed in one corner on the reverse, leaving plenty of space for a message, so she had written it large using a broad-nibbed calligraphy pen and spiky, assertive letters.

No sign of day yet.

How much did he know?

Probably everything.

In which case, was he watching her now? Waiting in the open, above her on the mountain, to see what she would do? He had flushed her out, but she was resolute that she would not run.

Almost resolute.

Rebecca had switched off her torch when she reached the hut to save the batteries, but had no doubt he could see in the dark anyway.

Beyond the horizon, where the sea would be moving, the sky was edging towards dawn. Not much longer to wait.

I'll have eggs for breakfast.

Shapes took form out of the dark, trees and the hillside and the broken walls of the hut. A breeze ruffled Rebecca's hair, and somewhere a small animal cried. There were clouds overhead, and Rebecca realised that the moment of half-light had passed and day had arrived, and the monolith behind the rubble had not moved.

She took a long breath; her hands were trembling.

The postcard.

Not needing the torch now, Rebecca clambered between the rocks, scouring the site for a good place. She wanted it to stay dry and she didn't have a cloche.

The best she could find was a slit between the stones of the soundest wall and she propped it there, an inch or two projecting, a flash of peacock and lime against the granite. Then, without a backward glance, she walked home to breakfast.

Nobody had been more surprised than herself when Rebecca fell in love with Skye. She had considered herself a city-dweller and proud of it; relished the busy-ness, the convenience of twenty-four/seven open hours, and most of all the cornucopia of museums and galleries within easy reach.

But the island had possessed her from the day she set foot on it; everything about it, from the landscape of seashores and snow-sifted mountains to the solitude, the sheep, and the damp, misty weather. Skye touched her somewhere deep inside where almost nothing else ever had, and immersing herself in the wild landscape, unaltered for centuries, was the best medicine for her soul that she knew.

So after breakfast, she put on her walking gear and set out for the Quiraing.

She needed to take stock, and walking was as good a way as any. Rebecca had discovered that although it didn't help her to think, it did clear her mind of accumulated rubbish so that when she stopped, she could concentrate on what mattered. And anyway, she loved it.

She had become much fitter. She rambled about on the hills for an hour or more most days, and the gradient and rough terrain had honed her balance and judgement. She could climb without getting puffed and skip down afterwards, stepping from boulder to boulder without putting a foot wrong. It was exhilarating.

There was a hollow in the rock formation known as The Prison where, reputedly, medieval clansmen had corralled their cattle to keep them safe from raiders. It was grassy and gentle, and a favourite picnic spot for tourists, although not usually in January.

Rebecca found her preferred seat, a more or less flat slab of stone, and gazed back down the slope she had just climbed. Far below was the tumbledown hut with the monolith inside and, beyond, the roof tiles of her house.

She and Connor had stood here the day they discovered the hut. She had drawn it back in London with no knowledge of it at all.

Drawing had been at the root of everything.

She had been drawing at the V&A the day she met Michael, who had been drawing too. She had lost track of time and discovered, on snapping back to the present, that her sketchbook had been overrun with images of vines.

It was the first hint of what was to come; the first inkling.

Since that afternoon it seemed to Rebecca her life had never truly been her own. Oh, she could control the little things, of course; she could decide where to go and who to meet and what to do. But the arc of her existence was drawn by a thread, and the thread would not let her go. Memories haunted her of matters she could never speak about except to Michael and Connor, less on account of secrecy than for the fear of being thought insane.

And Michael had gone now, so only Connor was left, submerged in university life in Oxford, making up for lost time.

It was hard knowing what she knew, while the BBC made documentaries on wacky theories about time travel and altered states of existence, and the bookshop in Portree filled its window with paperbacks and picture books about the island's fairy legends.

Rebecca was naturally sceptical, and it had taken physical proof of the most dramatic kind before she had truly started to believe that there could be another world, invisible to us, and that it was possible, sometimes, to move between the two. The idea terrified her, always had, and she knew with granite-like certainty that she would never try it.

But Connor had, and come back. And Michael had, and stayed.

Beyond her house was the sea. On a day like today, misty and moist, it was scarcely visible, a soft-focus line beneath the low cloud drawn with chalk and smudged with a finger, but Rebecca felt its presence, ever moving, never changing, waves reaching across the pebbles and drawing back every few seconds as they had for millions of years.

Millions of years of seconds.

I am *now,* in this second, Rebecca thought; and now again; and now. In this second, and now this one, I am sitting on the mountainside, and I assume that soon I will stand up and leave. But I don't know when. And I don't know what will happen next.

More seconds passing. There was a small rustle away to the right where some minor creature moved, encouraged by her stillness.

Her backside was becoming numb.

Was the prowler, the pirate, what she suspected? It was difficult to find another solution. But what did he want?

Another rustle. Rebecca glanced round, but could see only the vertical rock walls of the Prison, and the silent grasses, and the sky.

There was an itch between her shoulders she would never be able to reach through the layers, and her seat was definitely uncomfortable now. She stood up and shook out her legs, got the blood flowing. She had work to do, and after that she'd have another look at that box in case Connor was right.

At the hut she clambered over the rubble and stood inside. There was enough light to see, but even so Rebecca checked with her fingers.

The card had gone.

Guillermo, Liam, Gwilym, Billy, Will sat on the flat rock and breathed the sky. He could smell grass and rabbit droppings and, more distantly, sheep, and over them all, the salt of the sea. Birds were calling, but so far off even he couldn't see them. The air fed his skin. It was plain why she was here.

He watched her, ant-like far below, enter the barn and emerge again, and then disappear behind the shrubs to her house. He smiled.

The card was in his breast pocket. He drew it out and looked again at the angry, demanding letters.

WHY?

Not yet, Rebecca, not yet.
But with every day that passed he became more sure she was the one he was seeking.

Chapter Thirteen

Geoffrey Foster looked at the risotto congealing, glue-like, on the plate. The boy had called while he was eating, admittedly rather late, and it had been a long conversation. He could microwave it, he supposed...

It went down the waste disposal unit and he ground some coffee. Coffee was good for thinking.

The boy had been surprisingly easy to talk with.

Hardly a boy, now, of course, but Geoffrey had thought of him that way, if he thought of him at all, for too long to change.

Connor. Call him Connor.

Connor said he had called to apologise.

'Apologise?'

'For the Dons. Professor Peregrine and Professor Viator and Professor Lloyd. Especially Professor Lloyd.'

The shrunken, reptilian one, with the beady stare. The one Geoffrey had suspected of laughing at him secretly all through the interview.

They had got the wrong end of the stick, Connor told him. They had not understood the extent of Geoffrey's knowledge or the nature of his involvement, and had naturally wanted to head him off.

Naturally.

But they had been mischievous and naughty and should not have wasted his time.

Geoffrey's hackles lay down a little. He took the phone into the sitting room and put his feet up. 'So how's life? You're at Cardinal's, are you?' he asked. One generally had to invest in a little chitchat before people opened up.

They had talked for nearly half an hour, and though Geoffrey was unable to coax Connor into speaking about his experience in that other place (and Geoffrey didn't mean Cambridge), the boy was unexpectedly forthcoming about the gaps and where they were. One in Vermont, apparently, and one slap bang on the river at Oxford of all places, right opposite the college boathouses.

Lewis Carroll had come into it too; it seemed the rabbit hole idea had not been entirely original.

The boy had also listened politely while Geoffrey expounded about the physics aspect, although it was unlikely he understood much. It was pretty esoteric stuff.

By the time the call finished Geoffrey felt as though he had been conversing with a colleague.

In the bottom drawer of his desk in the study lay a stack of playing cards bundled together in an elastic band. They had drifted into Foster's thoughts while he was talking, and when he finished he went to fetch them.

They were not a deck of cards but individuals from many different decks, most of them very old. He had found them amongst Uriel Passenger's peculiar collection of antiques and tat that Michael Seward had put in storage, and for some reason – he wasn't quite sure why – he had removed them and kept them.

He had been a little uneasy about it at the time; this conversation with Connor had made it worse.

He took off the elastic band and flipped through the cards. Every one was the Queen of Clubs, and the styles and colours flashed by like a simple animation: classical Grecian robes, nineteen-twenties gowns, Art Deco and a few novelty designs as well as the most common Tudor garb. He couldn't imagine them having any value.

But he had never admitted to taking them. Truth was he had never admitted to going to the storage unit at all. It had always surprised him that Michael Seward had allowed him access so readily; he had put it down to the man's obvious depression at the time, and congratulated himself on his own good luck.

He supposed he ought to feel bad about that knife, too, but somehow that had become his in a way these cards had not.

On impulse, Geoffrey tore out a sheet of notepaper and began to write.

No more cards had appeared. For three days Rebecca's skin had prickled. Her eyes were constantly looking, checking, her mouth dry, her heartbeat fast, but nothing; not even one saying *Why not?*

The mirror remained a mirror. There were no footsteps at

night, or at least none that woke her, and she did not dream. But it was difficult to work. Her breathing tightened when she picked up pencil or pen, or even charcoal, that loosest of media. So far there had been no unsettling absences, no loss of control, but she observed a new sinuousness to her drawing that was not intentional. These days, when she looked at her sketchbooks, she frowned.

Walking was about the only time her muscles really loosened up, and she ventured farther each day, striding vigorously, drinking the cold air, going high where she had to clamber with her hands on the rocks, and all the time memorising the views as if she needed to learn them and keep them safe in her soul. The mild, moist weather had moved on, opening the door for a cold front, and snow was promised – less frequent on Skye, with its island microclimate, than one might expect.

Coming back down on the fourth day, tired and refreshed, she reached her door at the same time as the postman.

'Hi!'

'Hallo there! Been for a walk?' Roddy was a cheerful, weathered guy in his fifties who wore shorts eleven months out of twelve. He handed her the small bundle of mail in an elastic band.

'Thanks. Yes. Heavy skies though.' Rebecca riffled through the envelopes, checking postmarks.

'Aye, well, snow's on the way.' The postman paused as he opened the door of his van. 'Oh, and Will says Hi.'

Rebecca, distracted by the mail, said vaguely, 'Will?'

'Will. Your man. Said to tell you. Cheers!'

Rebecca's head snapped up. 'What? *Who?*'

But the door had slammed and Roddy had started the engine. Rebecca stood frozen on the step as the van disappeared down the drive.

The mail consisted of a bank statement, a catalogue of art materials, and two padded envelopes, one of them addressed to her in Aunty Edie's hand and with *Please Do Not Bend!* written above the address. That was quick!

Rebecca did not recognise the handwriting on the smaller

envelope. She flipped it over but found no return address; the postmark was Cheltenham. Rebecca didn't know anyone in Cheltenham. She bit her lip.

Hold on.

Her heart was still clunking from the postman's parting words. She put the kettle on first and made very strong tea, and then took the mail to the sitting room to open.

Mystery package first. She slit the top, and upended it. A pack of cards dropped out, and a sheet of notepaper.

Rebecca,
Returning these cards to you in case they are of interest. They came out of the Ashendon collection.
Kind regards,
Geoffrey Foster

What did he mean by "came out of the Ashendon collection"? He made it sound as if they had fallen unaccountably into his lap.

Rebecca picked up the pack of cards, held together by an elastic band, and turned it face up. The top card was the Queen of Clubs, an earlier version of the modern Tudor design, and softer, less geometric. Her eyes met Rebecca's.

Slowly Rebecca brought in her left hand and tipped the top of the card towards her. The next card was the Queen of Clubs too.

Rebecca freed the cards from the elastic band and fanned them out. A spread of Queens from what looked like a vast range of nationalities and periods stared back at her, all of them blank-eyed and implacable, all of them overshadowed by the symbol of the Club, which always looked so much more like a cloverleaf than a weapon.

Well, of course. Although why on earth Geoffrey Foster had taken them was beyond her imagining.

Will says Hi.

She didn't want to see these cards.

Across the room sat the carved box that she had to open, even though she had already opened and shut it dozens of times. Rebecca scraped the Queens back into a stack and dropped them into the box on top of the Jack of Hearts, who was still avoiding her gaze.

Let them swamp him.

She closed the lid and ran her thumb over the lock plate, smooth beside the rough, carved wood...although not entirely smooth. The metal was engraved with the name of the lock maker, scrolling letters with elaborate curlicues: *Sheriton and Son.* The name had been bothering her and she didn't know why.

Aunty Edie's letter was much longer, and Rebecca skimmed through, reading what was relevant and saving the rest for later. There were three photographs folded inside, all of them curved and brittle with age.

The smallest was a group: an old woman in a heavy dress seated on a wooden chair, and a younger man standing behind her. He wore a dark suit buttoned high, and rested one hand on the back of the chair. There were flowers in a vase on a small table to the side.

According to Aunty Edie's letter, this was Emily Seward with her son, Gabriel, photographed in 1912. Gabriel, Rebecca knew, had been Michael's grandfather.

The middle photograph was clearer, cleaner, showing a slim woman wearing a blouse and wide-legged trousers, leaning artfully alongside a nineteen-thirties car – the kind you'd instinctively want to call a *motor*car. The door of the car was open, and her arm was draped along the top. Her dark hair was drawn back, and she was not smiling so much as laughing, Rebecca thought.

This was Cicely, Emily's granddaughter, the fun-loving, wilful girl who had travelled the world and then come home to be killed working in a soup kitchen in the Blitz. *I know you asked for Emily,* Rebecca's aunt had written, *but you ought to have a picture of Cicely too, and this is my favourite.*

The largest photograph was almost A4 in size: a studio portrait of a woman in the high-necked, high-waisted bodice of the nineteenth century; eighteen-sixties or seventies, Rebecca guessed. The focus was soft, making her centre-parted hair cloudy and her eyes dreamy, but even so the gaze was direct. The woman had chosen not to turn her eyes elegantly away but to look into the camera lens straight.

Had the photographer argued with her? Had he been

uncomfortable? This was Emily, Rebecca felt sure, although her aunt had written cautiously: *I cannot tell you for certain, but if it is not Emily Seward then I don't know who it is.*

Rebecca met the steady stare. The woman was, perhaps, forty? It was difficult to gauge. She was not a beauty, but she was attractive.

Are you Emily? Rebecca thought. Did you meet a fairy man and fall in love with him?

The woman in the photograph would never speak. Rebecca sighed. From a practical point of view the photograph was useless: no jewellery was being worn apart from a cameo brooch at the throat. She was as far from finding Emily's necklace as ever.

Chapter Fourteen

Rebecca rang all the auction houses and dealers of period jewellery she could find on the Web and, depending on the outfit, they were either aloof, sympathetic or brisk, but the result was always the same: nobody had heard of Emily Seward's necklace.

However, she did manage to place the locksmiths, Sheriton and Son. Problem was that they weren't locksmiths at all but clockmakers; she had recognised the name from a carriage clock that had become significant years ago when she first met Michael.

Why would a clockmaker branch out into locks?

She set the box down on the kitchen table and unlocked it. She raised the lid and watched the mechanism move as she turned the key.

It wasn't even that smooth; there was a glitchy point part way through, where the rods that had to slide apart seemed to stick for a moment before moving on.

Rebecca folded her arms and thought.

The library was hosting a story-reading session in the children's corner and Rebecca came across young mothers in the book stacks who had escaped; lots of potential for barked ankles on empty buggies.

She had called first to enquire about books on locks and the staff had put a couple under the counter for her, but since she was here she might as well change her fiction at the same time. She carefully skirted a sleeping baby in a pushchair and smiled at the mother, wearing tartan leggings and looking like a kid. It seemed incredible to Rebecca that someone younger than herself could already have children – terrifying, in fact. But she had turned twenty-five in October and was forced to admit it was possible.

She was reaching for a new book by one of her preferred authors when someone close by said, 'Good.'

A man's voice, not a woman's. Rebecca glanced up, but saw only the child-mother, who caught her eye. Rebecca said, 'Did you say something?'

'No. It was that guy.'

'That guy?'

'The one that was here just now.'

Rebecca walked quickly round the end of the shelves and scanned the room. There were a couple of pensioners, no-one else. She walked along the wall, glancing between the stacks: no guy.

He had sounded so close.

Rebecca twitched her shoulders to ease a prickle and returned to her place. It had been just some guy talking to himself.

Do I believe that?

Probably not.

She selected her remaining books in haste, choosing not to analyse why, and dumped the pile on the counter to be scanned. The assistant handed her card back and said, 'Oh, there's a message for you, Miss Mulligan.'

Rebecca froze. She became acutely conscious of her skin inside her clothes, and of the way her ribs rose and fell as her breath went in and out.

The woman located the note and read aloud: 'It's from Will. He said he was in a hurry but to tell you, good.'

'Good?'

'Yes, that's all it says.'

Rebecca said carefully, 'When was this left?'

'Five minutes ago or so. He said he didn't have time to go back and find you.'

'What did he look like?'

Rebecca watched the curtain fall. 'Er...I can't really...dark hair, I think...'

'It doesn't matter.'

It did, but it couldn't be helped. Rebecca shoved the books into her bag and headed for the car park. He wasn't a prowler any more but a stalker, and she had enough now to take to the police; but she knew she wouldn't.

Precisely what about her doings at the library was good? She doubted strongly that it was her choice of fiction.

Rebecca slogged her way through the books on lock manufacture, getting bits here and there, missing quite a lot more.

It would all have made more sense, she thought, had she physical components in front of her, but theory by itself was a struggle.

Apparently locks could be made to have a double function, although usually that was pretty obvious and made them clunky affairs. But if a clockmaker were to attempt such a thing…

The mirror must have been delivered to her for a reason. With trepidation, Rebecca held the box up to the glass, turning it this way and that, holding the lid open so that the void inside could be seen, presenting the lock mechanism for reflection.

Enlightenment remained elusive. She put the cards back and considered. Then, with far more trepidation, she extracted the Victorian Jack of Hearts – or rather Knave of Hearts, as the corners were marked *Kn* – and turned it to face the mirror.

She held her breath. Once upon a time she had suffered a truly disturbing illusion this way which had resulted in her fainting for the first time in her life.

But apart from looking over his left shoulder instead of his right, the Jack was unaltered.

With relief, Rebecca let out her breath.

What remained? Emily's necklace and Uriel's knife.

She opened the carved box to drop the Jack of Hearts on top of the gaggle of Queens, and thought, *What was Geoffrey Foster doing in Matlock?*

He was washing his hands and it took him a few moments to get to his mobile. 'Foster.'

'Did you take a knife from the Ashendon stuff in Matlock?'

The question snapped out of the phone and out of the blue. Startled, Geoffrey Foster said, 'Yes. No.'

Too late, the damage was done.

'You did!'

Hellfire and damnation. 'Yes,' Geoffrey said, 'it is true, I did – take – a small pocket knife. I–'

'And the necklace?'

'Necklace!' Righteous indignation rose. 'I don't have anything other than the knife. Certainly no jewellery.'

Rebecca – it could only be her – said suspiciously, 'Really?

Did you see one when you were plundering the collection?'

'I wasn't plundering. I simply thought it would be sensible–'

'But did you see one?'

'–to have some idea of–'

'A necklace? *Any* necklaces?'

'No.'

There was a pause. Geoffrey cleared his throat. She had caught him on the hop and he had mismanaged the conversation so far, but he could try to claw back the situation.

'I had the wood from the knife handle radiocarbon dated,' he said.

'You did *what?*'

'I thought it would be useful. And it was.'

Rebecca grunted. 'So?'

She was still suspicious. Geoffrey said, 'They accused me of time wasting and fraud and threw me out.' That should defuse her, at least a bit; self-deprecation was a powerful weapon.

'Why?'

'First, they couldn't identify the species of wood. Second, the stuff had a higher concentration of Carbon 14 than could possibly be present in anything that wasn't already a fossil. Therefore I must have tampered with it.'

'Although you didn't.'

'Correct.'

Geoffrey waited, letting her think. Undeniably he was in the wrong, and bluster wouldn't help; but a little cool reflection on her part might.

Rebecca said, 'How much of the knife is left?'

'Oh, all of it. It only needed a sliver. Two millimetres.'

'And you've got it now?'

Foster slipped his hand into his pocket. 'Yes.'

Her next question surprised him.

'Describe it to me.'

Geoffrey brought out the knife and turned it over in his hand. 'It's simple enough. The blade folds into the handle. The handle is wood, grey wood, carved with a botanical design.' He heard a small snort from the phone. 'And the blade is short, curved. Decent edge to it actually. Engraved with the same pattern. And there are a couple of–'

'No name anywhere?'

'Name? No. There are–'

'Not *Sheriton and Son?*'

'No, no name at all. It has got–'

'It doesn't have a key hidden in the handle, I suppose?'

The girl was raving. 'No,' Foster said firmly. 'No key. Why? What do you want to unlock?'

But Rebecca was asking questions, not answering them, and she sounded exasperated. 'Is there anything at all unusual about it? Anything – I don't know – anything you can't see a reason for?'

And finally Geoffrey got his chance.

'Yes. The notches,' he said.

The wind had been escalating throughout the day and by dusk was booming and battering around Rebecca's house as if it were trying to dismantle it. She was reminded of a Ted Hughes poem she had always loved, and felt her house was indeed far out at sea, especially with that great glass prow of a window.

Then just as she was settling into a concert on Radio 3, there was a thump and everything went black.

By the dim light of her mobile phone, Rebecca lifted the hatch of the circuit breaker unit and found an orderly row of switches all pointing up. The fault was not with her.

A minute later Maggie Davenport rang. They were out too, and the Grahams farther up.

Candle time.

Rebecca went round with matches, setting thick, creamy church candles on the mantelpiece above the wood-burner and on the oak chest that had once served as a coffee table in Michael's London flat. The room became visible once more in the illumination of flames, which is always so different from even dimmed electric lamps. Pools of wavering light around the candles chased away soft shadows to huddle in the farthest corners. The low beat and crackle as the flames shuddered sounded intimate while the wind thrummed and sighed beyond the windows.

It was possible to read, but not really comfortable; besides, candlelight instils an atmosphere so unlike ordinary life, so redolent of times past and ways gone, that eventually Rebecca simply sat, her book open but ignored, and gave herself to her senses, her eyes and ears soaking up the strangeness.

Even the smell of the room had changed with the back-of-the-throat, honey scent of the molten wax. She became aware of herself becoming aware of herself: her existence, moment by moment, in the dark house, breathing in and breathing out, and waiting...

It was like leaving the business of life behind and falling slowly, slowly, down a long, dark, embracing tunnel...

The power did not return and Rebecca went to bed by the light of a slim white candle wedged firmly into a brass candlestick, which she stood on the tiled windowsill while she brushed her teeth and then set by her bed while she undressed. She was crossing the rug to put her watch on the chest of drawers when the gleam from the maple mirror caught her eye.

Seconds stopped. Motionless, Rebecca stared into the glass as if into a picture, and her reflected self, if it was herself, stared back; but not as Rebecca knew herself to be.

The reflection appeared not in jeans and sweater but in a dress – or rather, she thought, not a dress but a gown. It had a close-fitting bodice which shaped to a gentle point below the waist, and a full, flowing skirt to the ankles; the sleeves were puffed at the shoulders but then grew close and extended past the wrists, and the neckline echoed the waist, downward pointing, revealing her collarbones but not her cleavage.

It was, Rebecca thought, a beautiful dress and dark, dark blue: midnight on the lake. There was a gentle sheen highlighting the folds, suggesting velvet or silk. It seemed to her that she could feel the weight of the fabric at her shoulders and hips.

Her hair was loose, not plaited, and formed a dark cloud around her face. There were ornaments in it, stars she thought at first, but then, looking closer, saw them to be tiny golden vine leaves glinting.

Rebecca drew back a step and watched the figure in the mirror do the same. She turned her head, and saw the movement reflected.

It is me, she thought.

Slowly, she raised her hands to unfasten the fine chain around her neck and watched her reflected self raise her hands too. She lifted the chain down, the swinging vine leaf shimmering in the candlelight without and the candlelight within the mirror, and saw, one by one, the golden vine leaf ornaments in her hair wink out.

How can this be?

Rebecca dragged her eyes from the glass and looked down at her clothes, stroking the denim with her hand, feeling its smooth close fit, and then looked up again.

The gown had gone, and so had the cloud of hair, and only herself, in jeans and sweater and plait, stood before her, with eyes wide and pupils black.

The candle flame guttered, and dark swallowed the room.

Chapter Fifteen

Rebecca woke to harsh light and voices downstairs. After a moment of panicky disorientation she realised she had forgotten to switch off the radio and lamps after the power cut.

She crossed in front of the maple mirror with caution and saw herself, wary in her night things.

She paused and looked again, critically, at her reflection. She rarely bothered with this sort of thing. At twenty-five Rebecca still thought of herself as a girl; yes, sure, an adult, but 'girl' was the word that came trippingly to her tongue. Yet last night it had been a woman who met her gaze in the mirror – that person in the blue gown, mysterious in the candlelight, had not been a girl by any definition.

Now, Rebecca leaned inward and searched for signs of that other version of herself, of the authority and coolness, and was not sure she found them. What she did see was caution, and shadows under her eyes from not having slept well. She had dreamed again of the man on the hillside in the night, and the wind had blown his hair and sucked away her voice when she tried to call.

Rebecca dressed, noticing that her wardrobe consisted almost entirely of trousers of one kind or another, and slipped her watch on. She fastened the vine leaf chain around her neck, watching herself in the maple mirror, challenging the cloudy-haired woman to return. Then she pulled a sweatshirt over the top and the vine leaf was hidden.

She grilled bacon for breakfast in celebration of electricity, and ate it looking at the photograph of the mystery woman propped against her glass of orange juice.

Are you Emily? Did you have Uriel's child?

The woman in the high-necked blouse gazed back at her, level and true, like the midnight woman of the maple mirror. If she was indeed Emily Seward, then she was Cicely's grandmother: Cicely the wild child, the dark-haired beauty who had sought adventure instead of marriage and had returned with stories which so enchanted her little nieces that seventy years later Aunty Edie would tell them to Rebecca.

Had Cicely's blood borne those other-worldly genes? Was

that why Emily had chosen her to be the recipient of her necklace?

You must have it now, Aunty Edie had told Rebecca, when she gave her the gold chain, and *Keep wearing the necklace*, Michael had said later, although how he had known she had it she never found out.

And so she wore it. It was so fine, the vine leaf so flat, that she could wear it beneath a high-necked top without it making a bump. Fastening it around her neck every morning had become as automatic as putting on her watch. It had become a part of her: Rebecca's necklace now, just as once it had been Cicely's necklace.

The instructions had been precise: *Open Michael's box, Use Uriel's knife*, and *Wear Emily's necklace*.

Wear, not *Find*.

Open Michael's box, not *dump it on a shelf and stare at it.*

Use Uriel's knife, not *sit fuming over the arrogance, selfishness and sheer bloody nerve of Geoffrey Foster's having swiped it in the first place.*

The knife arrived by recorded delivery and Rebecca had waited in for it. She noticed that yet again the post was delivered by someone who was not Roddy, so asking him about this 'Will' who claimed to be her 'man' was still not possible.

She took the package inside to tear open.

Inside the envelope was a lot of bubble plastic. Rebecca snipped her way in and finally held Uriel Passenger's knife in her palm.

It was as Foster had described: carved and engraved with a pattern of vine tendrils, the blade gleaming silver, the wood silvery grey and worn smooth. There was, she saw to her disgust, a corner that was deeper grey where the wood had been sliced away.

Cut into the top edge of the blade were two rectangular notches. Breathing a little tight, Rebecca brought the carved box to the table and lifted the lid. She turned the key in the lock and watched the two rods slide apart, noticing as always the small judder half way through.

The thickness of the rods matched the width of the notches

exactly.

Rebecca laid the knife blade alongside the rods, parallel to the edge of the box, and turned the key until the rods lined up with the notches. She slid the blade into place so that the rods were now held captive, and turned the key further.

For a moment there was resistance, and fleetingly Rebecca wondered how much force she could safely use. Then the key tilted and turned again, there was a scrape of wooden parts sliding in the base of the box, and she saw, with triumph and trepidation, the flat wood that she had thought was the bottom of the box begin to lift.

Connor was right. There needed only the shallowest of spaces to contain an object of importance, if that object were a single sheet of paper. Or even three.

Rebecca drew out the contents of the hidden compartment, locked away from the light of day for many decades, and laid them gently on the table.

One she recognised at once, having its twin in the box Michael had given her. It was the Queen of Clubs, or rather of Clover, but hand-painted by an artist from a world that was at once both far, far away and, as Michael had so disturbingly described it, just next door. The Queen sat on her throne in three-quarter profile, her white arms bare, her skirts billowing, her imperious gaze grazing Rebecca's shoulder.

The second was another card, also hand-painted, quite probably by the same artist, but this time a Jack. He wore a doublet and a dagger, and as in a regular deck he too was depicted turned a quarter aside; but his hair was black and his brow was stern. In the corner was painted the heart-shaped leaf of a vine.

The third item was a sheet of paper, folded. Rebecca opened it with care, conscious of its fragility for it was certainly very old. It had discoloured to a pale brown like tea stains, and was so dry it crackled when she touched it.

So great was her concentration on unfolding it without causing damage that she did not immediately notice what it bore. But when she did, her heart almost stopped.

Chapter Sixteen

Term had begun and Connor had moved back to his room in College. He had been lucky in the draw for accommodation, and although other rooms were larger, his was in a prime location, on Main Quad on the second floor and facing north towards the chapel. During services after dark the stained glass windows across the lawn glowed scarlet and blue and gold.

But when Rebecca called he had his back to the window, seated at the built-in desk. He saw her name on the screen and clicked to save his work. He hoped it would not be a long call; he wanted to get this finished tonight.

'Hi.'

'Hi.' Rebecca dived straight into business. 'I'm calling to let you know you don't need to think about the necklace any more. Or the knife.'

'Really? You've found them?' Connor swivelled to sit sideways on his chair with his back to the screen so as not to be distracted while Rebecca spoke. He crossed his legs and swung his foot.

'Well, I've already got the necklace. It's that gold vine leaf Aunty Edie passed on to me.'

'How do you know?'

'I'm pretty sure. There was a…I'm pretty sure.'

Connor stopped moving his foot. 'What about the knife?'

'Would you believe Geoffrey Foster had it?' She sounded disgusted.

'You're kidding.'

'That time he was caretaking the cottage – when Michael had to go up to Aberfeldy – he wheedled permission out of Michael and let himself in. Honestly!'

Connor's foot began to swing again. 'Wow.'

'You don't sound appalled,' Rebecca's voice said in accusation.

'No, I am. That was unforgivable. An awful thing to do.' But he found he was fighting a smile. The old twister. 'Did he tell you he had the knife, then?'

'I guessed,' Rebecca said shortly. 'He'd chopped off a chunk and had it radiocarbon tested.'

'*Really?* And?'

'The readings were off the graph. They threw him out for falsifying the material and wasting their time.'

Connor laughed.

'It isn't funny,' Rebecca said sharply.

'Oh come on. It is, quite!'

Rebecca growled. Connor said, 'Anyway, I presume you got it off him?'

'Yes.'

'And did it unlock the box?'

Rebecca's voice was suddenly cagey again. 'Yes, actually. Quite cunning.'

There was a pause.

'And?' Connor prompted yet again. This was not the Rebecca he knew, bounding in full of importance to grab the spotlight and reveal how clever she'd been. Something was up.

'Well, you were right. There's a false base.'

After a moment Connor asked, 'Anything inside?' This was hard work.

'Just some papers. Cards. Two cards.'

'What kind of cards?'

He heard her take a breath. 'One of them was a Queen of Clubs very like yours. The other was a Jack of Hearts. They match.'

Connor said, 'The Queen of Clover and the Knave of Vines.'

'Yes. I think of him as the Jack of Hearts though. Um…'

'Yes?'

'Nothing. That's it.'

'Nothing else in the box?'

'No. Nothing.'

Connor waited, silent, allowing her the opportunity, but she didn't take it. Instead, after a few moments, she said, 'How are the Dons? Missing the scones, are you?'

They talked for five minutes or so, shallow chat that skipped over the deeper matter of their relationship, and Connor wondered when – or even whether – she would realise that she had never told him she had taken the Queen of Clover card from his coat pocket three years ago, although he had long guessed it.

And he wondered about the third thing she had found in the hidden compartment of the carved box.

'Well, better let you go,' she said at last.

'Rebecca, are you alright?'

'Yes, of course.'

Connor said, 'I'm always here, you know that, don't you?'

'Of course.'

'If you want me, I'll always come.'

There was a pause.

'Yes. Yes, I know,' Rebecca said.

Open Michael's box.
She had.
Use Uriel's knife.
She did.
Wear Emily's necklace.
She was.

And now, written in thick, black ink on the decorated back of a playing card, *Find the Jack of Hearts.*

But she already had found the Jack of Hearts, in the carved box. The instruction was too late. What had gone wrong?

The latest message had been in the niche between stones in the hut, where Rebecca had left her scrap of defiant retaliation. She had formed the habit of checking each time she went for a walk, and knew it must have arrived in the last twenty hours.

She retained enough detachment to realise how bizarre it was that she had adjusted so quickly to being stalked. In London, at Ashendon, on Skye, in a delivery van, in the library, chatting to the postman, this guy, this – man – was watching her, keeping close, waiting for…what?

He was probably on the hillside now, monitoring her movements, preparing his own next step, silhouetted against the sky whether it was pale or dark, his hair blown about by the wind.

She had no doubt that he was the man in her dream.

She ought to be terrified, but somehow she wasn't; shivery, yes, and sometimes a bit queasy in her stomach, but it seemed to her that the threat was not physical.

She did not intend to tell the police.

Nor did she intend to tell Connor. It had been tempting on the phone, carefully skirting around the third item in the hidden compartment, not mentioning the latest message, but it didn't feel right. Connor was not involved in this, she knew. This was down to her, alone.

On the other hand, she wasn't at all sure how successful she had been at dissembling; she suspected not very. Connor knew her too well.

Find the Jack of Hearts.

Assuming the message was not late, then there was a further Jack of Hearts to run down. What it could be, she had no idea. There was a kind of logical progression so far: first the modern Waddingtons Jack at Ashendon; then the older, Victorian design she had found in Uriel Passenger's collection of bric-a-brac in the storage unit at Matlock; and now the other-worldly painting of the Knave of Vines. Surely nothing could top that?

Yet she had to find another one. And it really was 'find' this time, with no margin for interpreting it differently. She had to hunt this Jack of Hearts down and she hadn't the slightest idea where to start.

Would she have to resort to asking Connor after all? Or the Dons, who were an uncanny bunch in possession of a great deal of extraordinary and unlikely information?

I'll think about it.

But while she was thinking, an email popped up on her screen from Connor, and what he was asking threw all her thoughts into disarray again.

Chapter Seventeen

The other students living on Connor's staircase included a linguist, an historian and a physicist. The physicist was called Joe. Connor knocked on his door.

Half an hour later he had some idea about how lenses and crossed polarisers and light interact, and had been introduced to the strange Dirac experiment; true, some of it was hazy, but it was a starting point.

He emailed Rebecca, and shortly afterwards received her reply.

I do, actually. After all that searching for the box and then the key I know the exact position of the entire contents of the cottage. It's in one of the square baskets on the bottom bookshelf. It's still wrapped in that brocade.
Why?

Of course there would be a Why. Connor sent back: *Just a thought. Thanks,* and called Mrs Dixon at the hotel.

High on the hill, sitting on her slab of rock, Rebecca leaned her chin in her gloved hands and thought.

Or tried to.

The climb up here should have swept her busy mind clear, but it hadn't swept very clean today. She wanted to attend to the Jack of Hearts business, but Connor's email kept worming back in.

Why did he want the telescope? If it was just a case of using it to magnify something it would be easier to borrow one locally. He must want their particular telescope, and that was what bothered her.

The seemingly random group of objects they had traced and collected years ago had been supposed to have had a dual function. Most of them had fulfilled this; the telescope had not. Neither had the spool of thread, but perhaps because Rebecca worked with thread herself this had never concerned her; thread could be used for a dozen tasks. But the telescope had never revealed its primary use, and that had always niggled.

If they had only needed a tube of a certain diameter, why not something much simpler and cheaper, like a length of dowel? Surely for a telescope to be needed, the act of looking through it ought to come into play?

But it never had.

And now Connor was interested in it, and wasn't telling her the reason.

The wind was still rolling around, sometimes taking a nap only to wake with renewed energy; its sighing had become a constant background even indoors.

A distant sheep bleated.

Somewhere on the mountain, Rebecca thought, he might be watching me; and in her mind's eye she saw again the brittle, folded paper and the impossible thing that was drawn on it.

Watching her, he sensed that part of her mind was occupied on a different puzzle, the wrong puzzle, and bent his thoughts towards her.

Rebecca, find the Jack of Hearts.

Because that was all that was left now.

An idea was brewing in her innermost mind – no, in her innermost guts. It was a visceral, deep-in-her-body feeling, not like a thought at all, and made her want to clutch her arms and fold at the waist as if she had stomach cramps. It made her tremble.

It had been hinted to her once that she was the Queen of Clubs – or *a* Queen of Clubs. If you wanted to be pedantic, that should be the Queen of Clover. Playing cards were common, allowing for a degree of variation, to many different cultures, and there was no denying that the symbol of the Clubs was considerably closer in appearance to a cloverleaf than a blunt instrument.

So suppose that the Jack of Hearts she had to find was not a card at all, but a person.

There could then be no doubt which person.

Rebecca searched on-line. She Googled 'playing cards' and

was presented with dozens of images of the court cards and the history of their development.

Then she Googled 'Jack of Hearts' and leapt straight to song lyrics. She was not the first to interpret the character as a man.

She thought again of the ancient paper with its vertical fold, now placed carefully inside a book on art history where it was protected, and where her eyes could not stumble upon it accidentally.

Rebecca read through the words to the Bob Dylan song. It was plain the character was sharp, cool, fiendishly attractive and wild. She stared at the wall and saw again the pirate on the South Bank, felt again the jolt of his smile.

An actor better than any other, anywhere.

Spanish, Scots or Cockney. And now she knew what he looked like.

Rebecca covered her face with her hands and groaned.

He turned his back on the lit windows of the house and strode along the road towards the inn where he would sleep that night.

The way was downhill and the walking was easy.

He missed the pirate coat. He missed the way it swung with his stride, and its vast pockets.

He began to whistle.

Chapter Eighteen

Rebecca woke in the early hours and sat up immediately. Eyes wide, she waited for her night vision to arrive, for the shadows to appear looming out of the dark. But she was alert, not alarmed, and had not woken because of sounds outside or because she had dreamed.

She had been woken by a thought.

Drawing the duvet up round her shoulders, she ran over the idea in her head. She was sure she had remembered correctly. What confounded her was why she had not remembered before.

Oh well, better late than never.

She switched on the bedside lamp, squinting in the sudden brightness, and fished for her slippers.

Downstairs she opened her laptop and searched her email folders. *There.*

When Michael had decided to take that terrible, irreversible step of vanishing into the World Invisible, he had taken care to make matters as easy as possible for those he left behind. When Rebecca had recovered from the shock sufficiently to open the envelope he had given her, she found a sheet of paper listing his solicitor, banking details, insurance and so on, and stating that he had arranged for her and Connor to have legal power of attorney over all his affairs.

He had also sent her information by email, including a handful of Word documents of which one had been his catalogue of Uriel Passenger's journals.

Their mutual ancestor, the troublemaker who had given them their fairy genes, had been a compulsive diarist, and there were over a hundred and fifty handwritten notebooks at Ashendon which she and Connor had barely dipped into. Michael had spent years reading them and making notes on the contents.

How could she have forgotten this?

Digging out the emails, Rebecca recognised in herself the telltale signs of regret and distress – her hollow stomach, her brows pressing into a frown – and guessed the truth. Reading Michael's last messages to her awoke the grief, and she had probably buried the memory to protect herself.

The envelope she took from him that bleak, frosty dawn had held two letters as well, one for her and one for Connor, handwritten and in their own, separate envelopes.

You know how much I owe you, he had written in hers, *and you know that I know.*

That, too, lay in the base of her jewellery box.

The catalogue file was in the folder where Rebecca had stashed all the documents Michael had emailed to her, and was a chronological list of the journals with notes on their contents. Rebecca searched for 'Queen' and quickly realised that was going to throw up interminable references to the royal family, beginning, ridiculously, with Victoria.

She switched to 'Queen of' and struck gold. Within a couple of minutes she realised she badly needed Uriel's journal for 1871. But it was nearly five hundred miles away.

Connor read Rebecca's email and replied. A minute later his phone rang.

'I can't do that,' Rebecca's voice said.

'Of course you can.'

'It will mean she's tramping about in there all over again.'

'Rebecca, what do you think she's going to do? She's got a hotel to run. The cottage isn't of any interest to her. She'll just go in, get the book, and lock up again.'

'Mm.'

Connor listened to Rebecca considering his words; her scepticism was almost palpable.

'I wish I'd thought of this before. I wish I'd asked her to get it at the same time as she got the telescope for you.'

'Yes, but you didn't. I'm sure she won't mind. So long as we don't keep doing it.'

He knew Rebecca was coming round. Her only other option, after all, was driving a thousand-mile round trip.

'What did you do about the postage costs?' she asked.

'I sent her some flowers.'

The postage had been an awkward amount, too small to warrant a cheque but too much to be ignored, or at least too much for Connor to ignore. And there had been her time and trouble. He had arranged for some lilies to be delivered, and hoped she liked them.

'Oh. That was nice.'

Rebecca's voice had lifted a fraction; a corner had been turned.

'Well, okay, I suppose I'll have to ask her, then. What kind of flowers did you get, so I don't get the same?'

Just before she rang off, Rebecca asked, 'What are you doing with the telescope?'

'Thinking about it,' Connor said. 'Bye.'

'Of course I don't mind,' Bridget Dixon said. 'Can it wait until Friday? I'll be going to the Post Office then.'

'Friday's fine,' Rebecca said, because she could hardly say anything else. Frustrating, though.

'I presume you didn't have any more trouble with that Spanish guest, Garcia?'

'No, none at all,' Rebecca lied. 'Never saw him again.'

Oh well...the last bit was true.

The wind had subsided and still, damp weather had settled over the island: typical Skye weather, Rebecca thought, milder than the Scottish mainland and laden with moisture. It was an Isle of Water, the coast fringed with inlets, the ever-seething ocean never more than five miles away.

And on Rebecca's doorstep, nearly. She stood on the shore and stared out towards the smaller island of Rona, while droplets formed out of the mist and settled on her hair and coat. There was not a breath of movement in the heavy air; it felt as if the island were waiting.

In Portree the art students were preparing for their Highers later in the year, and the island's craft co-operative was showing in the An Tuireann Arts Centre. Rebecca had declined to take part this time, claiming pressure of work but in reality preoccupied.

In Oxford, Connor was attending lectures and writing essays

and doing something with the telescope that, irritatingly, he wouldn't tell her about.

In the secret, windowless room in Ashendon Cottage, for a few minutes each day, two beams of light passed by one another, safely deflected by angled prisms so that they could not intersect.

Somewhere, probably not far away, was a man Rebecca now knew she would recognise should she be given the chance again. She had asked Steph to send her jpegs of the photos she had taken on the South Bank on New Year's Day. One of them, taken while Rebecca was watching the fire-eaters, included the pirate, and brought up large on the laptop screen it left Rebecca no room to doubt any more.

The likeness was exact. And if that long-ago, far-away artist had known and drawn how Rebecca would look so far in the future, then she had no doubt he, or perhaps she, had known her companion in the picture too, standing to one side, his hand on the back of the chair in which she sat with her skirts flowing and her hair long, as if he were her attendant, or her brother.

Or her consort.

Chapter Nineteen

Rebecca had been waiting and reached the door seconds after the bell rang.

'Roddy!' She scratched the stylus on the electronic box in an approximation of her signature. 'Did you have a good break?'

'Aye, thanks, went to my dad's in Dundee.'

'Have you seen Will recently?'

'Will?'

'You know, Will,' Rebecca prompted. She swallowed. 'My man.'

'Oh, no...I don't think...I've...well...'

Rebecca watched the process of the postman losing focus as he stood before her. Extraordinary.

'Never mind,' she said briskly. 'Thanks.'

Dusk was settling like a blanket. Rebecca switched on the lamps and made herself comfortable. She began to read.

Uriel Passenger's journals were not daily diaries but casual notebooks in which he recorded his impressions of the world he inhabited. Sometimes he filled ten pages in a day, sometimes weeks passed without comment. Some entries described events, public and private, and some merely followed abstract thought.

He wrote in ink which had faded to brown, using a spidery, forward-sloping cursive style that was not easy to decipher out of context. Rebecca quickly realised that skimming pages on the lookout for individual words would get her nowhere, and reluctantly began to read from the beginning.

But as on a hot August day years before, when strains of distant footfalls and voices had drifted through an open window with the warm scents of garden flowers and herbs, the musings of the man who had been more alien than any sane person would ever believe drew her in. Just as on that distant summer day she had forgotten about codes and keys, now she forgot about cards and characters and gave herself instead to the events of a year in the middle of Victoria's reign as seen through the eyes of the man who was an outsider in every possible respect.

He wrote well, with an uncluttered style less laden with punctuation than Victorian novels tend to be, and with an ear for balance and clarity. In other words, it read modern.

Had he spoken modern too? Rebecca began to wonder whether Uriel Passenger had ever managed to fit in. Had he been picked out, remarked upon, skirted around with delicate caution? She knew he had become a recluse, that when his mad collection clogged up the manor house he withdrew to the tiny cottage, hidden by trees from the grounds. Had that been eccentricity or a considered retreat?

Reading the journal was a pleasure, at any rate. He had not dwelt much on the political activity of the day, but he did mention items of news that caught his attention: in February there had been terrible gales that had taken twenty-eight ships beneath the North Sea, and at the end of March Queen Victoria had launched the Royal Albert Hall with a concert involving a choir of a thousand.

After an hour of reading Rebecca caught her breath and sat up. *Mr Dodgson has published again,* Uriel wrote. *A looking glass this time, and a game of chess. Nothing to be concerned about, they tell me, but I shall pay a visit in any case. I hope they are being discreet.*

Stomach jumping, Rebecca raised her eyes to digest the implications.

The windows were completely dark now – no street lamps disturbed the night sky here. She marked the page with a scrap of paper and went round closing curtains.

There was little doubt who 'they' were, but finding them in the faded, nineteenth-century script delivered a jolt nonetheless.

And she had eaten their buns.

Once upon a time Rebecca had wondered how three ancient professors could linger on in the cloisters and common rooms of Oxford University without being rumbled, but no longer. Connor called it 'Skill', somehow giving it a capital letter, and Rebecca had no doubt as to its efficacy. The Jack of Hearts was currently wielding it with resounding effect, so why not the Dons at the Ferry House?

Fairies! Rebecca thought, and turned the oven on.

It was past eight when Rebecca reached the words she had

been waiting for. She had switched on the lamp at her side but neglected the others and the walls and corners lurked in clotted shadow beyond the island of light centred on the page.

Rebecca set down her coffee mug and read the words slowly, with concentration, because this, she felt convinced, was at the heart of all that had happened to her, and was still happening.

As on the hillside, she had a strong sense of her position in time – of the seconds passing: *now,* and *now,* and *now.* At this moment, where she was living and breathing and feeling the texture of the paper under her fingertips, she did not know what she would find written on the pages that followed. In the sentences and paragraphs ahead, which she would be reading shortly, lay information that would answer questions, provide reasons, and even, perhaps, explain why her life had taken the course it had.

It was unimaginable. It would be momentous. And she needed to prepare herself to receive it.

Taking a deep breath, Rebecca straightened her back and flexed her fingers. She switched position, refreshing muscles tired from inactivity, and licked her lips, and swallowed. She raised her eyes and looked across the room to the curtains she had closed on the world outside, and to the shelves where her books stood leaning away from the box of carved wood wherein the Jack of Hearts waited for her to discover the truth.

Now, and this second now, I still don't know.

But it couldn't continue, this not knowing.

Because of Michael and Connor, because of her dreams, because she couldn't bear not knowing any longer even though it might change her life and rob her of her future, Rebecca began to read.

Connor was halfway across the threshold when he hesitated.

'Forgotten your key?' Joe asked.

'Just a sec.'

Connor glanced back at his room. What was it?

He checked his phone.

'Hang on. Sorry.'

He jiggled the mouse to wake up the screen of his laptop. No emails.

What, then?

For a moment he stood, frowning, searching his senses, while Joe watched from the landing.

'Problem?'

Connor shook himself and smiled. 'No. Sorry. Let's go.'

But he closed down his computer first so that if an email arrived it would definitely come straight to his mobile.

In the parlour of the house screened by tall trees on the north bank of the Thames at Oxford, the Dons were watching the re-run of a lengthy literary adaptation. The early scenes took place in the nineteen-twenties, and on screen the quarter-peals rang over cobbled lanes where mortarboards outnumbered motorcars.

Professor Peregrine said, 'Too much sunshine. I recall there was much more rain.'

Professor Viator said, 'He got the idea for the bear from that poet fellow. Such affectation. He left it behind after one of my lectures, you know, and I should have thrown it away. The inhabitants of Slough did not deserve it.'

No-one replied. After a hundred and sixty years there's not much new to say. But then Professor Peregrine glanced up sharply and met the eyes of his fellows.

There was a pause, and the characters on the television set spoke to inattentive ears.

'Is that—?'

'I think—'

'She's off!' Professor Lloyd, like a gleeful tortoise, waved his claws in excitement. 'I always said she'd get there, and she has!'

But the television screen distracted him.

'Oh look, there's Julia. She is a *poppet!*'

Silent in a corner of the snug, watching the customers at the bar, a man who had no need of a hood to help him pass unnoticed lifted his head a fraction, as if listening.

He smiled.

Then, the smile passing, he lowered his eyes in reflection.

Chapter Twenty

In the pool of lamplight, to the soft crackle and whump of the wood burner, Rebecca read.

They use our cards here, Uriel had written more than one hundred and forty years ago. *The names are different, but the characters remain: the king, the queen, and the knave. But in their games the king outranks the queen.*

Michael had told her that playing cards of simple numbers and court cards in suits appeared in cultures all over the world, and she had understood that they were known in the World Invisible too. It seemed strange, though, that Uriel at least considered them to have originated there.

What was stranger was that some of the cards represented real people; or rather, real figures.

The King of Thorns, whose symbol resembled the sharp points of the suit of Diamonds, had once held power but seen it eroded over generations until he bore a mainly ceremonial role, more figurehead than leader; Rebecca, reading between the spidery brown lines, detected that he had been gradually reduced to a puppet under the control of others, and now, Uriel wrote, the rank was no longer filled or used at all. The King was not dead but defunct.

The Queen of Clover was considered the receptacle of wisdom, the decision-maker, the wielder of power over people and property.

And the Knave of Vines – the Jack of Hearts – was her servant; or at least, the servant of royalty. That was the original meaning of the word *knave*, and the overlay of trickster and rogue had come later. The fifteenth-century text that linked species of hawk to rank had allotted a kestrel to a serving boy, not a rascal.

The Knave of Vines was more than that, though. As Rebecca read on she began to form an image of dynamism, the protector of the realm, the one man in whom resided responsibility for the wellbeing of everyone and for the world itself. If there were unrest in the streets, he imposed order; if there were famine in the fields, he brought relief; if there were attacks from marauders, he marshalled resistance. The Knave was at the centre of all that happened, a powerhouse of energy, clear-sighted and capable down to his very fingertips.

It was quite an image.

But there was more.

It became clear to me, Uriel wrote, *that fresh blood was needed to replace what had become too dilute for the Queen of Clover to fulfil her function.*

He meant fresh blood from a different world – the Real World, although it was becoming increasingly difficult for Rebecca to make this distinction.

The Queen of Clover had a duty to maintain justice in the absence of anything Rebecca would recognise as a legal system. Quite how she achieved this Uriel did not say. However, he had been convinced of the need to travel through the gap between the worlds to search for a suitable candidate, and what he found had filled him with dismay.

It has ever been a poor land for growing, that I knew, but it had become still poorer, and contaminated with the outpourings of filth from areas given over entirely to the making of things from metal. Whole tracts of productive soil are sealed over with stone for the building of structures many storeys high, all filled with the engines of manufacture and the workers who must operate them. I found people living together so densely they had never seen open fields.

What must he have thought by the time he died, in the early twenty-first century, Rebecca wondered.

I have met and spoken with souls who have never milked a cow.

Oh, horror! Rebecca thought of the clinical production line that was the modern milking parlour.

But worst of all by far is the abominable exploitation of children in the pursuit of financial wealth.

Uriel Passenger had been so shocked by the corruption he saw, from child labour and gin palaces to debtors' prisons and public executions, that he had switched the focus of his mission from finding a new Queen of Clover to learning how England's once green and pleasant land had become so besmirched, so that he could take steps to prevent the same happening to his home.

That was why he had stayed. That was why he had inveigled himself into the society of the thinkers, the movers and shakers of the day, beginning with Oxford. And that, Rebecca read with dawning amazement, was why at the age of fifteen Connor had walked through the gap at Ashendon straight into a prison.

The wall he encountered had been built on the command of Uriel Passenger, Knave of Vines, Royal Factotum, Chief of Security and Defender of the Realm. *Should anyone strange ever appear in the enclosed forest*, he had told the people who lived beyond the wall, *feed him, clothe him, but keep him contained.*

Connor had been imprisoned because he might be an intellectual contaminant.

Rebecca read on. In 1871 Uriel had yet to build the manor at Ashendon, probably, she hazarded, because even with his expert wielding of Skill it must have taken time to gather sufficient funds. But he already had plans.

I intend to launch these objects upon this world. When they merge once again, we shall have a new Queen of Clover. The dice shall decide.

Rebecca said aloud, 'The box and the necklace and the knife!'

She guessed right. Uriel continued, explaining the method by which he would dispose of the tokens.

The gold necklace and the carved box he would give to Emily Seward, with instructions that the necklace should be handed down through the female line and the carved box, with its secret compartment, through the male. His own pocket knife, with its handle carved from the wood of the most sacred tree in the World Invisible, he would lock away in a cabinet in full view.

Rebecca lifted her eyes. *Lock away in a cabinet in full view.* It was an elegant solution to hiding something you wanted eventually to be discovered by the right person, and it was not the first time he had used the idea.

Just as Uriel would build Ashendon to house his personal collection and conceal the key to the carved box, so he and his associates had already founded the Museum of South Kensington, later to be renamed the Victoria and Albert Museum, in order to conceal the seven elements of the key needed to access Ashendon.

It was beautiful: circular, sophisticated, and self-contained. It was even witty. It was surely imagined by a creative, cunning and mischievous individual.

It occurred to Rebecca that she had only ever pictured Uriel Passenger at the end of his extraordinarily long life, a wizened, reclusive old man. But in his youth he had wooed and won Emily Seward and then gone on to woo and win at least one other woman to Rebecca's certain knowledge. He had been a fairy, for heaven's sake – a being from another plane of existence, rare and exotic and able to work magic! He must have been dynamite...

A Knave of Vines, that could entwine a woman's mind and take root in her soul...The Jack of Hearts, than whom there was no better actor anywhere, and who stole the tarts beneath the noses of everyone in the court...

A pirate whose glance had been a shock of electricity.

And he was waiting for her to find him.

Chapter Twenty-One

It was one o'clock when Rebecca went to bed. She paused as she passed the maple mirror, but the lady in the midnight gown was not there.

She slept uneasily, her firm mattress seeming too soft, the duvet too bulky. Sometime in the early hours she realised she was awake again, and lay with her eyes open in the dark.

After a minute or two she sat up and switched on the lamp to its dimmest setting – still bright to her eyes.

The mirror waited against the wall, its smooth face at this angle black and featureless.

Rebecca rose and stood before it again, examining her reflection in cotton night clothes, her hair pulling loose from the plait she slept in. Clearly she had been turning on her pillow.

After a moment she crossed to the chest and lifted the gold vine leaf necklace. She held it up in front of the glass, and then carefully fastened it around her neck.

Her reflection stared back, solemn and watchful, her hair still drawn back, her legs still in the loose cotton trousers.

So it wasn't the necklace.

Rebecca bit her lip.

She went downstairs and rummaged, to return with the candlestick and box of matches. She turned off her bedside lamp and stood before the maple mirror again, and in the reflected candlelight, pale against the thundercloud of her hair, the face of the other Rebecca, the enchanted Rebecca, looked back.

She willed her heart not to race, breathed slowly from her diaphragm. It was an illusion, nothing to fear. Rebecca raised her hand and touched the cold glass with her fingertips, and her midnight self did the same...

Of course.

This is my reflection, she told herself silently, *she – I – might look different, but we are one person, not two.*

She dragged her eyes away from the eyes in the mirror and looked instead at the rest of the figure. She had never taken much interest in her looks, and for many years had worn her hair cropped ultra-short for reasons of economy. She did not use make up and more or less lived in jeans.

Until Connor – and come to that, since Connor too – men had not featured in her life either. At school she had once been told she was scary, and had been inclined to scorn teenage boys who were so easily put off. After dropping out of art college she had worked so hard to forge herself a career that social life had dropped off the register, and she had to admit she was living a rather reclusive life now on Skye.

Still, she had eyes and ears. She was aware that she was attractive, and could even look really good if she bothered. It was just that bothering was too much...bother.

But the girl, no, *woman* in the mirror was, indisputably, beautiful, in which case then she, Rebecca, must also be beautiful. It was something to think about; it put a new slant on matters.

The dress was gorgeous, designed with an eye to the essence of femininity that had been revisited time and time again over the centuries. The cut, with the full sleeves, close bodice, plunging waistline and gathered skirts, resembled costume from the mid-sixteenth, late eighteenth and mid-nineteenth centuries: Hans Holbein, Joseph Gainsborough, and the costume gallery at the V&A. There was no frippery, though, no lace or ribbons or embroidery, but unadorned night-blue silk and those simple, exquisite shapes.

Looking closer, Rebecca's attention was caught by the shadows beyond her reflection, and narrowed her eyes.

In the bedroom behind her, she knew, was her wardrobe – a simple, undecorated, functional piece with wide, plain doors. But in the dark beyond her reflected self were hints of something else, something with details that caught the faint candlelight and stirred it. Something like...leaves?

Rebecca threw a swift glance over her shoulder. Just the wardrobe. She returned to the reflection.

Definitely leaves.

Well, that's typical, she thought, and realised wryly that she had come a long way if she could be reacting quite so sardonically to this supernatural stuff.

Still, it was true that rampant foliage seemed to be a recurring symbol of the World Invisible. Her adventures had begun with the vines carved on the ivory casket in the V&A, the day she first met Michael and saw the vine tattoo on his wrist. Vines had been involved in the riddle of Skye, too, and here she was, wearing a vine leaf charm all her waking hours.

Was her mirror-self outdoors or indoors? Was a forest growing in her room this very night? Would vines hang from her ceiling, and would there be wild things beyond her walls?

The sharp, shocking wail of a newborn baby made Rebecca leap in her skin before she recognised it as the bark of a fox in the night. When she turned back, the maple mirror showed her familiar self, startled and slender in her thin night clothes and staring like a deer.

Rebecca extinguished the candle.

Four days later, Rebecca felt herself as far from resolution as ever.

She could not find the Jack of Hearts.

She had left a message in the wall of the hut, of course, but it had not moved. That was frustrating.

She had tried once more to nail down Roddy the postman about the mysterious Will, and even Maggie Davenport about the delivery driver, broaching the subject with heart in mouth lest she raise unwanted questions, but to no avail. They both barely remembered the incidents now, let alone the man, and showed a ludicrous lack of curiosity about Rebecca's interest.

She had dawdled in the public library, scoured the marketplace, loitered on the quay in Portree and stared out to sea. She had taken a deckchair and a book and staked out the broken-down barn. She had even stood on the hillside above her house and shouted *YOU are the Jack of Hearts!* into the wind, but apart from the turning tail of a startled sheep there had been no response.

What else could be done?

She fetched the other-world Queen of Clover from her jewellery box and the other-world Knave of Vines from the carved box, leaving the gaggle of queens to complain amongst themselves, and laid them side-by-side on the table.

They remained docile and domestic, promising nothing.

The Queen gazed past her shoulder, coolly distant as always, and the Knave looked either towards the Queen or away from her, depending on which side he was put. Intuitively she felt he should be watching the Queen, but at the moment it seemed to Rebecca he had turned his back.

Connor called and Rebecca spent the entire conversation weighing up whether to mention the matter to him, and then didn't. Nor did she consider more than fleetingly taking the business to the Ferry House. Without a clear idea why, she was quite sure this was her problem to solve, and neither Connor nor the Dons could help her.

Or maybe should help her.

She reread Uriel's journal, lingering over the meaning of each sentence, trying to guess what he might have known but withheld. There must be something here that should tell her what to do, because otherwise what was the point of it all?

But what?

By the weekend Rebecca felt she was going mad. Her preoccupation with this one problem had taken over all her waking hour; her sleeping ones too, as she dreamed again and again of the man and the wind and the sky. And the only idea she had managed to dredge up, the sole stratagem she had concocted, was so crazy it terrified her.

After stocking up at the supermarket in Portree, she bought cod and chips from the shop on the quay and ate from the paper, sitting on a bench overlooking the rows of moored boats. She had waited while a fresh batch of fish was being fried and the batter was crisp and delicious but damagingly hot; she waved each chunk in the salt air to cool it before putting it in her mouth. The waves slapped against the harbour wall and a diver was preparing equipment at the seaward end.

Rebecca thought.

The Knave was her henchman. His job was to serve her. That must include keeping her safe.

So if she put herself in danger, would he not surface in order to save her?

Wild, stupid, reckless idea. But it could work...

So what kind of danger? If it involved just a bit of risk, something that might result in a sprained ankle for example, it would be unlikely to flush him out. Yet if it were to be true, urgent danger, it would require her to place an insane amount of trust in a theory she had no way of testing first.

Impossible.

Rebecca scrunched up the fish paper and dropped it in the bin as she left the harbour.

But the idea, having germinated, grew.

Suppose she could find a way, invent a scenario that would be seriously hazardous yet not life-threatening? It would be a calculated game of brinksmanship. Could she think of some situation where her local knowledge might give her just a whisper of an advantage over the outsider?

Could she have the best of both worlds? Could she step forward into danger while leaving the way open to save herself should she need to? Take him to the cliff-edge without quite stepping off?

Could she *cheat* the Jack of Hearts?

Frowning, churning over the ideas in her mind, focused fiercely on achieving the impossible, Rebecca waited for the cars to pass and stepped forward into the road without ever seeing the motorcycle.

Chapter Twenty-Two

Frowning, churning ideas over in his mind, Connor stared at the slim brass telescope lying on top of his essay.

After a while he picked it up again, turned it over a couple of times, and then raised it to his eye.

This was becoming more than a habit; this was teetering on the edge of obsessive-compulsive. Still, he pointed it towards the window and adjusted the focus until the strips of leading between the shapes of stained glass were reasonably sharp. He moved the telescope in micro-stages along the coloured robes to the face, and suddenly an eye appeared, filling the lens, affronted and glaring.

The Saint was broad-shouldered and bearded, brandishing an improbably hefty key, which meant he must be Peter. Connor ignored him and roamed down the vertical folds of his robe to where the cloth was depicted as crumpling at his feet, and wondered again what the dark, whiskery visage could belong to that stared from behind the figure. He had found the uncanny, bestial face the first time he looked at the window through the telescope, never having noticed it before, and now it nagged at him.

Connor put the telescope down again and yawned. He had been working hard, head down, for ten days in order to get sufficiently ahead, and once he'd handed this in he would have a few days' grace – enough to cover a long weekend in the Peak District. He could have left tonight if he'd wanted, delivering the essay on the way, but tomorrow was Professor Viator's lecture on Shakespeare's missing years, and he couldn't resist sitting in again.

It was an annual fixture, and was received differently every time, or so the Professor told him in his customary stern tone which belied the wicked humour Connor now knew to lurk beneath. Some years the intake sat bemused; some years they rustled uneasily but were too shy to protest. Some years people got up and walked out; sometimes hecklers emerged. And once in a while, rarely but interestingly, the zeitgeist was such that enough of the audience swallowed it to begin to sway their more sceptical colleagues.

The lecture had a reputation; students came to it who had nothing to do with the English faculty. The walls bulged, standing room only, and Professor Viator would speak without notes until he had finished and then leave.

He never took questions.

Last year Connor had nudged the girl next to him and whispered, 'What do you think?'

She had grinned. 'Complete bollocks. Talk about being away with the fairies.'

Connor rolled the telescope back and forth with his middle finger. The Dons were of the opinion it was the Oxford gap the young Will Shakespeare had stumbled through. It was certainly the most likely, pretty much half-way between the burgeoning London theatre scene and his family in Stratford-upon-Avon. Connor wondered wryly, as he had often wondered before, whether he too might have had his muse touched by the wonders of Faerie if he hadn't had the ill luck to blunder straight into prison.

Which brought him back to the present.

He stowed the telescope safely in his rucksack and looked up the times of trains. Maybe this summer he'd take driving lessons, but for the time being he was on public transport.

'What do you think?' Connor asked the boy next to him.

'It's crazy but, you know, it kind of adds up. How else did he get all that learning and knowledge and wisdom? How else could he have turned out so unique?'

Different every year.

Connor left Oxford within an hour of the lecture finishing and arrived at Ashendon a little before nine, starving. He paid off the taxi, let the hotel receptionist know he'd be around, and tripped over a gardener's cloche on his way to the cottage door.

Rebecca! Although it wasn't like her to be so careless – and what would she have been doing with a cloche anyway? He moved it safely aside and let himself in.

He was relieved to find the can of baked beans he had been

counting on still in the cupboard, and he chipped and levered a couple of slices off the loaf from the freezer and put them under the grill while he checked the rest of the cottage.

All fine, of course. In the small parlour at the back, the wall of speckled mirrors offered up his reflection in a patchwork of frames. He lifted down the three that shielded the low door and ducked his head inside. The small, windowless room was dark and still.

Good.

Connor went back to stir the beans.

Uriel Passenger had never mentioned the telescope, of that Connor was sure. Michael had read his way through every journal in the cottage – he had lived there for three years, after all – and Connor trusted the catalogue he had compiled. Still, he couldn't resist lifting a book or two, or three, or four, from the shelves and dipping in, skimming the spidery script, searching for clues.

It was useless, of course. Part of the problem was that even when you could not find what you wanted, what you did find instead was enthralling. It was like one great big, devilish literary trap: once you started reading it was almost impossible to stop.

Connor did manage to stop at midnight, when the carriage clock on the mantelpiece chimed. Rebecca must have wound it, although that wasn't like her either. If he set his alarm he could catch a couple of hours' sleep and hopefully be fresh enough at twenty past two.

He didn't bother undressing, and filled the kettle ready for making coffee when he woke. He expected a struggle but in the event, after the first half-minute, it wasn't so bad, perhaps because his mind was occupied with the nitty-gritty of camera lenses and polarisation; that and Shakespeare's fairies. A wood near Athens, or the river at Oxford?

He was surprised how hard his heart was beating, given he wasn't going to *do* anything.

Wearing his coat over his sweater because the temperature outside was below freezing and the hidden room was unheated, Connor lodged himself against one wall and waited, telescope in hand, for his eyes to adjust.

Softly, slowly, the dark inched back and the faintest of light became detectable in the closed room. A line glimmered between the prisms which had been set with such precision on the lecterns – barely a trace since it was, after all, night-time, but steady and true as it was deflected down, along, and up again in the pattern designed more than a century ago.

It was, you had to admit, an elegant solution.

Connor checked the time on his phone, careful to shield the screen. A minute or less. He lifted the telescope and trained it on the area he'd need.

And there it was suddenly: a thread of light, strong and fierce, entering the room from the opposite wall and exiting through the wall at his shoulder.

Connor instinctively moved aside, allowing it more space. The light beam was thin in the way that sheet metal is thin, or a laser beam.

His mouth was dry. Licking his lips, Connor raised the telescope again and searched for, and found, the light being reflected from the prism; and what he saw made his breath catch.

So what he had in mind might work.

A moment later the room returned to utter blackness. Connor felt his way to the door and slipped out.

Chapter Twenty-Three

It was like standing in a whirlwind. Rebecca's bag was whipped in front of her, jerking her shoulder and slapping her ribs, and at the same time she was yanked backwards by something hard round her waist so that she stumbled and lost her balance. There seemed to be a lot of noise, and she felt something solid against her shoulder blades, which was a relief because without it she'd have fallen.

With a screech of rubber the motorcycle that had come from nowhere slewed to a stop away to her left, and Rebecca saw the rider twist round. His helmet visor concealed his face but his body language was unmistakable: pure outrage.

Her bag swung against her once more and came to rest. Incredibly, that was all that had been hit by the motorbike; she herself was untouched.

I was nearly killed.

And yet here she stood, upright on her two feet, undamaged, with the rest of her life still intact.

Her heart was hammering though.

He could have been killed as well.

Rebecca took a shaky breath and opened her mouth to apologise, only to have her words stall in her throat as someone else did the job, using a light baritone voice that nevertheless vibrated in her ear.

'So sorry. Really sorry. I turned my back for a second and she just…She can't help it. Are you alright?'

*Turned my back…She can't help it…*Rebecca, shock receding and senses returning, felt afresh the solid wall that had stopped her from falling and which was still in light contact with her back even now. She made a bid to turn round, but found her waist was still encircled.

'What the–' Her words trickled away as she realised she was being walked.

'*Step.*'

Rebecca stepped up the kerb onto the pavement, and finally became free…was made free…he freed her. It had nothing to do with her own efforts, and in fact once detached she became aware how badly her legs were shaking.

Settling her bag strap firmly on her shoulder, she took the step backwards that was vital for her dignity and sense of self before looking at the face of her saviour.

Quick and intent, eyes sharp and brows raised, one side of his mouth lifted in silent humour and shockingly, tremblingly close, the Jack of Hearts looked back.

'I found you!' Rebecca said, without warning herself first.

'You found me,' the Knave of Vines said. 'And now you need tea.'

They walked side by side to the café above the harbour, and somehow Rebecca went through the door first and then somehow the choice of table was made on her behalf, and the chair.

She was being managed. She sat down and then stood up again.

'Actually, do you mind if we swap sides?'

They swapped, solemnly, and Rebecca wondered if he knew why.

Probably.

Or realised how very small her protest felt.

Probably.

Irritated but for the present resigned, Rebecca busied herself folding her coat on the empty chair next to her and wondered whether she was ready yet to meet his eyes. She risked a quick glance and thought probably not.

The café was a favourite of hers, and the familiarity of the warm, bright-coloured walls, the blackboard menus and the background hubbub of cutlery and conversation soothed her.

She ordered black coffee, not tea. Her stomach was still queasy after the shock, although how much of that was down to her near miss with the motorbike and how much to being saved she wasn't sure.

I am having coffee with a fairy, she thought, and stared into the dark liquid, too hot yet to drink.

'Why were you so difficult to find?' she asked. Her voice croaked a bit, but she ignored that.

'Part of the test.'

'*Test?*' Rebecca looked up then.

'Of course. I have to be sure. There is only so much information that can be obtained from research, and there's a point after which observation becomes critical. It's an important choice, Rebecca. A big thing. This is not a game.'

He didn't talk like a fairy. On the other hand, why should she know how a fairy would talk?

This is not a game.

She was standing on the brink now. Instinct told Rebecca that if she said the obvious words now, let the conversation run, *did not stop him*, then matters would be revealed to her that would change her understanding of the world and her place in it more deeply even than all the events of the past six years.

She was poised on the cliff edge, able as yet to back away from the void beyond and continue her life as Rebecca Mulligan, artist and illustrator and citizen of Skye, undisturbed – relatively – by the realm of magic and wonder that had touched her.

But the void tugged.

If I allow him to talk, Rebecca thought, *I'll never be the same again.*

But all her questions would be answered, and she would know.

Rebecca said, 'What is not a game?'

And the Knave of Vines told her.

Fresh coffee arrived, and later, when the fish and chips had settled, a dish of warm flatbread which they shared. Rebecca had no idea whether it contained leeks or tomatoes or what kind of cheese. She was vaguely aware of customers arriving at the table next to theirs and later leaving, and of the waitress clearing the empty plates away and wiping the surface, and still she sat at the window overlooking the sea listening to the stuff of dreams and legend.

Always over coffee, she thought, this stuff always happens

over coffee. At first it had been mugs of instant coffee in the tiny office behind Michael's London studio, when he had told her of a world just next door where magic existed and of the strangers who sometimes stumbled here. Then it had been the café upstairs in Blackwells Bookshop in Oxford, where Connor had recounted a little – only ever a little – of what had happened to him on the far side of the gap between worlds.

And now, once again, she sat over coffee listening to a man with dark, dark eyes and a voice that licked around her, speaking of wonders.

Wasn't he concerned they'd be overheard?

'We won't be,' he said.

'Won't be how? Can't anyone else hear you? Or are you scrambling the language?' While he was this close to her, Rebecca was ready to believe anything.

'They'll hear but the words will just slip away.'

'In other words, you're magicking everyone here, just like you've been magicking people all along!'

He smiled. Rebecca's skin fizzed and her stomach took a dive. The very business of getting through, second after second, minute after minute, with him three feet from her was wearing her out. She desperately needed either to turn her back and walk away or climb into his lap, and she wasn't at all sure which it was going to be. How *could* Bridget Dixon, and Maggie Davenport, and those women in the library, and even Steph on New Year's Day, not have remembered him?

Rebecca said, 'So you're just turning it off for me.'

'I don't need to. It doesn't work on you. That's how I knew who you are.' Then he added, 'Can be.'

It was logical. The system of formal arbitration he had described would fall apart utterly if the Queen of Clover, as arbiter, could be influenced. *Skill* Connor had called it, and it seemed almost everybody in that other world possessed it at least to some degree.

Connor had understood that their nature, these people that Rebecca balked at calling fairies, was casual, vague, easily distracted to a level which here would be called negligent. It was as if they lacked the focus to commit crime. That, coupled with the astonishing fertility of the place leading to an abundance of food for all, resulted in a society that was really not very materialistic. It sounded idyllic to Rebecca, who considered she herself had become much less materialistic since moving to Skye.

Inevitably there were occasional disputes, and these were resolved by bringing them before the Queen of Clover, who listened to the arguments from both sides and then made a decision by which everybody always abided. It took place in public, and if either party resisted or, heaven forbid, disobeyed the ruling, he or she would be ostracized and would never be able to do business again.

It sounded elegant, efficient, and trouble-free. But of course it wasn't, not entirely.

'The stories tell that the best decision-makers have always been those who came from farther away than it was possible to travel. Some of us interpret that to mean here.'

'Uriel Passenger did.'

'Yes.'

Rebecca thought about Emily Seward and her cool stare.

'But he didn't send anyone back for you.'

'No.'

Should Emily have been the occupant of that cold throne, weighing what was right and fair and delivering her judgements to be accepted and acted upon without dissent? Why did she not go? Fear? Disbelief? Or had Uriel discovered that she would not after all be immune to skilful influences worked upon her?

Was that why Uriel had abandoned her, baby and all, and gone to father the line that ended with poor, mad Celia Scanlon? But presumably Celia's ancestor had declined the offer too. Rebecca found herself wondering whether the bitter jealousy that had ruined Celia Scanlon's life had been a terrible misunderstanding all along; that the disinheritance she had learned from her mother had not related to property but to the status and rights her ancestor would have held had she taken up the opportunity to become Queen of Clover in the World Invisible.

Because there had to be benefits as well as duties, didn't there?

'Of course. Think of it as a contract. And there will be people who will help.'

'You?' Rebecca asked unguardedly, and immediately wished she hadn't.

The fairy man's bright eyes melted her bones. 'Every Queen of Clover has her Knave of Vines,' he said.

Chapter Twenty-Four

After Connor had left three voice messages and simply hung up half a dozen times after that, his call was finally picked up. He almost jumped.

'Rebecca!'

'Yes. What is it?'

On the spur of the moment he couldn't remember what it was; his original reason for wanting to speak to her had given way to anxiety about whether she was still there at all.

'How are you?' Lame, but he wanted to know.

'Fine. I'm fine. How are you?'

'Fine.'

Stupid conversation. Connor lurched to his senses. 'Oh yes! Did you get the journal?'

'Journal? Oh, right, of course. Yes, I did.'

In the room overlooking the quad, Connor frowned at the pin board above his desk, not seeing the timetables or notes or photographs, but picturing instead Rebecca, cool and competent and slightly scornful, the way she always had been, the way she was made to be, not at all the way she was sounding now.

She might say she was fine, but she wasn't.

'And?'

'And…it was…very interesting.'

'Rebecca, what's going on?'

'Nothing's going on.'

Connor waited, knowing there were times when simple silence had the power to unlock even mighty doors. He allowed Rebecca to pause and hear him waiting, and was rewarded.

'Well, there is something.' Rebecca paused again. 'I don't really want to talk about it. Yet.'

He could empathise with that. 'Are you alright, though? Forget *fine*, are you okay?'

'Yes. I am alright. I'm a bit…preoccupied, that's all.'

Again Connor gave her time but nothing more was forthcoming, and he said, 'Well, I'm going to Ashendon at the weekend, so do you need anything else from the cottage?'

'Oh. No, thanks. Not now.'

And that was unguarded too.

Rebecca finished the call and looked glumly at the screen before it blacked out. Plainly Connor guessed she was concealing something, and she felt bad evading his questions. She told herself that she was under no obligation to confide in him, and that anyway she would explain everything when she was ready, but it didn't make her feel any better. It was complicated, and came under the heading of People Stuff, at which she knew, in her heart, she was not especially talented.

She sighed and went through to the kitchen, where Will was chopping onions and celeriac and squash for a roasted vegetable medley she knew would be delicious.

They had settled into an easy domesticity that slightly alarmed Rebecca when she thought about it, so she thought about it as little as possible.

After that long, long talk in the café above the harbour, there had followed four days during which Will had left each evening to walk the three miles to the pub where he was staying, and then on the fifth day Rebecca suggested he might stay over. 'I'm sorry the back bedroom hasn't much of a view,' she had added, heading off any misunderstandings at the start, and then spent the next two nights horribly occupied by thoughts of the dividing wall.

By the third night she was exhausted and just slept.

The week had passed in a clichéd blur. How could he keep on talking like this without getting a sore throat? It was a mystery to her almost as great as how she was able to go on listening and taking it in.

Not all of it, of course; he had to repeat things sometimes.

'But there was someone doing the job when you left?' Rebecca asked, knowing this had been touched upon but unable quite to recall the details.

'Yes. But she is not fit. She can be influenced. It isn't working well.'

'And how will she feel if I waltz in?'

'She will be relieved and eager to leave.'

If I waltz in, she had said.

After a week the idea still seemed preposterous.

Will – not his real name, of course – had come specifically to find her and persuade her to go into the World Invisible and take up the duties of legal arbiter and law-maker, to settle disputes and mete out punishment.

Less *punishment,* more *recompense,* he said; she wouldn't be handing out prison terms.

'We don't lock people up,' Will told her.

'You locked Connor up,' Rebecca said.

'Alright, we don't lock people up usually. But that was to protect everyone.'

He had been afraid of contamination, both intellectual – as if Connor single-handedly would have started an industrial revolution – and also physical. The possibility of a minor infectious disease from this world running rampant through the vulnerable population of the other could not be ignored forever.

'Michael Seward went through,' Rebecca pointed out. 'And Jack spent time here and then returned. He could have been carrying infection.'

'I know. But the fact that isolated incidents have occurred without bringing disaster doesn't make it safe. You will be a risk too, but one we have to take.'

'What about the cats?'

'The *cats?*'

Rebecca shifted. Her question had raised the wild, amused delight that seemed to run like fire in his veins, always so close to the surface. She said, defensively, 'The Dons said cats can go to and fro between the worlds. Can't they, then?'

'No!' Will laughed, turning Rebecca's muscles to milk and her sinews to cotton. 'We have cats of our own, thank you, and they're the right size too!'

'And ours never slip across?'

'Maybe accidentally, once in a while. Not as a matter of life style.'

Rebecca was relieved. She had never felt comfortable with the idea and nowadays found it difficult to meet the stare of any cat she might pass in the street. She kept being reminded of the proverb about cats looking at queens.

Queens of Clover. Always the circle brought her back. Rebecca sighed.

'Did Michael tell you about me?' she had asked, early on.

'No. I've never met Michael.'

'Then how–'

'That's complicated, and it doesn't matter.'

What did matter, apparently, was that the stalking had all been part of the test, a way to discover whether she was truly made of the stuff necessary to be a good Queen of Clover.

'Wit, intelligence,' Will said, causing Rebecca to blush. 'Interest, involvement – you didn't ignore me and walk away. Perseverance – you could have given up. Self-reliance – you didn't seek help.'

'I spoke to Connor,' Rebecca said.

'But only at the start. Once it got weird you kept him out of it.'

'And you did make it get weird,' Rebecca said dourly.

'Yes, I did.' His eyebrow flared, his grin pure wickedness. 'And courage – you have that.'

'Yes!' Rebecca sat up straight. 'I damn well have! You have no idea how frightened I was that night!'

'Oh I do.'

It seemed she possessed everything required by a Queen of Clover, including that most vital quality of all: immunity. The Queen must be proof against all attempts to influence her; magic – Skill – simply must not work on her, ever.

'Nobody else noticed me or remembered me,' Will told her, 'only you.'

Far from switching it off for her, he had been using all his strength to wield his Skill against her from the start. 'But you picked me out of the crowd, every time. Even when I wasn't within sight.'

Rebecca remembered the itch between her shoulder blades. It seemed to her that she had been living with the supernatural, or at least the awareness that it existed, for so long she had forgotten to find it strange. He seemed so powerful to her, so full of life force, so electric, and yet only she felt it. Not even Steph...

'Steph,' she said, before the thought had fully formed in her mind. She looked at Will and saw him watching her with intent. She said slowly, 'Steph could never remember my dream.'

'Of course not.'

'But why? It was my dream, not yours.'

Will said, 'How did she react when you told her about Michael? Ashendon? The gaps?'

'As if I were talking about – I don't know – groceries. Shoes. The next-door neighbours.'

'And yet you were speaking of marvels.'

Rebecca looked at him, and he looked back, waiting. She said, 'It's been as if…as if Skill were being used.'

Will smiled.

'But I don't have Skill. I can't use it. I've never even been there.'

Will said, 'As if you needed any more proof.'

Chapter Twenty-Five

It took Connor less than half an hour to set everything up. He had to use an extension lead from the parlour of course, but Michael had had the cottage rewired two years ago on grounds of safety and there was no risk of overloading the system.

The tripod he had bought from the camera shop worked well. He drafted in one of the kitchen chairs and a few books, and did his best to approximate the positioning so that only small adjustments would be needed when he fine-tuned it later.

He set an alarm for one forty-five in the morning.

Rebecca gave up trying to sleep and checked the time. It was a quarter to two. She slipped into her dressing gown and went downstairs to make a drink, only to find the kitchen lit and Will leaning against the cupboard where she kept the mugs.

Damn.

'Can't sleep either?' he asked. He turned his back to reach for a second mug, and Rebecca found she was drawing her cotton gown closer round her. She tied the belt more securely.

'Coffee?' Will asked.

'Tea.'

She wasn't going to say 'please' when it was her tea and her mug. And her hot water.

He had on a tee-shirt of some indeterminate khaki-ish shade, soft from wear, and grey bottoms; his feet were bare despite the wood floor. Rebecca watched the movement of his shoulder blades as he poured water into the mugs, and thought about his skin underneath the thin cotton. Her own skin felt raw and hot; she shivered.

Will, Liam, Guillermo, they were all versions of the name William. She had looked it up. 'William' meant 'defender of the realm'. Was he actually defending his realm or was it a random choice, just a common enough name to fit in anywhere?

'Garcia' meant 'like a fox', but like in which ways? Not colouring, not in this case. Clever, lithe and beautiful? Or cunning, predatory and sly?

He handed Rebecca her mug. 'Careful, I over-filled it.'
Yes, mustn't scald the Queen of Clover.

Rebecca said, 'What is your surname?' She read his quirked eyebrow and added, 'I mean what are you using here on Skye?'

'Good question for the middle of the night. Fox.'

He was smiling with one side of his face only.

Rebecca's hand wobbled and the coffee slopped.

'Ow! Damn.'

She crossed to the sink and let some of the drink tip away, ran the tap and mopped up. There seemed to be even less air in the kitchen than there had been in her bedroom, and she was having to breathe at the top of her lungs, her chest and shoulders tight.

She concentrated on wiping the rim of the mug and did not realise he had moved until she felt his fingertips touch the nape of her neck beneath her night-time plait of hair. But when he did, in the instant that his fingers came into contact with her skin and stroked the two inches downwards to the collar of her robe, her bones and all the soft tissue that wrapped them slackened and blurred. Her breath escaped her in a sound she was powerless to prevent, neither a whimper nor a sigh but something in between, and as she turned round she knew it was already too late.

She knew what would happen, and she knew it was inevitable, so it was no surprise at all when it did.

By twenty past two Connor was propped against the wall in the dark room, weighing the thesaurus in his right hand. It was a fat paperback, and although it hurt to do this to any book, there was a duplicate copy in hardback on the shelves in the parlour. This one would have to be sacrificed.

It was a clearer night with less cloud, and the soft, thin beam was a little less faint. He waited, staring, for the moment when reality would crack and the alien light would appear.

And there it was – brighter and hotter than the moonlight, a thin, anxious line piercing the wall and travelling through the space made for it.

Immediately Connor was in motion. With his left hand he removed one of the prisms mounted on its stand, so that the beam of moonlight was no longer safely deflected downwards. Freed, it cut straight across the space and collided – if you can talk about light beams colliding – with that of the other world.

Photons exploded. Heart racing, his breath tight, Connor ignored the writhing forms that danced in front of him to toss the book through the dazzle, and then swiftly replaced the prism.

Order was restored. The forms vanished, the glare was gone, and only the two pencil lines of light remained, moving politely past one another.

Connor counted the seconds, waiting for his pulse to settle, and then at last the alien light beam removed itself and darkness flowed back.

Finished.

Connor returned to the parlour and woke up his laptop. He clicked on the surveillance icon and opened the new application that ran the wireless IP camera.

A few moments later an image appeared on the screen of a stone wall, bare and very dark, quickly followed by a second picture of the same room much brighter, the stones of the wall clear-cut and sharply in focus.

The third image revealed the thesaurus lying on the ground, upside down as it had landed. The pages were a wreck but the spine faced him and Connor could read the title without difficulty.

The connection to the hotel's wireless network functioned perfectly. His crazy idea was going to work.

Rebecca lay awake and alert, her brain a mess of tangled and knotted thought that wrapped around her and squeezed her, refusing to grant her respite.

Her eyes were wide open in the dark.

She was sure he was asleep.

Taking care to move quietly, Rebecca rolled from under the duvet and felt about for her slippers. It wouldn't be a quick sortie for a drink this time.

With the kitchen door closed behind her, she began to breathe more easily, although she took care to be quiet with the cupboard doors. When the hot chocolate was made she took it through to the studio and tucked her feet under her on the saggy sofa she had inherited from Michael.

This is your thinking place, she told herself, *so think!*

It was still only four o'clock; she had plenty of time. Gradually solitude, silence and the high empty space of the two-storey studio worked their quiet healing on the twisted fibres of her thoughts, smoothing them and straightening them and laying them out tidily for her to examine. She grew chilly, and pulled the bright woven throw around her. Wrapping up to keep warm had long been her preferred state; she always hated being hot in summer.

When she had drunk the tea she reached for her pad and began to write a list, and as she wrote, numbering the points and leaving a blank line between each, she realised with a little shock – but to be honest not much – that her brain was producing counter-arguments without any conscious effort on her part at all.

I will not do this because:

1 *It is nothing to do with me and is none of my business.*

That should have been true but Rebecca knew it wasn't. Ever since the day six years ago when Michael saw what she had been drawing at the V&A and told her that Fairyland was real, she had been involved one way and another with the rifts between the worlds. At times she felt it to be really unfair that the responsibility had somehow been dumped across her shoulders like a yoke, and had toyed with the idea of slipping out from under it and letting someone else deal with the fallout.

But she never had. Over and over, when push came to shove, she had rolled up her metaphorical sleeves and dealt with things. Dealing with things was something she believed she was good at, and – to be brutally honest with herself – she felt it compensated for not being good with people. She felt it balanced the scales a little.

2 *I wouldn't know how to do it anyway – I am an artist, not a lawyer.*

Except that what Will had described sounded a lot like common sense, and she considered she had plenty of that. She wouldn't need to be trained up or Will would have said so (wouldn't he?). It sounded as though the primary requirement, once it was known that she was immune to Skill, was to think straight and to want affairs to be tidy. Rebecca took pride in her capacity for straight thinking, and untidiness irritated her. She liked things finished and filed away, not lingering scruffily in the pending tray. If she were Queen of Clover, she'd get on with the job.

3   *I don't have time because I have a commission with a deadline to meet.*

True, but it was a long way off and Will was asking for only five days. Only five days to begin with. That was what she was weighing up at present, because that was all she could imagine; and she could, she knew, afford to take a five-day holiday.

4   *I'm not good at learning languages.*

Undeniably true. Still, Will had dismissed this problem more than once. 'You'll cope,' he said, 'believe me.' So assuming he was right...

5   *I might do it wrong.*

She was forced to allow this to be a possibility. On the other hand, anyone might do anything wrong. The world – either of them, presumably – was full of people doing things wrong, and most of the time it wasn't irrevocable. It is how you learn. And since she hadn't asked for the job it would be ungrateful in the extreme for them to hold the odd slip-up against her.

6   *I wouldn't have time to draw.*

Oh tosh, there's *always* time to draw. She would make time. They could lump it.

7   *I might not be able to find the way back.*

Very scary prospect. But Will would be there, and she would take immense care to mark the spot. Leave a trail of breadcrumbs perhaps. No, truly, she would take whatever measures were necessary to ensure she could return safely.

   Rebecca reviewed what she had written and what had rushed through her head in response. She knew, from the stillness and the calm within her, that her mind was making itself up, as if it were independent of her. Already it was just a case of how much influence she cared to exert to alter its course.
   She noticed what her pencil had been doing – drawing, of course, as it always did in spare moments – and saw the big sleeves and tight bodice and the stars all around.
   Carefully and slowly, in nice, neat, uniform script, she wrote:

8   *I do not have the right clothes.*

Chapter Twenty-Six

There was one other argument for not going and Rebecca was fully conscious of it. It was that she was afraid. But that went without saying and therefore she did not write it down. Knowing it was bad enough; reading it in black-and-white was something she could spare herself.

She had never understood how first Connor and then Michael could have stepped across into another plane of existence, utterly unknown, and from which there was no assured means of return. The gaps opened once every twenty-four hours for a few moments only, and who knew what might happen to you in such a place while you waited for the way to open again? Marauding bands of wild tallixers would probably be the least of her worries.

The shifting shadows and flickering forms she had glimpsed through the clashing light had weakened her sinews each time and made her feel faint, even when she knew she could stay safely back from the brink and that the gap would close in a minute or two. How *could* Connor and Michael have walked into them? It was something she would never understand.

And yet here she stood, on the brink herself not of the other world, not yet, but of a decision which would take her there just as surely. And she knew what was driving her, at least in part.

Once, when she was a teenager and still at school, Rebecca had allowed herself to get drunk. Not rolling drunk, not staggering and sick, but enough red wine at a party, just enough, for her to realise that she was laughing too much, talking too much, using her hands to gesticulate a little too extravagantly. The following day, remembering, she had made up her mind never to drink that much again, and she never had. It was the insult to her pride in retaining control, of her vulnerability once unable to judge her actions and words, which hurt and frightened her.

And now Will had made her drunk again, not with alcohol but with his proximity. She had loved Michael secretly, from afar; she had fallen in love with Connor for himself. Neither did she regret for an instant. But Will was different. He drew from her a response which was fierce and ungovernable, as if a storm had broken out within her, thunder and lightning in her blood, more than she could control and far more than she wanted.

If she applied logic it didn't necessarily make sense; allowing him to take her into his own foreign world was hardly the obvious way to avoid intimacy. But she couldn't live with him here, in her house, and she had no confidence in her ability to throw him out. What was he going to do – shrug and walk away? This was the Jack of Hearts, for heaven's sake, on a vital and long-term mission. But if she complied, did as he asked, took this five-day challenge…

It wasn't even a week. She would be back by the end of the month and it would all be in the past.

Including Will.

Rebecca sat on the stairs with her phone in her hand. She told herself she was getting her thoughts straight and deciding what to say, but really she was summoning courage.

Will had gone. She had given him her decision and watched him drop his gaze, his head bowed: the Jack of Hearts, face down. Then he had lifted it again and that desperate, crazy smile was back in his eyes so that Rebecca had to take a tight grip on herself.

She told him she wanted twenty-four hours alone to prepare, and was relieved to meet no argument. Where he had gone she didn't know – back to bed-and-breakfast at the pub probably, although who knew how far a fairy man might walk? She had laundered clothes and checked the fridge and decided what to pack, and shut down her laptop and unplugged the television set from the wall. Now all she needed to do was call Connor.

Rebecca bit her top lip and pressed the key.

It seemed to Connor that he knew it was Rebecca even while the phone was still in his pocket. He almost didn't bother to check the screen.

'Hi, Rebecca.'

'Hi.' She sounded cagey. 'How are you?'

Formalities first.

'I'm fine. You?'

'I'm fine. Listen. You're not at Ashendon, are you?'

Cagey but diving in.

Connor said, 'No, Oxford.'

'And you're not thinking of–'

'I'm not going back for a while,' Connor said. 'Don't worry, I won't be there.'

He heard her voice sharpen. 'Won't be there when?'

Perhaps he was going too far, but he could only trust his instincts, and his instincts were telling him to plough on.

'When you go through, Rebecca. I know you're going through.'

There was silence. Connor glanced fleetingly at the clock above his desk and then swivelled to turn his back to it. Rebecca had called at an inconvenient time and he might end up late for his lecture, but this was too important.

'How could you know…'

The uncertainty in her voice touched his heart. She was so sure always, held such confidence in her own judgement, and she seemed like a waif without it. Connor said gently, 'Just a feeling. I don't know. I think I've suspected for a while.'

He heard her make a bid for lightness. 'Longer than I have then.'

That might well be. She wasn't too practised at looking within herself.

He said, 'You remember the telescope?'

'Telescope? Of course.'

'Well, when you get there you'll see what I've done with it.'

The distraction worked; her voice picked up energy, and as he explained, some of the shadow lifted.

Astonishment helped, too!

'You're kidding! And it works?'

'It works perfectly. I'll email you an image if you like.'

'No, it's okay, I believe you. Wow, though.'

'Yes, wow.'

'And so,' Rebecca said, more successful with the lightness this time, 'you'll be keeping an eye out for me.'

'Yes,' Connor said. 'I will always keep an eye out for you.'

* * *

What do you take to Fairyland? Rebecca had asked herself this question before, wondering what Michael had stowed in his rucksack. Now it was her turn to pack.

Tee-shirts and underwear; you can't face the unknown with confidence if you don't have clean underwear. Sneakers, because she would be wearing walking boots and presumably at some point they would go indoors. An A4 sketchbook, pencils and a small field box of watercolours, because even though Connor said they had paper, who knew what quality it would be, or how long before she had some of it in her hand?

A toothbrush, a comb, and a few spare elastics in case she lost the one holding her plait now; she didn't want loose hair getting in her way. A scrap of paper with Connor's phone number on it; he was more like next-of-kin to her now than her stepfather, buried in Suffolk with his herd of British Blues, and daft or not, she felt better for having it.

And sandwiches. How banal. But it seemed wise to make provision for a couple of meals, at least.

Rebecca fastened the flap and shoved a bottle of water in the net pocket. Keys for Ashendon clipped to her belt, milk poured down the sink, Maggie Davenport informed that she'd be away for a week. *Don't worry, I'm not expecting any deliveries.*

All she had to do now was drive to Matlock with only the gear lever between herself and Will.

Rebecca shook her head and shut the door.

At ten past two Rebecca shut the door and stood in the darkness of the hidden room, waiting for her eyes to adjust to the low gloom of the beam of moonlight that travelled across the space, careful to stand well clear of the contraption Connor had left.

However had he thought of it? The telescope, clamped to a tripod, pointed at the place where the light beam from the world invisible entered the prism.

The lenses in the telescope were polarised, he had discovered, and there were two of them. That meant that when adjusted to the correct relationship, at right angles to one another, then what you saw when looking through was flat black. Nothing at all.

But Connor had asked questions and learned about something called the Three Polarisers Experiment and the quantum theory explanation, all of which had led to his discovering that although when their telescope was rotated correctly it cut out all the normal light, nevertheless light from the Other World was still able to come through.

And this meant that if you looked at the faint trace of otherworld light that escaped from the prism, you saw everything.

That was amazing in itself, but he had gone further. There was now a security spy camera on a pile of books which peered straight into the eyepiece of the telescope. It was monitoring all the time, and if it detected movement, or a sudden change in light level – in other words, the kind of effect a housebreaker would cause – then it took a photograph and zipped it straight to the computer that was running it – in this case, Connor's.

He had told her he could read the cover of the book he had thrown through, so if she wanted to send him a message, she need only write it – large – and prop it facing the gap for the camera to record it and Connor to be notified. Telegraphy, almost. Security.

'Don't touch anything!' she had warned Will, who laughed, which made her cross.

He stood next to her now. The tension must be touching even him, for he was silent and seemed preoccupied.

Rebecca's breathing was tight and shivery.

Five days, it's only for five days.

Standing here on the edge she found it difficult to remember how much she had wanted Will away. Now, he was a rock, her champion, an armoured truck that would keep her safe in face of the unknown, and it was all she could do not to reach out and grasp his hand.

Two twenty.

The keys were in a drawer in the dresser. She had been worried about getting locked in, and had fussed over the best place for them to stay for the five days. Displacement activity.

She had thrown away half a pint of milk from the carton they brought with them as well. Such a waste.

What am I doing here? I always said I'd never do this. Why am I doing this?

Rebecca opened her mouth to say...what? That she had changed her mind? That Will could go through by himself? That she was too afraid to do what Michael and Connor had each done, and she no longer cared who knew?

And then the light swelled as the thin beam entered, and her words died in her throat.

Will dislodged one prism, and Rebecca whimpered as the light exploded, the colours and shapes writhing and reaching for her. She was rooted, unable to feel her feet much less move them. Her skin had turned to ice.

Will said something; he was tugging at her.

'What?' She could hardly breathe.

'Quick!'

He was holding her rucksack strap. She said, 'Don't we have to go? We have to go!' She felt faint, starved of oxygen, her lips numb.

'I know. Give me the bag, quick – best if I take it.'

Rebecca, bewildered and dizzy, slipped her arms free and released the rucksack. It might well be better if he took it – she was having to concentrate just to balance on her feet.

'Now!'

The room was beating with the sub-sonic throb she remembered, the dazzle red against her eyes. Appalled by her own actions, Rebecca took a step towards the threshold between worlds and felt Will's hand firm on her back.

She groped behind, fingers searching for him, but found only space. He was there, she knew he was there because she could feel the push between her shoulders, but she didn't seem able to find him...

'Will?'

'Go!'

And as she stepped into the light she felt him shove so that she stumbled forward, landing with a thud on her hands and knees...

...in daylight.

'*Will!*'

She scrambled to her feet and spun round, but the room was empty all around her, and Will, her rucksack, Ashendon Cottage and everything she had ever known had vanished.

DOWN THE RABBIT HOLE

Chapter Twenty-Seven

The first day: five days left

Rebecca sat down, very carefully, sinking to one knee at a time and steadying herself with her hands on the floor. She was shaking, and the beats of her heart were like body blows from within. Her ears and throat and most of all her collarbone winced under the onslaught. She couldn't breathe.

This is a panic attack. Just a panic attack. Sit still and wait.

She never had panic attacks.

Don't think about it.

Rebecca closed her eyes and tried desperately not to think about what had happened to her or where she was.

It was impossible.

She opened her eyes again and shuffled to one side of the door, and then sat with her back to the stone wall and waited for her metabolism to right itself.

Breathe.

Rebecca breathed, and as her heart rate gradually steadied she was aware of her thinking-brain wriggling free from the blanket of fear and shaking itself and getting down to work. It began to take notice of what her eyes were seeing and her ears were hearing, and started, little by little, to formulate possible courses of action.

The walls of the room were unadorned stone, just as in the cottage, but the floor here was simply bare earth; not beaten down, though, like the floor of a hovel that was lived in, but merely devoid of grass.

Not enough light for grass to grow except the half-metre inside the doorway, Rebecca thought, and then thought: *I'm thinking again! About time!* Blind terror did not align with her opinion of herself at all.

She took a deep breath and flexed her shoulders. Better, although still fluttery in her abdomen.

Ignore it.

Let's be practical.

Yes, Rebecca thought, let's.

The light streaming in through the open doorway was certainly not moonlight. As far as she could recall, Connor had never mentioned what time of day he had landed in, either going or returning, and Rebecca had never asked. She realised now, with a sick little feeling of regret, that there was a book-load of questions she could have asked which would have made her feel less unprepared now. But of course she had never dreamed – never nightmared – that she would find herself here, alone, needing information. Even when she had decided to come, to take that desperate step off the cliff, she had assumed she would be escorted by a native who would take care of all the business stuff.

Rebecca thought grimly of the hand that had stripped her of her rucksack and then pushed her through the gap. What an unspeakably foul thing to do. What a treacherous swine.

I'll just stick here and go back tomorrow when the gap opens. Stuff him.

She could wait it out. There was a roof. She'd be hungry and thirsty, but she'd manage. It was what they had agreed to do in five days' time anyway – return here, wait for the light to burst forth, and walk back into Ashendon Cottage in time for breakfast.

Except the thing that would have made that possible was the prism being out of position throughout their absence, allowing the light beams to continue to mingle and the way to remain open. But if Will had replaced the prism then the light beams would move elegantly around each other and the way would be closed to her. And for sure he would have replaced it.

A little jump of fright hopped in Rebecca's chest, and she stamped on it, quick, before it could take hold.

What Will had or hadn't done didn't matter because Connor had rigged up his amazing communication channel, just for her. All she had to do was write a message and prop it in front of the light beams for it to pop up on his laptop screen, and she knew with certainty he would come for her then, no matter what lectures he might miss.

The book Connor had thrown in was lying in the middle of the room, its pages crumpled beneath its weight where it had landed, marking the spot for her to position her message. But she had no paper on which to write a message, nor pen to write it with, because that had all been in the rucksack of which Will had so basely deprived her.

Rebecca thought rude words and tried to concentrate.

In her hip pocket, today as every day, reposed a small, postcard-sized sketchbook with a short clutch pencil slotted into the spiral binding. It was as much part of Rebecca as her wrist watch and, for the last few years, the gold vine leaf necklace; just now it carried the hand-painted Queen of Clover card she had stolen from Connor too, sandwiched safely between its sheets; she had decided to bring it from Skye at the last minute, extracting it from her jewellery box after everything else was packed. Now she slid the book out and flipped through the pages.

Over half were already used. Unlike the larger sketchbook she had chosen specially, this was just her current pocket book, for emergency sketching on the fly. Text written on one of these pages would be too small for Connor to read through the telescope and the camera, and if she were to tear out a batch she would have no way to stick them together. She'd also have none left for actual drawing.

Would that matter? The room was sheltered so no breeze would ruffle the papers. She tried to ignore the prospect of having nothing to draw on.

Rebecca envisaged herself arranging the patchwork of torn out sheets and blocking in the letters. What would she write? *Come and get me* ? *Don't trust Will* ? Or simply *HELP!!!* ?

She riffled the pages. Will was squatting in the cottage this very minute. He had probably dismantled the Wallace-and-Grommet arrangement on the chair in the hidden room and her message would never reach Connor anyway. What would Connor do when he saw the camera had cut out? Zoom up to Ashendon and fight it out? Unlikely images danced through her brain of two astonishingly handsome men indulging in fisticuffs because of her, and, amazingly, she snorted with laughter.

Rebecca shivered, then rubbed her face and flexed her fingers. She tore out a single precious page from the sketchbook. She wrote, read it back, and signed her name. Then she rescued the abandoned book – it was a thesaurus – and placed the sheet of paper inside, positioning it so that two inches peeped out over the top, and placed the book neatly back on the ground.

Then she stepped over the threshold into the sunlight that awaited her.

Deep in the leaf mould, beneath the stands of bracken, something twitched, scratched, and sniffed.

It shrank still further back, until tree bark met the humped spine.

In the shadows under the trees, it faced the clearing and the hut, and watched.

Chapter Twenty-Eight

The stone room was, as Connor had said, an anomaly planted in the middle of a forest. 'Shared space', Michael had once called it. In Ashendon Cottage the room had a regular ceiling and a pitched and tiled roof above it. Here the four stone walls were covered over by thatch and the door was simply three stout planks of wood joined vertically, with a loop of twine threaded through a hole near the edge. From inside the room you could push it open or pull it to behind you, but whoever had last used the gap had left it ajar.

The room stood in a small clearing, the trees allowing it perhaps six feet or so all round, and here the grass was up to Rebecca's knees and feathery with seed heads. The pearly light falling into the clearing had a morningish quality to it, but there was no dew. It was also considerably milder than it had been in Derbyshire, and Rebecca shrugged off her jacket and tied it round her waist by the sleeves. She felt she wanted her hands free, just in case, although just in case of what she hoped not to find out.

When Connor came through here six years ago, he had walked through the trees until he came to a wall too high to climb, and then followed that wall to a door. But which direction had he taken?

Rebecca stood in the long grass and searched with her eyes for some indication of a path between the gnarled, green-grey tree trunks that surrounded her.

And there it was, ahead and to the left: a space between two wide trees that was not completely filled in with tightly packed, small-leaved undergrowth. With a brief glance back at the stone hut, its dark interior just visible through the slanting door, Rebecca swallowed and set off into the wood.

The way was level, apart from the spreading roots that crossed the path, and the canopy was dense enough for the forest floor to be mostly clear. The ground felt spongy under Rebecca's soles, a thick mat of leaves fallen in previous generations, and the scent of damp bark and bitter sap pervaded the air she breathed. No pine, though; the forest was deciduous, and the leaves above her were immature and pale green. It was late spring; no wonder she was warm.

Don't take sweaters, Will had said, *it won't be very cold.*

Little had she guessed he was setting her up for a solo trip.

Bastard.

And yet...

The thought of what she was doing right now had terrified her before. If Will had been with her, would she be leading the way through these trees or following meekly behind, staring only at his back?

That's no excuse.

No, but it was a thought...

But not one she had time for at present. Even as it occurred to her, she saw the glimpse of stone ahead. Half a minute later she had reached the wall and realised there was a fresh question to be asked.

Left or right?

The ground was clear in both directions, but Rebecca, without knowing why, felt more comfortable turning left and set off again keeping the wall on her right.

Now she could smell stone as well as bark, and was surprised to discover stone actually had a smell. Was this because of the world she was now in, she wondered, or should she put it down to the adrenalin coursing through her veins and heightening all her senses? For the moment it was at least an empowering dose of adrenalin, not a shivery, debilitating dose, and Rebecca was conscious of her personal need to keep moving. She instinctively knew that pausing would be a seriously bad idea, and when she found this door she would have to batter on it and hope they came very quickly indeed to let her out.

They...

Rebecca broke into a jog, despite the narrowness of the path and the frequency of the roots, in order to refocus her thoughts away from the people she was going to find herself facing so soon.

And then she had reached the door, the wood soft and grey like the great doors of the Oxford colleges, and with a black iron knocker, just as Connor had described.

So Rebecca lifted the plain, iron handle and was about to let it fall on the plate when she noticed the slim pencil-width of air between the edge of the door and the rough wooden door jamb.

The door was not closed. She could push it open for herself and walk through. She replaced the knocker quietly, thankful not to have announced her arrival after all.

Never pause, never stop.

But it was too late, and she had. On the brink of yet another threshold, Rebecca hesitated, trying to recall what Connor had told her of his arrival here.

He had knocked, he said, and someone had come and opened the door for him. That happened quite quickly, she'd gathered. Somebody had to have been close enough to hear his knock, and Rebecca felt that must have been pretty close.

What was on the other side of the door?

The sky above the wall looked clear, so not more trees, or at least not immediately. The farmstead where Connor had been incarcerated? Was she about to meet his captors, his guards?

Her stomach churned and she bit her lip. Stupid, stupid to have stopped – starting again was always so hard.

Will must know what he was doing. He wouldn't have shoved her here by herself if she was going to end up imprisoned.

Or was that part of the test? To see if she could get herself free?

Damn! Damn!

Rebecca listened, and heard only the whisper of leaves in the open air, the distant call of birds and the close-by crackle of something small – she hoped small – in the undergrowth.

She laid her palm on the fibrous wood.

There is a saying: if you cannot *be*, then act *as if*. Right now, right here, Rebecca knew that she could not be as she would like to be – confident, self-assured and powerful. So she would have to act as if.

I am the Queen of Clover, she thought, *and that means something here.*

She pushed the door open and walked through.

* * *

There was broad sunshine on the other side of the door and for a moment Rebecca paused again, although reluctantly, to get her bearings and take stock. Shading her eyes from the sun with her hands, she took in the landscape before her.

Around the wall grass grew, right up to the stones, broad-bladed and verdant and so dense that the earth was invisible, even looking straight down. The grassland spread in all directions, inclining gently downwards to Rebecca's right and gently upwards again to her left. To the right, perhaps a hundred metres away, a dark hedge formed one boundary of an enclosure and cattle, or something very like cattle, could be glimpsed grazing the hill beyond. Still farther, Rebecca could make out what looked like a roof.

Connor's farm?

Ahead of her, the ground was level and looked as if it led to a track or even a road running crossways to her. It seemed likely it wound its way to the farm. To her left, the land climbed smoothly to new trees, their bushy tops marching steadily higher and higher so that what Rebecca saw was a great bank of foliage.

Something, whether a buried half-memory or the words to a song she did not know, or even a scent she was not aware she could detect, seemed to want to guide her. Rebecca turned her back on the farmstead and the road and, lifting her feet high over the long grass, headed for the forest.

Or was it a wood?

Within a few feet of her having struggled through the bracken-like undergrowth fringing the trees, the sunlight and fresh air had been left behind, replaced by the closeness of bark and leaf mould. The sounds under the canopy were short-range sounds, like twigs snapping underfoot and the dry rustle of dead leaves.

Rebecca set her palms against trunks as she wound between them, wondering how old they were, and whether if they looked like oaks then they were, in fact, oaks. They were squat, with trunks wider than she could have hugged, although she wasn't given to hugging trees, with deep fissures in the bark and branches that jutted out at right-angles to the trunk and to each other. She kept having to duck to avoid taking a twig in the eye.

The ground beneath the forest carpet humped and dipped, with ancient roots lying in wait as if hoping to trip her, and the bark left a film of green moss on her hands. Rebecca misjudged a step and stubbed her foot on a stump, and it occurred to her that perhaps coming into the wood had been a poor choice after all.

But soon after that the thick, gnarled oaks gave way to taller, smoother trees whose branches spread elegantly at an angle above Rebecca's head, so that she could walk straight without worrying about losing her sight. The forest floor became more level and the space between the trunks a little wider. The fallen leaves here were larger, and Rebecca's feet in her walking boots swished through the dry reminders of previous seasons.

There was birdsong, but not close by, and the loudest sounds seemed to be those made by herself. Rebecca halted, pausing to listen, hardly afraid she would be tempted to stay stalled in the middle of a wood, and became aware of her own breathing, a little rougher now that the ground had begun seriously to climb.

She set off again, weaving between columns belted by horizontal bands of lichen, marking their change from polished nut-brown to cool grey, noticing the way they were wound about by the delicate embroidery of ivy tendrils, the trunks becoming ever more slender, the branches ever closer to vertical, until she walked beneath arches which soared like fan vaulting in a cathedral, and with that image, suddenly knew what lay ahead.

She had been here before, not in the flesh but in spirit. She had dreamed these trees, these spaces, this floor, and she had dreamed what waited for her beyond the perpendicular columns.

Even as she thought this she saw just ahead, almost the same colour as the skins of the trees but smoother, the stone face of the castle.

Quickening her pace, anxious not to permit herself to stall again and anyway eager suddenly to see more of this, her dream made real, Rebecca set her foot confidently on the first, shallow step. As she did so, she remembered she had dreamed not only of trees and steps and corridors.

She had also dreamed of a curtain.

Chapter Twenty-Nine

This door really was closed and Rebecca reached for the knocker. It was fashioned in the shape of a woman's head, shoulders and arms emerging from a tree – a dryad, Rebecca thought, and immediately recalled the pert little mermaid decorating the Dons' door at the Ferry House.

She grasped the dryad and dropped her onto the plate three times.

Magic number three.

She imagined the sound waves flowing along passages, rebounding off stone and sinking into tapestries. There would be tapestries, she felt sure, and floor coverings made from rushes plaited into strips and sewn together. How far would the sound need to travel before it was heard? How long would it take for someone to come to the door and open it?

Once upon a time she had stood on a different doorstep, waiting for a different door knock to be heard and answered, and had thought too late of using her mobile to let a friend know where she was.

No chance of that now. She would be no more alone inside the castle than she was outside; she was vulnerable everywhere here.

Wrong! Thinking like that was the short route to disaster. She was the Queen of Clover, damn it, and people had better watch out!

But she wished the wretched door would open. She was raising her hand to knock again, when it did. After a slight judder the door swung smoothly inwards and Rebecca found herself face to face at last with one of the inhabitants of the impossible world she had entered.

She – it was a she – was looking down on Rebecca, but only because there was another step at the threshold. Rebecca guessed they were probably about the same height, and age too, although she knew looks could be deceptive here. For some reason, probably story-telling tradition, Rebecca had anticipated an ancient retainer, or at least a servant, and a man; if the woman who stood in the doorway was a servant, then servants here had grand ideas about appropriate clothing.

She was red-haired, and that was a surprise too. Rebecca had expected to find a nation of black-haired, white-skinned, black-eyed people.

What else had she got wrong?

She opened her mouth to speak, but was beaten to it by the woman and the flow of watery syllables she let fall, and Rebecca remembered with a little rush of despair the most vital thing of all.

She had a language to learn. So much for *I am your Queen of Clover – let me pass!*

But she could draw. Rebecca reached automatically for the small sketchbook in her pocket, and as she brought it up, the card inside it slipped out and dropped, edge on, landing face up exactly across the threshold, two corners outside the castle, two corners inside. Before Rebecca could move the woman had bent and retrieved it, and Rebecca watched her examine the picture.

Then she raised her eyes to Rebecca.

Rebecca said gamely, 'Me. That's me. I also am the Queen of Clover.'

She felt ridiculous, gabbling pointlessly in a language that would be heard merely as a string of random noise; and yet the woman smiled, her eyes as well as her mouth, and spoke again, and this time Rebecca had no doubt about what she was saying.

Yes, the fairy woman was telling her, *yes, I know.*

Her name was Lorian, and Rebecca liked her immediately. Despite the language barrier they seemed able to laugh together, and naturally too, not a forced, social kind of laughter. That there was anything to laugh about at all amazed Rebecca, and it seemed auspicious that the first person she should meet should be so easy, so *nice*.

Just as she had dreamed, there were plaited rushes on the floors and tapestries on the walls, huge vistas of forests and meadows and hills providing a backdrop for riders on horses, carrying hawks on their wrists, and more people on foot with dogs.

Hounds. When you are hunting, dogs are called hounds.

Rebecca was reminded of the Devonshire Hunting Tapestries at the V&A, and was suddenly swept back to the day, years earlier, when she had stood in the dim gallery where the tapestries were then housed and listened to a man with haunted, haunting eyes speaking about somewhere impossible.

Now Michael was here, in the impossible place, himself, and against all the odds, so was she.

For a moment Rebecca could have laughed, or cried.

Then a thought struck her and she narrowed her eyes, trying to see detail as they passed along the pictures. She realised she had instinctively called them 'horses' and 'hawks' but they might not be quite that. The tallixer that had slipped accidentally through the Oxford gap had had no direct equivalent in the normal world.

But if these weren't horses, the difference was beyond her eye, and the same with the hawks, or falcons, or whatever they were, and with the dogs – hounds – too. But one of the scenes showed the quarry to be a tallixer, of that Rebecca had no doubt, and another included, in the far distance between the trees, a dainty white unicorn.

There was another animal she did not recognise slipping out of the side of one scene, an unusually sophisticated image out of keeping with the general style of draughtsmanship. It was a brown, whiskery thing that seemed to be throwing a glance backwards over its hunched shoulders as it slipped away.

Perhaps it was a pet. It couldn't be the quarry at any rate, because nobody was paying it any attention. Very ugly pet, though.

Lorian had led her round corners and up stairs and beneath archways to arrive finally at a door between tall, narrow tapestries of stylised trees laden with both blossom and berries. Rebecca, obeying her guide's gesture, lifted the latch and entered to find herself in instant domesticity.

It was a sitting room, and it was lovely.

One couldn't forget that it was a room in a castle. The walls were smooth cut stone, silvery pale, and the windows opposite the door were grouped lancets, steeply pointed, the stone transoms slender like twigs and, like twigs, dividing asymmetrically, carved into a semblance of a living branch spanning the space.

But the walls were lined with shelves built from wood the colour of oatmeal, and there were couches covered with blankets of woven wool in buttermilk, cloud blue and grey. There was a low chest bearing a round, shallow basket full of fruit, and a terracotta jug holding a cascade of tiny white flowers like baby's breath. The air smelled deeply fragrant, flowers mixed with herbs mixed with the airing-cupboard scent of warm wool.

Rebecca was entranced.

Lorian gave her a little push and said something which almost certainly meant 'Go on!'

Moving gingerly, as if not yet sure she was entitled, Rebecca crossed the room, skirting the chest, to the door between shelves on the left-hand wall. A heavy velvet curtain had been swept to one side and roped back, presumably a draught excluder in cold weather. Rebecca opened the door and found herself in a room very like the first but this time furnished with a bed, which was huge and dressed in warm white. There were cupboards instead of shelves, and more flowers.

Rebecca glanced at Lorian, who nodded. So she crossed the floor and, once again, pushed open a door into a new space which this time literally stole her breath. She stood on the threshold motionless.

Lorian laughed.

Rebecca drank in the huge, multi-paned windows that filled the wall, and the sunlight that poured through them, and began to breathe again. She took in the empty, white walls, the uncovered floorboards, the drawing table with its slanting surface, the plan chests of wide, shallow drawers and the conker-red box on top, and turned at last to Lorian. 'It's a studio,' she said.

They had prepared a studio for her. How? *Why?*

She walked to the windows and looked out over the forest canopy, and saw rolling pasture beyond and, farther still, the smoky blue foothills of moorland rising to land higher yet. It was a landscape that had been portrayed in countless picture books over decades if not centuries – a landscape of pastoral idyll, where grass was green and skies were blue and roads were dry, dusty, and empty of traffic: Fairyland. She stood in a castle on a promontory in Narnia, in Middle-earth, in Shakespeare's wood near Athens, in Camelot.

She was existing, breathing, her heart beating, her senses

working, in a plane of existence imagined by almost everyone at some point, and it was real.

Rebecca turned round, facing Lorian across the studio that was now hers. 'It's lovely,' she said. 'Thank you.'

Chapter Thirty

'Two hours,' Rebecca said, holding up two fingers. 'See you in two hours, then,' and she closed the door.

She didn't know why she was talking like this since Lorian could not possibly understand, but it seemed to be what they were doing. She talked in English, Lorian talked in whatever language was used here, and they smiled a lot and gestured. It had been working surprisingly well all day.

She leaned against the door, taking pleasure in the luxury of solitude and privacy. Both had always been essentials in her life and she had enjoyed living alone. Now she had a short while for them to work their magic and refresh her before she ventured out into this alien world again.

Just how short, she had no idea – she didn't even know how time here operated. She had two somethings, but no way of knowing how long that was. She hadn't seen a clock yet.

There was a key on the inside of the door, with a handle wrought like a cloverleaf. She turned it and listened to the lock mechanism snick. Bliss.

Right, to business.

Rebecca set the jug of gypsophila or whatever it was on the floor and lifted the lid of the chest.

Blankets. Blankets and also a herby, citrus scent that was familiar.

She closed the lid and replaced the jug.

There was a tall cupboard against the wall which revealed itself to be a wardrobe full of things that weren't trousers. Rebecca sucked in her lips and considered. She was, she knew, dressed inappropriately. The other women all wore skirts, and skirts with a period feel, although not specific to any period or culture Rebecca was aware of. If pressed, she might have hazarded seventeenth-century European, but not English – the detail was not quite right, either the neckline or the cut of the sleeves or the way they were laced.

The clothes hanging here, in tawny brown, claret and ochre, looked more in keeping with her surroundings, and she had little doubt they would fit her.

But she was not tempted. Surrendering her trousers would leave her feeling vulnerable, and that must be avoided at all cost.

The shelves bore books with leather or cloth covers, but intriguing though they were, Rebecca had something more pressing in mind and left them for later.

On the plan chest in the studio was a box made from dark red wood with a grain like the contours of a map, and Rebecca's heart had leapt when she first saw it a few hours ago. The thick wooden hinges, curiously curved, hugged the lid in a style at once familiar and poignant.

Rebecca's fingertips stroked the wood and then lifted the lid. At once the scent she expected rose to meet her, but stronger – rosemary and lemon, mingled with a distant note of honey. The box had been made more recently than the chest and had been finished, Rebecca guessed, with beeswax.

Like the one she had at home, in her bedroom, this was a jewellery box. There were two trays of small compartments, lined with close-piled velvet, black as a raven's wing. In one of them lay a twinkling of golden vine leaves, cousins of the one she wore under her tee-shirt. Rebecca lifted a leaf and the others came too, evenly spaced along a wire so fine it might have been thread.

They were beautiful, but there was no clasp and Rebecca could not see how they could be worn. She laid them back with care, and removed the tray to look beneath.

The second tray was empty. She took that out too, and in the space under that was a pair of long-nosed tweezers, which was bizarre, and a photograph laid face down. Rebecca turned it over and felt her heart contract.

It was Connor and herself, and for a moment she could not remember where or when; summer, certainly, because they were in short sleeves and there were sharp-edged shadows falling across the slatted outdoor table at which they sat. Her hair was cropped spiky and short, but Connor's was long, hooked behind his ears.

Then she knew. The table was the one outside the hostel where they had all stayed in the days leading to their discovery of Ashendon House. Connor, beautiful even then, was only sixteen or so, coping with an abusive home life and desperate to escape.

Rebecca looked closely at his face, printed on the paper. He must have been plotting even then to use the gap, if they found it, and neither she nor Michael had suspected a thing.

She had a vague memory of Michael having snatched a photo or two on his phone. She had no idea it was anything other than an idle notion. Yet this had been given a place in his single rucksack with which he had entered a new life here.

She had no picture of Michael at all.

She wished he had left a letter for her here.

Rebecca replaced the photograph, and the tweezers, and replaced the trays, slotting them neatly in. The gold vine leaves winked at her as she closed the lid.

When Lorian knocked on her door Rebecca was ready. She had plaited her hair afresh, and she had unzipped her fleece from its waterproof jacket so that it could serve as a cardigan, because it was cooler within the stone walls than it had felt outdoors. She could do nothing about her walking boots and was feeling aggrieved all over again at having had her carefully packed rucksack whipped away by the duplicitous Will.

But she had equipped herself with a sketchbook and pencils. The paper in the studio was all loose, but Rebecca had folded and torn a couple of large sheets into signatures and stitched them together into a simple pamphlet. It was a rough-and-ready way to produce a sketchbook, but perfectly practical.

With drawing materials to hand, she felt buoyant and enthused as she followed Lorian through the passages, noting with satisfaction that some of the tapestries were already looking familiar. With a left turn and a short flight of steps, they arrived outside the chamber Rebecca had begun to think of as the classroom, and Lorian opened the door.

A tall man, bald but not old, stood to greet her, and Rebecca smiled brightly. There was a stack of documents on the table between them; they looked like drawings, which was intriguing. So perhaps not more language, then.

The people here were wasting no time. Within minutes of her arrival Lorian had whisked her into this room and begun to teach her words and phrases. It was her first language lesson since

GCSEs and she had feared the worst, but in the event she was surprised to find she found the early steps easy. The sounds were comfortable in her mouth and the vocabulary remarkably easy to remember, which was a relief although puzzling. She had become so engrossed she had not noticed the time passing and had been pleasantly surprised when they broke for food.

Wholemeal bread in dumpy, round loaves with seeds scattered on top, sharp, strong cheese, and green apples with bite, like Granny Smiths but without such tough skin. Delicious.

There was also milk which was slightly sour, and Rebecca had downed the whole glass thinking it to be a sort of yogurt drink before it was withdrawn. A serving maid did this, with unmistakably dismayed gestures which suggested it was not after all intended to be sour. It was replaced by apple juice, and that was delicious too. Very promising.

Now Rebecca took her seat and leaned forward, trying to see the thin, precise lines of ink on the paper that was projecting from half way down the stack.

Her tutor laid aside the top sheet and revealed the truth. The papers were maps. Rebecca began to smile.

The milk was sour at dinner too, although that was small hardship for Rebecca, who was not accustomed to drinking milk with a cooked meal. But already, astonishingly, she was picking out snippets of sense from the flow of talk around her, and it seemed all was not right in the pantry.

Lorian sat with her at the table in the small hall where they had taken lunch, and Mathias, her geography tutor, sat facing her, as he had all afternoon. They were waited on by a different woman, older and tougher than the tongue-tied girl at midday, and she seemed indignant rather than defensive about the milk having been spoiled.

The meal was thick, steaming slices of some kind of meat roasted, with tender green vegetables and plums. Rebecca tasted these separately, just to be sure, and they were – she'd have staked money on it – plums.

Afterwards someone came and measured her feet and legs,

which was a touch weird, and then they repaired to a room with a hearth a cow could have lain down in. There were great, sagging sofa affairs laden with cushions embroidered with chain stitch and Cretan stitch in coloured wools, and Rebecca felt sufficiently relaxed to shed her annoying boots and curl her legs underneath her.

Another new person arrived: a boy who just for a fleeting moment reminded Rebecca of the young Connor as he had been in the photograph in Michael's box, although with none of that Connor's watchfulness and secrecy. He settled himself at one side of the hearth and began to read from a hefty, leather-bound book. Rebecca paid attention at first and tried to pick out words she had learned, but it was like playing pig-in-the-middle with people much taller than you, and she had no chance of catching the ball. Besides, she had begun to feel sleepy, which was not surprising after the day she had had, and leaned her head on her hand on the round arm of the sofa.

Sometime later she felt a touch on her shoulder and opened her eyes. Lorian was bending over her.

'Sleep?'

I know that word!

'Yes,' Rebecca said, carefully. 'Sleep!'

Lorian waited while she pulled herself together, and they padded through the quiet castle to the Queen of Clover's private apartment, Rebecca's boots swinging from her hand.

The sun was setting, crimson and gold, beyond the lancet windows; her rooms faced west. A nightshirt lay folded on the bed, simply cut and without lace, and Rebecca undressed. There was a bathroom with a claw-footed tub and brass taps the far side of the studio, and Rebecca found a toothbrush of sorts and a small box of powder, the mintiness of which was a shock of the mundane at the end of her fantastical day. Then she checked the lock on the door and climbed into bed.

She lay, enveloped in sheets that smelled of gardens, and the soft light from the windows faded and turned the furniture to clumps of shadow.

I did it, Rebecca thought. *I am here. Even if I didn't do it on my own.*

It was a cliché, but it seemed to have been days since she had stood in Ashendon Cottage waiting for the gap to open.

She would never, not ever, forget the feel of Will's hand on her back, launching her through the light.

On the other hand, she could have stayed huddling in the hut until the next night, but she hadn't.

Rebecca had never been one to talk down her achievements.

Alright, I did do it on my own. Sort of.

The mattress was comfortable and the covers warm. Rebecca closed her eyes.

Just before sleep took her she thought she heard a crash and a cry, but it was distant, softened by walls and passages, and someone else, she felt, would deal with it.

She slept.

Chapter Thirty-One

The second day: four days left

Rebecca woke to daylight but a rather flat daylight. That's what you get if your room faces west: stupendous sunsets, dull dawns. Never mind.

Lorian arrived at her door shortly after she had finished dressing and at once put her hands on her hips in a frankly confrontational manner. Rebecca didn't catch much of what she said but it didn't matter; the point was made loud and clear by the direction of her eyes: downwards to Rebecca's feet and up again no higher than her waist.

Rebecca set her mouth. 'No.' She had learned that one. She too put her hands on her hips.

I am the Queen of Clover and I'll wear what I like.

She waited for Lorian's eyes to meet hers, and was highly satisfied to see their resigned expression when they did. *Okay,* Lorian's raised eyebrows seemed to say. *For now.*

'For now' was fine. She'd be out of here in four days anyway. Rebecca walked with the fairy woman down the stairs and past an open door from beyond which drifted the sounds of construction – planks of wood clunking into place and hammering.

'What–'

Lorian took her arm and moved her on. The vocabulary eluded Rebecca, but the gist of it seemed to be *nothing to worry about.* Her companion seemed a little harassed, though, and apparently the milk had soured again.

All was not quite purring like clockwork in the state of Denmark.

Now that was a thought: could she ask about Shakespeare?

After breakfast there was another language lesson – understandably a priority – in which Rebecca again found herself lost quite contentedly. Once upon a time her worst nightmare would have been a language lesson *held entirely in that foreign language,* yet here she was, tottering happily along after her teacher, repeating the syllables she could manage, having a stab at the ones she couldn't, even beginning haltingly to string together

her own.

In fact, it was fun.

The lists of vocabulary Lorian gave her to learn were dauntingly long but transpired to be much stickier than French or German had ever been; 'stickier' as in 'able to stay stuck in her brain'.

I'm turning into Steph, she thought. *Bring on the Mandarin!*

The lesson was interrupted by the arrival of a man whom even Rebecca registered instantly as someone of status. He had knocked first, it wasn't that, but as he entered the room he brought with him a presence, as if there were an assumption that business would stop for him, whatever that business might be. Rebecca wasn't sure she liked it.

He was handsome, with the longish hair everyone seemed to wear here, smooth features and an easy smile, and there was an embroidered detail of entwining tendrils, like vines, at the collar of his jacket which caught Rebecca's notice even before he spoke.

As usual she could not pick up the individual words but only an approximation of what he said, which was to excuse his interruption of the lesson. But then Lorian introduced him with a title Rebecca had already learned.

'Rebecca,' she said, smiling and standing up, 'this is Robert, Knave of Vines.'

'This is Robert, Knave of Vines,' and tufted ears sharpened, and a blackish tongue licked pointed teeth, and in the passages above the throne room, amongst the dust balls and the cobwebs, something sniggered.

The hammering was still going on as they passed the door.

'What is it?' she asked, and noticed the question had sprung forth as a phrase rather than individual words. She'd have preferred to ask 'What's going on in there, what happened last night?', but 'What is it?' would do for now.

The Knave of Vines (*'Call me Robin'*) flapped his hand dismissively. 'Not important.'

Rebecca felt she was being led to believe that it was routine maintenance. That might or might not be so, but it was true she didn't know where the crash last night had taken place.

They were touring the castle, and Robert – Robin – talked history as they walked. He kept his language simple, and checked in with her constantly to ensure she was keeping up. It was very different from Lorian's habit of running off at full speed, leaving Rebecca to trail behind picking up one word in ten. This felt like early practice at catching a ball and, like a three-year-old child, Rebecca missed some, nearly caught a few more, and even succeeded in holding on to one every now and then. It took determination and focus.

From time to time she composed and enunciated a question of her own.

'Where is the...very big room with the...chair for the queen?'

Hall and *throne* had yet to feature in Lorian's lists of vocabulary. She also suspected she had said 'chair *by* the queen'.

Her escort – perhaps that was not a good word – looked down at her with a faint smile. Rebecca stuffed her hands in the pockets of her fleece and glared back. It was probably not called for, and there was none of the electricity that had emanated from Will, but he was undeniably good looking and from time to time he found a way to make contact with her – his hand on her back through a doorway or touching her shoulder to gain her attention – and she had no, absolutely no intention of allowing anything more.

Absolutely none.

That seemingly obligatory half-smile ever present, Robin guided her along a passage she had yet to see. It was wider than most, with windows at intervals along the left side, narrow lancets in pairs set higher than Rebecca's head. The sunlight fell in regular shafts across the floor, setting dust motes dancing and drawing the colour out of the tapestries opposite.

Sunshine on dyed fibres made Rebecca uneasy. We are so used to textiles being protected by gloom and closed curtains, she thought, and to seeing them already faded to fawns and soft blue-green. Here the wool – presumably it was wool – remained steeped in colour, scarlet and emerald and gold, even violet. Different chemistry? Or simply a continuing supply of replacements? More questions she did not have the language to ask.

She was so interested in the colours that the subject matter escaped her notice at first; then she registered the central figure that featured in each hanging and took a step backwards in mild shock.

'Oh, that's–'

She spoke in English, but Robin replied in his own language. 'Yes, that's you.'

Well, in a manner of speaking, Rebecca thought. She moved closer again, peering. Each tapestry depicted the Queen of Clover – *a* Queen of Clover – seated on a throne and actively presiding. The image immediately before her also showed two men, one each side of the throne, and a cow with a calf between them. The cow was rich ginger, delicate like a Jersey, and wore a studded collar. The calf, very sweet, was lying down with its little hooves tucked tidily away.

An ownership dispute? Who did the calf belong to? Something like that, probably.

Rebecca moved slowly along the line, trying to interpret the scenes. Some were fairly straightforward, others mystifying. A great barrel of liquid – it had to be liquid because there was a tap near the bottom – with apple trees in the background suggested disagreement about title, or perhaps quality. But what could be made of an angry looking man brandishing a scroll of paper? Libel? Breach of copyright? Really bad prose?

One tapestry showed a young woman holding a baby and another reaching poignantly towards them, her arms bare, her expression pleading. Rebecca's thoughts leapt to the Bible story of the judgement of Solomon, and she shivered. Libel was one thing; the idea that she might also have to arbitrate over parentage was chilling.

The sequence of images was interrupted twice by doors which Robin ignored. Rebecca tapped on one and asked her usual question, 'What is it?'

'For waiting.'

An antechamber: a place to corral suppliants before admitting them into The Presence.

Quite right too.

At the end of the passage was a great door ornamented with scrolling ironwork and flanked by pillars decorated with mosaic in a flowing botanical design. The rush matting ended in a bound edge before a wide, shallow step. The message was unmistakable.

The doorway possessed gravitas; standing here you were about to enter a place of importance.

The Knave of Vines turned the key, opened the doors and stood aside. Rebecca stepped cautiously forward.

'Did you enjoy your history lesson?' Lorian asked, passing a basket of bread. The rolls were small and dense, the dough having failed to rise properly, which was disappointing.

Rebecca replied, 'Yes, thank you, very good,' before she even thought about it. Wow!

'More words this afternoon, but we can go outside if you like.'

Rebecca got most of that, too, even at Lorian's heedless pace. Or perhaps not heedless; sometimes you need two approaches: full-speed and impressionistic as well as slow and meticulous. It was hard to believe anything here was being left to chance. They were prepared to receive her and raring to begin her education.

She was being equipped, she realised, to fulfil a function, and it made her anxious sometimes. It was a lot of trouble for someone who was staying less than a week. One and a half days had slipped under the bridge already, only three and a half to go.

Robin had not asked her to sit in – or was it on? – the throne, which was a relief. It was also a relief to find the smoke-blue curtains at the far end of the hall hanging motionless and without any disturbing bulges. But the room had been cold, with no covering over the tiled floor, and Rebecca had not wanted to linger there.

Now she cut herself some cheese and said, 'The tapestries at the throne room.'

'Ah yes, interesting? Did you like them?'

'Very interesting.' Rebecca left the other question to hang. 'Does the colours...do the light...' She had no word for 'fade'. Hopeless. She tried another tack. 'Are the tapestries new? *Always* new?'

Lorian laughed and told the tale. It was pig-in-the-middle again, but Rebecca found she was able to snatch the ball much more often now, and usually she knew how to ask when she was left behind.

Some of the tapestries – not these, but others around the castle – were refreshed regularly, and there was a tidy cycle of re-use. Those in the main thoroughfares were moved on to the parlours, and those they were replacing were sent to the dining rooms, and thus the chain continued through staff rooms and offices until finally they were ejected from the castle and distributed to the weavers, presumably as continuing reference.

It was the story of the rag rug in nineteenth-century England – from best parlour to bedrooms to kitchen to privy, ending up on the compost heap to help next year's potatoes grow. But rag rugs were thrown together from scraps; it defied belief that anything so immensely labour-intensive and skilled as a tapestry should be regarded so casually.

'But these,' Rebecca asked. 'What about these tapestries? Don't they fade?'

No, said Lorian, because the hangings here and in the throne room were important enough to be protected.

'Protected how?'

With Skill, Lorian said.

Rebecca shrank slightly from the tapestry closest to her, unnerved by the knowledge that the reason the colours did not fade even in the strongest sunlight was because spells had been cast on them.

She was in a wild and uncharted country, and they did things very differently here.

Rebecca found she was excited about venturing beyond the castle walls.

Chapter Thirty-Two

Lorian was her guide and tutor, but they had an escort too. Behind them tramped a stubby man called Coll, who put to rest the notion that everyone here was good looking. He was their – her – bodyguard.

He was very short, not quite as tall even as Rebecca. Lorian, reading her mind, said, 'He is very strong, and well-known.'

Rebecca frowned. 'Is it danger out?' She had been taught the word for 'danger' already, and was now wondering whether there was a hidden text she should be aware of.

Lorian shook her head. 'No, no…he's just…well.'

Not a convincing reply.

Rebecca in her walking boots set a smart pace, exulting in the exercise after two days closeted and mostly sitting down. The air was fresh, moist, and scented with everything growing. And oh wow, everything here did grow.

Connor had warned her. *Sometimes it's like watching a stop-motion film,* he had said, describing the speed at which buds formed and burst, leaves unfolded and spread, fruit appeared and swelled and ripened. The hedge his captors had planted to imprison him had grown to an impenetrable barrier twelve feet high in a single season.

Through the wood the ground was passable because the canopy prevented undergrowth from thriving, but once beyond the trees the grass was knee-high, and they kept to a path that had clearly been mown to maintain it.

This was not the way Rebecca had come. Lorian had taken them out of a different door on the other side of the castle, and they were walking away from the stone wall and the isolated hut behind it. Rebecca acknowledged a slight unease in herself, but put it aside; there was a lot to explore and nothing to worry about. And even if there were, they had the very famous, very strong Coll.

She glanced behind her and smiled brightly. Coll stared back. He had remarkably low brows and it was difficult to imagine him laughing.

Oh well.

I'm a queen; perhaps he's shy.

It was a language lesson as well as a walk, and Lorian concentrated on vocabulary over grammar. Rebecca heard the words for *grass, tree, branch, leaf, bark, twig, root, bird, nest, egg, rabbit* (or something very similar), *squirrel, mouse, fox,* and once they were in the open, *cow, calf, bull, cattle, sheep, lamb, ewe, ram, goat, kid, deer, doe, stag, fawn* and *farm.*

A good number stayed in her head. It would have been delightful to believe she had, after all, a previously untapped talent for learning foreign languages, but it seemed much more likely that magic was at work. Fairyland was, after all, a magical place.

Rebecca touched Lorian's arm to get her to pause. 'I remember the words, all the words,' she said. 'Why?'

'You are the Queen of Clover.'

Rebecca opened her hands. 'And?'

'You have Skill.'

Her voice was so matter-of-fact, as if it were something anyone could learn. Perhaps anyone could.

'Everyone can learn – no, can everyone learn Skill?'

'Yes, but some people are very quick and others are slow. You are fast as...' Lorian used a word Rebecca did not know.

'Fast as?'

'Storm.' Lorian pointed at the sky and produced some astonishing sound impressions. 'Thunder. Lightning.'

'Got it.'

Fast as lightning. She was storming through the vocabulary. It was a pleasing image.

When they parted outside Rebecca's door, Lorian swaggled her skirts and did a twirl before looking pointedly at Rebecca's legs, encased in her trousers. She raised her eyebrows practically to her hairline.

Rebecca sighed. 'Maybe.'

Alone in her room, released from lessons for her precious two hours of down time, she opened the wardrobe and perused the clothes hanging there.

If it was just for dinner. There were some nice colours, subtle and deep.

Rebecca ruffled through, as one did when shopping, forming impressions, dismissing some and lingering over others. Eventually she pulled out something in deep, foresty green and held it up to herself in front of the mirror.

Her dark eyes looked back, seeming somehow less her own because of the strangeness of the gown. Rebecca stroked the velvet; it was rather gorgeous.

Just for tonight, then.

She spread out the gown on the bed and walked into the studio, where the light beyond the windowed wall was already softening to dusk. They had stayed out late.

Rebecca drifted, touching the drawing table, stroking the stacks of textured paper in the drawers, noting the colours of the inks in their jars, the pencils in their boxes. Her fingers itched to use them, but the light was fading and anyway she was tired. Learning so much was monopolising her energy and she had little left at the end of the day to use for creating.

Could she claim a day off? Come here after breakfast and lock the door on the demands of her duties and just draw?

Unlikely. But then, why should they have set all this up when she plainly would not be able to use it?

On the plan chest, Michael's lovely box seemed to glow in the light from the setting sun.

How could he not have left her a letter? She would have left a letter for him.

She took it on her lap, stroked the lid and then lifted it. So much nicer than the carved box she had found in Ashendon Cottage. She recalled that first command from Will, the scrap of paper slipped into her coat pocket by a pirate, and all the trouble it had caused her.

Open Michael's box.

Well, she had, eventually, although the secret compartment had eluded her for quite a while.

Carefully, Rebecca closed the box, and then turned it around and upside down. Her eyes searched for – what? A hint? A flaw? There were never any flaws in Michael's work.

If there were a hidden compartment in a box like this, where might it lie?

She removed the trays, the vine leaves gleaming against the black velvet, and the photograph and tweezers, and felt the interior walls and base with her fingertips, seeking an imperfection, an irregularity, anything that might point to something more than met the eye.

Nothing. And there was no space for even a slip of paper to be hidden under a false bottom.

Rebecca closed the box and considered the lid. She sent her fingers roving again, probing the planes and surfaces, feeling the thickness of the exposed hinges and how they were attached to the lid.

Suppose...

While researching secret compartments and puzzle boxes Rebecca had read about a dozen different mechanisms for concealing openings, some simple, some fabulously sophisticated. Such concealments had been commonplace for centuries, she had discovered, when legal documents could not reliably be left in banks and before safes became widespread. There were accounts of desks containing more than twenty separate secret spaces, some no larger than a thimble. Now she pressed the wood, moved a finger's breadth and pressed again, trying to be methodical, covering the area systematically, and suddenly she felt something shift.

She peered. Along the side of one hinge, where it joined the lid, a hairline crack had appeared, barely noticeable even now. But hairline it remained; either it had jammed – unlikely in Rebecca's opinion, knowing Michael's painstaking craftsmanship – or a further action was required before it would open.

She would need something extremely thin. Rebecca scanned the room from where she sat, trying to think whether she had seen anything here that she might use.

Or maybe...

Rebecca shifted and fished in her pocket. As well as her tiny sketchbook, she kept with her Uriel Passenger's pocket knife, for no good reason that she knew. Now she drew it out and opened the blade. It was broad but thin, with a fine point. Delicately Rebecca inserted it into the crack and jiggled it.

The crack widened, revealing a space behind.

But it was too small for even her little finger.

A pencil. Rebecca gazed about, and realised how dark the room had become. The shelves where the pencils lay were lost in shadow, and the windows were dusky and dim.

Lorian would be here any moment. She had to get ready.

It wrenched her to replace the hinge but she instinctively wanted to keep the compartment secret. She would have to leave it until later.

Furious, breathless, Rebecca flung off one set of clothes and struggled into another, relieved to find she was able to reach the buttons herself and would not be dependent on Lorian's help. Brushing out her hair so that she could plait it again tidily, she caught sight of herself in the mirror, candlelit now, and hesitated, knocked off-balance by – well, it seemed so bigheaded, but – by her beauty.

Or at least, the clothing's beauty. It was the dress, with its close-fitting bodice and wide skirts, that was beautiful. And her hair, perhaps.

Rebecca pushed her hair around and toyed with the idea of leaving it loose for a change. It looked quite good. She could have sworn it was longer than she had thought.

But I can't wear walking boots with this.

Lorian's knock snapped her attention back on track. She would have to go barefoot.

But when she opened the door, Lorian was holding a pair of shoes like ballet pumps, and the amazing truth was that they were deep, foresty green.

Chapter Thirty-Three

Snatching meaning out of conversation was one thing – there was context and proximity and eye contact to help. Following a story being read aloud was another. Besides, the sofa was comfortable and the dinner and the wine – which had been served tonight in place of milk – were having their own say. Rebecca allowed herself to drift.

Two down, three to go; she was almost half way through her stay. It felt like weeks.

That was odd. She had always been so sure, so convinced she would never come here, even when Michael had longed to go and Connor had plotted in secret. How strange that she should be feeling so comfortable so quickly.

Granted, she was ensconced in comparative luxury, accorded respect, and had an amiable guide at her disposal, but Rebecca suspected there was more to it than that.

The language business, for a start. Never had learning vocabulary been so easy; in fact it didn't really feeling like learning something new at all. It was more like being reminded of something she already knew but had forgotten. She had no doubt it was magic, by whatever name you wished to call it, but that was the only magic she had seen so far. Her vague fears about stardust and spells, people who vanished while you were blinking, or tried to turn you into a frog, now seemed way off the mark. Even the animals were familiar.

At least, most of them. Connor had told her there were unicorns, which struck a little spark of longing in her, and there were tallixers, of course. Were there also centaurs out beyond the pastures and meadows? Fauns? Giants? If she reached the seashore, might she meet a mermaid?

Rebecca reached for the makeshift sketch book she kept with her, even at dinner, and swiftly drew a centaur and a faun, and then a mermaid perched on a rock, provocatively combing her hair as if posing for a sculptor. She pushed it at Lorian, curled catlike in the next chair, and raised her eyebrows interrogatively.

Lorian looked, then returned the book to Rebecca with a shake of her head.

Okay. Greek imagination, then.

Rebecca thought, and then drew a dragon, the European kind, with a neat body, perky head and muscular legs, his webbed wings spread. She pushed that across.

This time Lorian nodded, adding a waggle of her hand which suggested there were reservations but, broadly, yes.

Rebecca had another thought and added flames and smoke belching from the dragon's mouth.

Lorian pulled a face but nodded again.

Wow.

The boy by the hearth chuntered on. He was probably reading well enough, but to Rebecca, able to understand only one word in three, it had become a drone. Rebecca drew a series of dragons, each proportionately larger compared to the man she added for scale. Her smallest was perhaps the size of a pony – surely dragons wouldn't be smaller than that? – and the largest more like a double-decker bus, but before she could get Lorian's input the gathering began to break up.

Time had flown. She had lost herself in her drawing, producing dragons flying, rampant, and curled in slumber, with details of scales and teeth and claws, rolling eyes and lolling tongues, and now it was time for bed.

More lessons tomorrow.

Lorian was waiting, but Rebecca had a proposal to make. She had been mulling it over while she drew, and suddenly felt energetic and determined.

'No, I will go alone, not you.'

Inelegantly expressed, but it did the trick. Lorian raised her eyebrows ('*Sure?*') and handed over the key. She patted Rebecca's arm. 'Goodnight.'

'Yes. Thank you. Goodnight.'

Absurdly excited, Rebecca set out along the passages, checking through the route in her head. Really, the castle was no worse than a stately home, or a huge country hotel. It was true that the archways and steps thrown in randomly at corners made it confusing, and of course the rooms were not numbered. Still, she was sure she would recognise each turn when it arrived, and predicting them correctly in advance was a boost to her confidence.

Someone had lit candles in the glass sconces on the walls. The castle must have a complement of staff she had yet to see. But the sconces were spaced far apart and Rebecca walked from pool of soft light into sooty shadow and out again, over and over.

The tapestries lining her way glowed, jewel-like, then faded into sombre monotone, and then were lost in the darkness before re-emerging under the light of the next candle. Woven faces and hands, pale against the dark robes and trees, stared out at her as she passed, watching her as if to judge her. *You call yourself Queen of Clover,* she could imagine them saying, *but are you really? Are you honestly up to the task? Can you cut it?*

'No-one's said anything so far about doing it at all,' Rebecca said aloud. 'And I'm only here for five days anyway.'

Her words sounded ringingly clear in the empty passage, and she wondered whether she had been wise. But it wasn't as if she had pretended anything different. Neither Lorian nor anyone else had yet broached the matter of how long she was to stay. She had not deceived.

Besides, what would they do if they did know – whoever 'they' were? She couldn't see Lorian going for her with a knife. It was probably all arranged anyway, put in place by Will before he went in search of her: *I'll find one and send her through,* he would have said. *She can have a five-day trial and we'll see how it goes.*

Although 'trial' wasn't a good word. Rebecca shivered. Trial *period*, that was better.

It was the clots of darkness, the shapes unseen that had begun to undermine her confidence. Once she was in her own rooms with the door locked she would feel better.

Rebecca quickened pace. The green shoes fitted her feet extremely well. Perhaps she would look into the possibility of bespoke shoes when she got home. These were low cut in front, with no retaining strap or bar, but they flexed with her and did not slip, and she was able to stride out without fear of stumbling.

The velvet skirt swung as she walked, its folds strange against her legs but not hampering her. Perhaps she might buy herself a dress sometime. For parties.

Rebecca turned the corner into the final stretch with relief.

Nearly there. She gripped her sketchbook against her hip and shifted the key in her other hand, ready to insert into the lock, and caught a glimpse, just for an instant, of something moving at the far end of the passage.

A deeper patch of shadow that darted.

Rebecca hesitated, peering forward, but she could see nothing more. Something had *seemed* to move, but had anything really? Dark can play tricks with one's mind.

She halted and listened, concentrating. She counted three seconds and then, faintly, heard a scuffle, a noise like something scraping on matting.

Footsteps? But shuffling ones...

And then silence. Rebecca waited, but there was nothing more.

Imagination.

Maybe.

Just someone up ahead, going round the corner.

Maybe; but what was that bad smell, like sulphur or something rotting?

Well, she couldn't stand there forever. Rebecca walked forward, slightly breathless now, and counted down the steps to her door: seven, six, five...She was aware of plugging in to her peripheral vision, and also that her hand was ever-so-slightly trembling as she fitted the key in the lock.

For one fleeting instant she played out a scenario where the key did not work; it was the wrong key, Lorian had made a mistake, and she could not open the door but was marooned in the passage, forced to retrace all those steps through the shadows with the shuffling thing behind her...

But it wasn't the wrong key. The handle rotated, the deadbolt retracted and the door opened. Rebecca stepped inside and closed the door thankfully. She turned the key and then slipped it into her pocket for safekeeping – tonight was not a good night to leave it in the lock.

And then something in the room behind her breathed.

* * *

Astonishing, the effect of adrenalin tipping into the blood stream: Rebecca's skin turned ice cold as every hair stood erect, and her heart made a single, sickening thud that she felt to the ends of her fingertips.

She slid round, the door hard behind her shoulder blades.

No candles had been lit, but neither had the curtains been drawn and there was moonlight falling into the room. The furniture and shelves, the hangings and the jug of baby's breath appeared soft-edged in the delicate light, surely more blue than moonlight ever was in Suffolk or London or even in Skye. And also soft-edged was the great hulk of the animal that occupied the floor between herself and the windows.

The lovely herbal scent Rebecca was growing accustomed to had gone, overpowered by the strong, musky odour of fur and skin.

It was a familiar smell.

Rebecca, eyes wide, stared at the shape that was, unmistakably, staring at her. As her eyes adjusted to the dim light, more detail appeared: a flat-skulled head and sharp ears, a length of muscled back and a heavy, waving tail. Into her thoughts came memories of a dry, cold night in the rural outskirts of Oxford, of Connor and a skinny teenager with next to no useful English, and a joint of raw meat dripping blood into the grass.

It was a tallixer, she was certain.

A major carnivore, Connor had once told her, *somewhere between a panther and a wolf.* The predator at the top of the food chain, a meat-eater from long canine teeth to retractable claws, and as wild as wild can be.

And less than twelve feet away from her.

A low sound had begun, a rumble that was almost sub-sonic, felt rather than heard. Rebecca fumbled, searching for the way into her pocket, mentally cursing the stupid, unnecessary folds of fabric that concealed it. *There.* She snatched out the key and promptly dropped it.

Whimpering, barely able to believe what was happening, Rebecca lowered herself to her knees and groped, only to knock the metal shaft with her finger so that it skated across the floorboards and vanished beneath a bookcase.

All the bad words she had ever heard leapt into her mind, but she didn't dare utter them. Angry, frustrated, frightened speech would, she instinctively knew, be a very, very bad idea.

Shaking, Rebecca laid her makeshift sketchbook on the floor in front of her knees and slid it carefully under the bookcase, taking it wide in the hope that the corner would reach behind the key and scoop it towards her.

Not wide enough. There was a rattle as the key was whisked still deeper into the dust.

She had lost it for good.

So.

She was going to die.

Better stand up, then.

Slowly Rebecca stood, and made the effort to breathe a little deeper. Her chest and shoulders felt tight as piano strings. She needed to loosen.

It was an animal. It was a wild animal. Animals sense emotions. Animals operate more on emotion than on weight or strength – anyone who has seen a cat turn on a dog three times its size knows that.

Show no fear.

Easy to say.

Rebecca's palms were clammy, but she forced her ribs to move, taking in air slowly and evenly.

What else did she know about tallixers?

Gira, Jack's tallixer, had been tame. That hadn't prevented her from doing serious damage to the Oxfordshire sheep population, but on the night they caught her they had not needed the supermarket meat they had brought with them as bait. She had fed recently and was not so greedy as to eat more than she needed.

This tallixer had not yet sprung on her, so perhaps it too had fed recently.

How had Jack tamed Gira in the first place? Rebecca had never thought to ask. Had he found her as a cub? Trapped her and trained her? Or was there some strange, illogical affinity between the two species that allowed for individuals sometimes to form a bond? It is a recurring element in myth, and I am, Rebecca thought, in the heart of a mythical land.

Still the tallixer had not sprung. Her life was continuing. Gradually it was becoming easier to breathe. But this stand-off couldn't last.

Rebecca said, 'Hallo,' and heard her own voice shockingly loud in the still air.

The tallixer did not move, but the rumbling ceased.

I can't get the key, Rebecca thought, and I can't just wait here to be killed. I might – just might – make it to the bedroom.

The way was clear. When she moved, the tallixer would probably attack and that would be that. But if it didn't; if it did indeed have a good, full tummy and wasn't afraid of her either – which was laughable when you thought about it – then perhaps, if she was blessed with extraordinarily good fortune, and if God and all His angels and saints and the Powers That Be, and also her own, personal Fairy Godmother – which might even be Lorian – were all, all of them, smiling on her, then she might, she just might, still be alive in two minutes' time.

Two minutes.

Rebecca did not want to walk backwards in the dark, but neither was it possible to turn her back on the tallixer. She moved sideways, crabwise, flicking her attention between her destination – the longed-for door to her bedroom – and the great wolf-cat watching her.

So far, so good. Half-way there and she wanted so badly to cry.

There was a chair out of place, skewed part round and interrupting her route to the door. She had left it like that this afternoon, having turned it to catch the westering sun, and as Rebecca stepped across to avoid it her foot in the delicate green shoe stubbed against something on the floor the moonlight had not reached.

Sideways as she was, off balance and distracted, Rebecca could not save herself. She teetered and almost caught the corner of the bookcase but did not quite, and fell, landing on her hip on the hard floor. Panic-stricken, she scrambled to her feet but it was too late.

The tallixer was at her side, waist-high and pungent. Rebecca gasped in despair, knowing she had lost the gambit, and then gasped again as the great round head pressed against her stomach.

The rumble started up again, and this time Rebecca knew it for what it was.

The tallixer was purring.

Chapter Thirty-Four

The third day: three days left

Rebecca woke with a jolt as if she had fallen, and lay, eyes wide, certain she should not move although not sure why.

Light was streaming into the room, revealing all the untidy detail of the night before: her velvet dress crumpled on the bed, one green shoe half way to the open door, and beyond, her sketchbook lying on the floor by the bookcase.

Oh yes.

Cautiously, Rebecca turned her head and met the golden gaze of the animal that had shared her bedroom for the past seven hours. The tallixer was awake also, sprawled casually in front of the wardrobe. It was a wide wardrobe but the tallixer was wider.

Rebecca swallowed and cleared her throat. Well, she hadn't been eaten while she slept. Just how she had managed to sleep at all was another matter.

Whatever had woken her was still going on; there were muffled sounds of dispute on the other side of the wall. Moving smoothly as if wading through syrup, she slid out of bed – the far side of the bed – and padded barefoot through the sitting room.

The tallixer, she was relieved to see, stayed behind.

There was a powerful stink of raw meat which Rebecca had not noticed before, possibly because the stink of the living tallixer had been even stronger. Now she wrinkled her nose and was disgusted to find what looked like half a goat lying bloody and mangled underneath the window, the rib cage and one hind leg still connected by ragged tissue, the other leg a metre away against the wall.

New mats would be called for. Still, she was the Queen so they would probably be forthcoming. In the meantime she dragged a chair in front of the mess so that it wouldn't shock Lorian when she came in.

The door to the outside world was locked.

Of course it was. Rebecca dropped to all fours and fished for the key under the bookcase, but although she could see it, lurking in the dim light, she could not reach it. She looked around for a tool, but there was nothing.

Blast.

The studio, then.

Steadying her breathing, Rebecca walked smoothly and nonchalantly (*Ha!*) back through the bedroom, carefully skirting the tip of the black, rope-like tail, and into the studio where there must, she was sure, be a ruler of some sort.

Yup – on the shelf, next to the inkbottles.

Back through the bedroom – this was definitely getting easier – and she had the key out and doing its job in moments. She poked her head round the door.

Three people were in the passage a few metres away, all of them looking fraught. Rebecca thought they looked frightened as well. Lorian was one of them, and she glanced round at the sound of Rebecca's door opening.

'*Anything wrong?*' Rebecca asked, and then realised she had slipped into English and followed up with, 'What is it?' – the catch-all question she was still using a lot.

Lorian flapped a hand in her direction and said something Rebecca caught only one word from, meaning *dirt* or *mess*, she wasn't quite sure which.

Rebecca retreated and began to dress, dithering over whether to put on her trousers as usual or to cave in and take one of the skirts. It partly depended on the schedule for the day. If she was going to be classroom-bound then she'd play ball and put on a skirt; if they were venturing outside she definitely wanted trousers.

She thought about Lorian's harassed face.

I can always change.

There was a simple, plain-woven skirt in cool grey-brown that appealed, but it looked ridiculous with a tee-shirt. In any case, it would be much nicer to wear something fresh, so Rebecca exchanged her two-day-old top for a long-sleeved blouse of cream-coloured cotton (it felt like cotton), and that then needed a bodice that was put on like a waistcoat and hooked up at the front, so that by the time Lorian knocked on the door Rebecca was back in the sitting room looking, she thought, like a person in Fairyland should.

She enjoyed the startled expression on her guide and mentor's face.

'Is this good?' she asked.

'Yes. Very good!' Lorian's mouth twitched with mild humour. Rebecca was pleased that the problem outside, whatever it was, could clearly not be too bad.

She did not yet have a word for *problem* or *trouble*, so she simply asked again, 'What is it?' and indicated the castle beyond her rooms. When she didn't understand the reply, she was amazed to see Lorian mime, with careful gestures, the act of defecating. 'Animal,' the fairy woman added at the end.

That was a relief.

'Yuck. Oh dear. A cat?'

There were cats about the castle, Rebecca passed one from time to time, and they were, as Connor had warned her, much larger than normal cats.

But Lorian shook her head. 'No, no. Much bigger animal.' She spread her arms wide and then patted the air in front of her waist.

'Wow, that big!' Rebecca was shocked. What on earth did they keep as pets here? Or had one of the milk goats strayed indoors? For the umpteenth time she asked, 'What is it?'

Lorian shrugged. 'I don't know. Lion. Wolf. Gryphon maybe.'

A *gryphon!*

'Tallixer, perhaps.'

Tallixer! Rebecca's mouth fell open. 'Oh,' she said, 'but–'

'Tallixers are big, wild animals,' Lorian was saying. 'They prey on cattle and sheep. Very dangerous. So you will stay in here until it is found.'

'Ah. Yes. Um.' Rebecca considered her friend. She didn't think Lorian was the screaming type, but you never really knew...

Perhaps she should lay down a little preparation. She wished she could use English. It occurred to her that Lorian seemed not to have noticed the smell of the carcass behind the chair.

'I know about tallixers,' she said. 'A tallixer came through the gap.'

'To *England?*'

'Yes. It was – not wild – and it was...safe.'

She thought she had said *safe*. Lorian was looking sceptical.

'And this tallixer, this tallixer here, the one you're talking about today, is...over there.'

Rebecca pointed at the door to the bedroom. Lorian looked obediently, and then shook her head. 'No, Rebecca, listen–'

'Yes, Lorian, really.'

Rebecca closed her hands over Lorian's and looked hard into her eyes. They were, she realised, a wonderful chestnut colour, almost amber. 'Come and look. Quietly.'

With a bit of luck the tallixer would have gone back to sleep. Rebecca led the fairy woman across the floor and unlatched the door. If the tallixer had not wanted to attack herself, it would not attack Lorian either, would it?

She would take a quick peek and be ready to slam the door shut if necessary.

'Quiet, now!'

Rebecca edged the door open. The tallixer was invisible behind the bed. Rebecca did not want to walk in with Lorian, just in case, so she cleared her throat and said, feeling stupidly self-conscious, 'Hallo?'

She paused, heavily aware of Lorian's scepticism at her side. Then, momentously, two black, tufted ears rose from behind the mattress, followed by the flat skull and pointed muzzle of the beast. The orange eyes gazed steadily into Rebecca's, and something was suddenly clutching Rebecca's arm tightly.

'It's alright, it was here all night.'

Rebecca realised she didn't know whether the tallixer was male or female.

The mouth opened in a yawn, wide and salmon pink, the tongue curling exquisitely behind sharp, curved teeth. Then the head disappeared behind the bed, there was the heft and scuffle of something heavy getting to its feet, and the great predator ambled into sight, tail waving from side to side.

Rebecca tentatively put out her hand and rubbed the close fur of the tallixer's head. It might be a beast but it was rather beautiful.

'Lorian,' she said, 'meet Beauty.'

Chapter Thirty-Five

Rebecca walked along the passages with Rangy Robin striding alongside her and her new pet padding languidly in their wake. She was getting used to having it – her, it was a her – behind her and out of sight, which had been difficult at first.

Still was for Robin; he was twitchy.

She was having a history lesson, although less GCSE than Victorian nursery version, where international relations post-second world war were ignored in favour of a sequence of stories about princes and battles and ships, cakes being burned, beards being pulled, crowns tumbling into muddy rivers and kings hiding in oak trees. The tales Robin told her were even more bizarre, concerning witches, dragons, dreams and spells, and everything in threes or sevens. It stretched Rebecca's credulity, even here in Fairyland, and she was feeling buoyant and bullish, possibly a knock-on from having been chosen as The One by a panther. Her language was coming on in leaps and bounds too, and always seemed to have improved during her sleep overnight: the wondrous power of latent learning.

'Do you have flying horses here?' she asked, interrupting and not caring.

'No. Horses don't fly.'

'Oh.' Disappointing.

'Dragons fly.'

'Ah!'

Rebecca brightened. She hadn't got as far as pinning down the size of a dragon last night, interrupted in her scale drawings. And that reminded her of another thing.

'I'd like to draw this afternoon,' she said, hoping she sounded firm. 'In my studio,' she added, in case she should be misunderstood and dragged off somewhere with a tiddly scrap of paper.

She was constantly tantalised by the gorgeous studio full of materials and light, and beginning to suffer from withdrawal symptoms; her hands twitched. Drawing was not just her business, nor her hobby; it was simply *what she did*. It always had been, for as far back as she could remember. For three days now – because the day of preparation at Ashendon had been sketch-free too – she had been restricted to tiny thumbnail scribbles in the pocket book she never left behind or the makeshift pamphlet, and if she wasn't allowed to make some big, sweeping lines soon she'd shrivel up. They'd find her in some dusty corner hunched in the foetal position, rocking and mewing and sucking her thumb.

Having made her demand, Rebecca braced herself for an argument; but none came.

Robin said, 'Naturally.'

She should have asked before.

They walked on, Robin talking now about the system of arbitration and why the Queen of Clover needed to be impervious to spells, and Rebecca wondering why he was telling her all this as if she didn't already know it. Will had been very thorough, and she had pointed this out twice already, but Robin smiled and went stolidly on.

In any case, Rebecca's thoughts were largely occupied with the tallixer. Was she really going to call her Beauty? The word had slipped out and was sticking, but it sounded corny to Rebecca, who would have preferred something witty and cool: Portia, for example, or Africa. Or Sid.

Of more interest, though, was how the beast had managed to get into the castle and then into Rebecca's private suite of rooms. Clearly someone had lured it there with the half-goat or whatever it was, but why on earth? And was Beauty a trained, domesticated tallixer this – person, for want of further information – had found, or was she wild as wild could be until tamed by the queenly power of Rebecca herself? It sounded idiotic, but it seemed to be the line everyone was taking.

Rebecca had never been a particularly animal-loving person. Having grown up on a dairy farm, she knew a thing or two about how to approach animals, absorbed through osmosis simply from being around them, but she had never hankered for her own pet, not a pony nor a puppy nor even a gerbil. If she had indeed been exerting some sort of magical influence over the tallixer last night, then it had been entirely subconscious. But perhaps that was how it worked.

Happily, other people had dealt with the smelly mess in her

sitting room just as they had with the droppings in the passage, and it was undeniable that being accompanied – respectfully, two paces behind – by so impressive and dangerous an animal gave a tremendous boost to her confidence.

They turned a corner into a passage unfamiliar to Rebecca, and she immediately slowed to look at the new tapestries. The colour balance here was different – predominantly blues, violets and greens with touches of red or gold used only sparingly as accents. They turned the grey stone a smoky mauve, like the bark of trees in a bluebell wood.

As in the approach to the throne room, there was a consistent theme running through the scenes here. Each tapestry was set indoors, indicated by a slice of column either side and a decorative canopy above, not unlike medieval memorial brasses in a church. But instead of a knight in mail and surcoat or a lady in crespine headdress, hands together in prayer, the people in these tapestries presented objects to the viewer: a harp, a book, a painting in a frame, a drum.

Was this a celebration of the arts, Rebecca wondered? A promotion of culture?

But then came a hanging in which a man in a gown with an embroidered hem held aloft a sheaf of fat-eared corn, and in the next, a woman brandished what looked like a butter churn.

Rebecca opened her mouth to frame a question, and then saw that Robin had moved on ahead apparently not noticing that his pupil had stopped.

Not much of a teacher. Not much of a Knave of Vines either, come to that. He was undeniably handsome but had none of the danger, the electricity, the *liveness* that had been the essence of Will and, Rebecca assumed, of Uriel Passenger also. It was hard to imagine women collapsing like dominos in Robin's wake. She had ceased to worry about her own safety in his presence, feeling about as much threatened by him as by Roddy the Skye postman.

She was about to set off after him when her attention was caught by a hanging in which a young woman with pale skin and black hair held up a box. The lid was open, but the box faced the woman, not Rebecca, and the contents, if any, were hidden from view. There were hinges angled over the lid, and Rebecca thought immediately of Michael's box in her studio.

She still hadn't got at whatever was lying in the tiny hidden compartment in the hinge. The business with Beauty had – unsurprisingly – distracted her.

Rats.

After lunch, then, before she started playing with paper and pencil.

Rebecca jogged to catch up with the man she was beginning to regard as a bit of a bore, and the tallixer swung into a loose-jointed trot behind.

Rebecca nursed a doubt as to whether Lorian would capsize as easily as Robin, and was frustrated to find yet another fuss going on at lunch; she didn't want her fairy in a bad mood when she announced she would be changing the schedule today in order to indulge herself in her studio.

There was trouble in the kitchen again, this time with something that had been left too long in the oven, and also someone had cut himself with a cooking knife, quite badly by the sound of it. Rebecca listened, trying to make sense from the strings of words, and in the meantime helped herself to slices of tough meat with blackened edges: the thing that had been forgotten in the oven, no doubt.

Lorian's face expressed anger and bemusement in more or less equal amounts. Rebecca cleared her throat.

'I'm going to draw this afternoon,' she said, buttering bread and avoiding the fairy woman's eyes.

'What? Oh yes. Of course.'

That was odd. *Alright-if-you-must,* was what Rebecca had expected, but Lorian, like Robin, had caved in immediately. Because she, Rebecca, was Queen? Did she have more authority here than she realised? It was something to think about.

'Has the goat been cleared out of my room?' Rebecca asked, not keen on sharing her afternoon with the stink of the day-old carcass.

Lorian nodded. 'All done. Don't worry.'

'Did you find out who threw it in there?' Rebecca asked.

'Threw it in?' Lorian looked vague. 'I think the tallixer just dragged it in.'

'*What?*'

Rebecca put down her cutlery. This morning the great mystery of the month had been who could have lured the wild animal into the castle, through the passages and up the stairs, under arches and round corners and in and out of corridors all the way to the Queen of Clover's private suite and then picked the lock, hurled the goat inside, and slammed the door – and locked it again – leaving the tallixer shut in.

And now Lorian was telling her it was all an accident.

'How on earth could Beauty have unlocked the door?' Rebecca demanded.

'Well...we probably forgot to lock it.'

'Rubbish!'

'Perhaps...' Lorian petered out, and then brightened as a tray of fruit arrived. 'Peaches!'

Peaches. Rebecca narrowed her eyes, watching the fairy woman as she helped them both to fuzzy, flame-coloured fruit, tallixer, goat, burned joint and knife wounds apparently forgotten, and for the first time she wondered seriously whether there was something here of which she should be aware.

Chapter Thirty-Six

Rebecca drew.

The paper was creamy and thick, the sheets slightly smaller than A3, with deckle edges and texture like Rebecca's favourite Bockingford watercolour paper. The pencils, soft, black graphite encased in unadorned wood, fitted her hand perfectly, and the slope of the drawing table was just right.

At first, images of the tapestries filled her mind's eye, and she drew perpendicular figures with sad eyes, long noses, and robes falling in vertical pleats. Then she moved on to architecture, drawing columns and pilasters, tall gothic arches, lancet windows and arrow slits. As she drew, her thinking, calculating brain quietened making way for her free-running, creative subconscious, and her drawings became looser, full of curves and coils, loops and spirals.

The sun eased its way westward, and the light pouring through the wide windows became ever more golden. Images flowed across the sheets of paper, sometimes solitary, like islands in a lake of space, sometimes overlapping so that lines merged and became confused: people and animals and trees and stones, feathers and leaves and blossoms, riverbanks and vineyards, cottages and towers and barns and even a watermill.

As she drew, engrossed in the delightful, sumptuous, enchanting business of laying a trail of graphite on dried wood pulp, the tension eased from her shoulders and neck and from her hands and fingers, and her busy mind relaxed and became tranquil. The strangeness of the place in which she found herself retreated, and her concentration narrowed to the detail at the point of her pencil, all the rest of the world forgotten. Only when she swept aside a sheet of paper to discover she had reached the bottom of the stack and no more was to hand, did she stop, and lean back, and stretch.

It was like waking up, but waking up gently after a long, sound, untroubled sleep. Rebecca yawned, stretched happily, and ran her fingers through her hair, luxuriating in the movement, the feel against her scalp. Then she stood up.

Coffee.

There was no coffee, but she had a carafe of water and the water here was remarkably refreshing, tasting neither of chlorine nor of sulphur but of some distant trace Rebecca had not been able to identify; something *green*, she thought...It tasted the way freshly cut grass smells.

There was also a slender bottle of pale amber cordial, which Rebecca had found to be unlike usual fruit cordials. It was thin and sharp, and she poured it into her glass now and diluted it from the carafe. Not coffee but pretty good; she could get used to it.

She yawned, and wandered over to the windows, where the sun was reddening as it sank, casting a pink-orange filter over the distant mountains.

I'd like to climb those.

But there wouldn't be time.

Rebecca sighed.

The tallixer was sprawled across an unlikely expanse of floor and the sunlight made stripes on her dark pelt. She had raised her head when Rebecca got up, but then let it drop back again with a grunt. The sun lifted glints of colour from her rich black coat: purple and indigo and deep, peacock green.

She really was a beauty.

With her toe, Rebecca touched just the tips of the hairs on the tip of the tallixer's tail, for no reason other than to test her relationship with the beast. The last three inches of the tail lifted in a little wave of protest and fell back again; the tallixer's eyes stayed closed.

Rebecca shook her head, a small movement: *Unbelievable.*

She went to the table and scraped the loose papers into a pile, and then took them, with her drink, to the sofa to appraise. She must have been drawing for three hours or more; she wanted to see what.

Rebecca tucked her feet up and worked her way through the sheets.

There was her usual mix of sprawling impressionism – broad, sweeping strokes made with the side of the pencil, the suggestion of form expressed through blocks of light and shade – and meticulous detail – pure line describing construction and mechanics and ornamentation. There were landscapes and buildings, figures and animals, objects and cloth, and some of it was recognisably something she had seen and some of it must have come from her imagination.

Drawing like this was not new to Rebecca. She had learned, somewhere along the line, how to restrain this aspect of her ability, keeping it tidily corralled behind a fence so that she could concentrate on work, and also how, when it was appropriate, to release it and open herself to its – temporary – influence. It was what she had done that night in Aunty Edie's house, after seeing Will for the first time in his disguise as a movie pirate, and it was what she had done today.

This was, however, wilder and weirder and simply *more* in sheer quantity than any other time she had experienced this. But then, it was the first time she had tried it in Fairyland.

Trees featured heavily, gnarled dwarf shapes with twisted trunks and hunched branches, and smooth, slender forms lifting graceful arms to the sky. She had drawn groups of trees, individual specimens of trees, details of trees, and even examples of wood grain, as if for an illustrated arboreal dictionary. She had been tree mad for several pages.

There were vines too, of course; frankly she would have suspected trickery if there were not. And there were flowers, round-petalled dog roses and apple blossom, dainty, intricate harebells and snowdrops, and cascading laburnum and honeysuckle

Animals too. Beauty featured on more than one page, sometimes portrayed realistically as if sketched from life, sometimes reduced to the stylised representation of a tallixer in lines resembling the curls and spirals of Celtic design, or the odd, semi-human notion of animals in medieval illuminations.

She had drawn herself, which was a first, and, unexpectedly and poignantly, both Michael and Connor – just figures expressed in a few economic lines, but unmistakable.

Rebecca closed her eyes for a moment, and then moved on.

A few pages in, her attention was caught by a whiskery, sharp-eared face drawn scrappily at the bottom corner. It was hard to make out exactly what it was, or what the face might belong to – a malformed man? a malformed fox? – and it made her feel uneasy.

The eyes looked shiftily aside, and there was something about the nose – snout – *muzzle* - that made you think you could hear it sniffing.

Not nice. Rebecca put the page aside, but the creature was there again on the next sheet, the tip of a hairy ear appearing from behind one side of a throne-like chair, and something which might have been the tuft at the end of a tail emerging from the other.

Rebecca shook herself and took a sip from her drink, and its clear sharpness chased away the bad taste suddenly in her mouth.

The next few drawings were very domestic: fires in hearths, curtains framing small-paned windows, jugs of milk and platters of fruit and baskets of eggs. Then the nasty little face cropped up again on a page full of disasters: a broken window; a ladder falling sideways from an apple tree; a bleating calf beside a cow with a shrunken udder; an empty cradle.

An empty cradle…That last made Rebecca shudder, and suddenly she didn't want to look at her drawings any longer. There was a world of difference between the tidy, cradle-in-waiting for a baby yet to be born which she had *not* drawn and the tip-tilted, abandoned cradle with its crumpled blanket which she had.

What had she been thinking of?

The light in the room was fading now and the pencil lines were no longer black on white but grey on grey. Lorian would come soon to take her to supper, and even as she thought this, a knock came at her door and Lorian's voice called her name.

Rebecca admitted the fairy woman, and changed with lightning speed into the green dress. Fortunately the creases from its night crumpled on her bed had fallen out after a few hours hanging properly in the wardrobe.

She ran a brush through her hair and then gathered the papers into a sheaf to take back to the studio.

As she dumped them on the plan chest, she saw Michael's box and remembered, with a little twist of shock, that once again she had forgotten to retrieve what was hiding in the hinge.

Damn and blast!

Why did she keep doing this?

Too late now. Tonight. There would be no wild tallixer in her room tonight – no new one, that was – and she would deal with the box as soon as supper was over.

Rebecca, with Lorian on her right and Beauty on her left, went down to dinner.

The story being read aloud that evening was about a soldier who had lost his heart to a water spirit and grew old searching lakes and streams in the hope of finding her again.

Rebecca understood almost every word.

Chapter Thirty-Seven

The fourth day: two days left

'Can we go past the front door?' Rebecca asked. 'I want to look at something.'

She didn't mean *past* exactly, more *via,* and she suspected she was the first person to use *front door* to mean the main entrance to the castle, but that didn't matter. The meaning, she was confident, was clear to Lorian, and she knew that, as always, her fluency had moved on a few notches overnight.

She more or less knew the way herself, but she had not ventured down the final passage since arriving at the castle three weeks ago.

Three weeks ago? Rubbish, three *days* ago.

Now she strode forward, not hampered at all by her skirt and eager to test her theory.

Like the improvement in her language skills, the idea had arrived overnight, hatching in her unconscious mind while she slept and stepping forth brightly when she wakened, yawning, in the wide bed.

It was a good one; it fitted the facts as she understood them, and would provide the answers to a lot of questions.

The tapestries were as she remembered, hunting scenes depicted in glowing greens and blues and chestnut-red. They were huge, the figures almost life-size, and the detail, now that she could take time to look properly, was exquisite. Rebecca, momentarily distracted from her purpose, leaned forward to examine the feathers of a hawk, speckled and barred and extended ready for flight. There was even a tiny woven reflection in his piercing eye and on the bells attached to his leg. How many man hours did such painstaking labour represent? How many sore fingers and aching backs?

Rebecca became aware of Lorian waiting patiently. She stepped back and scanned the walls. Yes, there was the flash of brilliance amongst the forest colours that was the charming little unicorn, and further along the black silhouette of the tallixer. And there, yes there, was what she thought she remembered.

'Lorian?' Rebecca gestured her friend forward. 'What's that?'
'What's what?'
'That. There. That face.'
'What face?'

Rebecca looked at the fairy woman, staring blankly at the edge of the hanging. 'There! Can't you see it? That patch of brown behind the flowers.'

Lorian peered closer, but Rebecca felt she was being humoured. 'There's no face there.'

Rebecca looked back at the image, and the slanting, narrow eyes returned her gaze insolently over its hairy shoulders. *Think she'll see me?* it seemed to suggest. *Haven't you learned anything yet?*

She had another try. 'What is it then? That patch of brown?'

Lorian shrugged. 'Dead leaves? I don't know, Rebecca. Does it matter?'

Did it matter? Rebecca twisted her mouth and considered. It did, but it was only confirmation of what she had by now begun to guess and it would be pointless to argue.

'No,' she said, 'no, not really. Breakfast?'

At table, the milk was fresh and had not soured, which rocked Rebecca's theory a little, but there had been an accident the night before in which all the fruit was dropped on the floor, and the bruising overnight made it pretty much inedible.

'How did that happen?' Rebecca asked.

'I'm not sure. The boy said he felt his ankles grabbed and fell over, but there was nothing that could have done that. He just slipped.'

Maybe.

'Are all the cows producing properly at the moment?'

She expected Lorian to be taken aback by that, both the abrupt change of subject and the sudden interest in the local farming industry, but she simply raised an eyebrow and answered the question.

'Not all of them. Two have a disease and dried up. We'll have enough milk for the castle, though. Don't worry.'

Oh, I won't worry, Rebecca thought. At least, not about milk.

'Lorian,' she said, placing her palms down on the table in

what she realised was a gesture of determination. 'I have some questions I'd really like answers with. I mean, of. No, I mean, to.'

'Of course. What are they?'

'No,' Rebecca said. 'Not here. In the study room.'

She was getting a taste for decision making.

'Okay, right.'

Lorian would have no idea what that meant, but Rebecca found beginning with 'okay, right' always made her feel focused and workmanlike. It sort of cleared the decks and made way for fresh business. She positioned her pad of paper on the table with the pencil next to it, because that always helped too.

She saw Lorian's eyebrows twitch again, but ignored them.

'First question. Did you find out who brought Beauty into the castle?'

'I don't think anyone did, did they? Didn't she just wander in?'

'Or who soured the milk?'

'It just went sour.'

'Burned the meat?'

Lorian shrugged, looking bewildered.

Rebecca said, 'Right. As I thought.' She drew a satisfyingly resolute tick against the first line on her pad.

'Now, about the studio. How did you know I am an artist?'

Lorian's expression shifted from bewilderment to confusion – a subtle shift perhaps, but distinct. 'How did I know…? Of course you are an artist!'

Rebecca's turn for confusion. 'Why *of course*? How could you have known before you met me?'

Lorian opened her hands. 'You are the Queen of Clover.'

Rebecca leaned back, illumination slowly dawning on her.

'You mean all Queens of Clover are artists? The Queen of Clover *has* to be an artist?'

'Of course.'

'Wow.'

That had not occurred to her at all. How extraordinary. The studio had not been set up for her, Rebecca Mulligan. It was simply an integral and essential part of the Queen's apartment.

That would be why there were oils, even though Rebecca never used that medium. She'd missed a trick there.

But now a new question was forming itself.

'Who designs the tapestries?'

Lorian opened her hands again. 'You. The Queens. Of course. Who else could do it?'

Yes, yes, everything was *of course,* but it was all new to Rebecca. Ideas flapped in her head like birds.

So the Queen held a monopoly on tapestry design and fine art of other kinds too. How horrible for everyone else. But leaving that aside, if the Queen was responsible for what appeared in the tapestries, then one of Rebecca's predecessors had included that nasty, whiskery face in the hunting tapestry even though Lorian and probably everyone else was blind to it.

Why would you make an image that only your successor could see?

So that she will know.

Rebecca felt suddenly nauseous, and as if a needle were pricking her spine. She flexed her shoulders and, for a tiny instant of time, thought she heard something far away, beyond the stone walls, sniggering…

She glanced at Lorian, sitting opposite.

'Did you just–?'

Rebecca petered out, leaving the question incomplete; it was pointless, the fairy woman's expression was bland and calm. She had not heard anything, or at least nothing – untoward.

The moment had passed anyway, and the nausea was retreating. Rebecca shook herself and refocused her attention.

The tapestries were a message, a means of communicating information to someone you would never meet.

She would need to study them, all of them, wherever they appeared in the castle, but she would lay a bet that the most important messages were in the tapestries hanging near the front door and on the approach to the throne room, those protected against fading by magic spells. It was all Rebecca could do not to leap up and get started there and then.

But she had more questions to ask Lorian first.

She took up her pencil again and checked her list.
'Alright. Now tell me about *Robert*.'

This time, this time...

Rebecca checked that the tip of Beauty's tail had made it safely inside, then she locked the door, pocketed the key, and went straight to the studio. At last she had remembered the secret compartment of Michael's box at a time when she could do something about it.

Provided she was quick. Robert would be calling for her in half an hour, but that should be long enough.

She opened out the blade of Uriel Passenger's knife. It was perfectly shaped for winkling open the compartment and she wondered whether that was all she would need it for. No doubt she'd find out; she just had to keep her mind open to possibilities.

The hinge released its secret and Rebecca reached in for the slip of rolled paper with the tweezers Michael had so thoughtfully left for her. The tweezers bit and a slim tube emerged, tied with a twist of silver thread. Rebecca untied the knot and opened the paper.

It was reluctant to uncurl and she had to hold it flat with her hands. How long ago had Michael put it away for her to find? It held script written in Michael's cursive hand using black-brown ink and an italic pen.

It was complete gibberish.

Xyuk Lyvywwu, Mi byly sio uly xymjcy ypylsnbcha...

How she hated codes.

Rebecca fished out her small sketchbook and copied out the first few lines, using block capitals instead of lower case. She hoped, she really did, that Michael hadn't overestimated her cipher-solving skills; it would be flattering but extremely unhelpful if he had.

Then she rerolled the paper, popped it back in its home, and replaced the hinge. It felt very cloak-and-dagger but she had to respect Michael's judgement until she had enough information to rely on her own.

XYUK LYVYWWU...She had an idea about that already, but

verifying it would take minutes she did not have right now.

Rebecca unbuttoned her bodice while she surveyed the contents of the wardrobe. Ideally she wanted something that was dramatically different in colour from what she had worn so far, yet not too noticeable; not scarlet, for example, or that lovely ochre like lichen on a dry stone wall.

There, that one. Rebecca shrugged off the bodice and reached for one of soft dove grey. It was almost the colour of the stone walls, so she would blend very nicely and unnoticeably, and it was quite unlike the dark brown she had been seen in all morning.

As she swapped skirts regret for her trousers pawed at her, but it was no good: not even scarlet would make her stand out as much as wearing trousers would.

She slipped into the brown shoes she had been wearing – more pairs in different colours had arrived in the wardrobe yesterday – and slid her sketchbook and pencil securely into the capacious skirt pocket along with the knife and her door key. She sent her fingers to her collar bone to check by feel that the gold vine leaf was secure on its chain under her blouse.

She probably had fifteen minutes before Robin arrived. That should be a reasonable head start.

Rebecca opened the door, quietly in case anyone should be passing.

The corridor was empty.

Rebecca stepped out, held the door for the tallixer to join her, then closed it softly and locked it.

Now all she had to do was remember the way.

Under the cobwebs, amongst the mouse bones, it stopped in mid-chew and stiffened, sniffing. The air hung heavy about it, waiting.

Then it began to eat again, crunching the small skeleton and licking the juices.

She wasn't ready yet.

Chapter Thirty-Eight

Ideas and images swirled in Rebecca's head, leaving no space to think about the route she must take, but that didn't seem to be a problem; her feet spun her round corners and up steps and through doorways without seeming to need direction. The layout of the castle had taken root in her brain just as the language had.

She saw no-one and heard only voices muted by distance. Her biggest fear, that she might cannon into the Knave of Vines on his way to fetch her, was gradually laid to rest as she climbed through the castle, leaving the office levels behind and venturing into the quieter, lonelier, farther reaches.

The throne room was this way. Each new passage was recognised by Rebecca from the tapestries hanging there, reassuring her that she was on track – always assuming no tapestries were duplicated. She didn't think they were.

It was another thing to consider, but first she needed thinking time; there was so much to get straight.

There was something amiss in the castle and its environs, that much was clear, and she was the only one who could see it. That was true for both the abstract and the concrete. Nobody was investigating the string of accidents and mishaps, and they all seemed to forget about what was going wrong alarmingly quickly. The vagueness Rebecca had observed in Lorian when she questioned her floated about everyone else too, even Rascally Robin – which of course gave her another layer of problem to deal with.

Crucially, nobody had seen the – creature – that had flickered fleetingly in Rebecca's peripheral vision that night outside her door, and Lorian had been utterly unable to see its image in the woven hunting scene. A pile of leaves, for heaven's sake!

All of which must mean it was magic, and Rebecca would have to deal with it alone and knowing nothing about such things. She didn't even have a word for it.

Evil spirit suggested exorcists and possession; this was flesh and blood and hair and bone, and skin – sagging, wrinkly skin. *Goblin:* that was more like it. Something with hands that could grip a boy's ankles and drag a goat carcass.

Not a nice word, though; Rebecca shivered.

Well, so far its deeds had been a nuisance rather than serious harm, although there was the knife accident, and the tallixer might have been meant to kill her. Rebecca rated that way above a nuisance.

She glanced down fondly at the smooth black head beside her. The venture hadn't succeeded which meant the goblin was fallible, and that in itself was reassuring. When you have very little to be reassured by, you grab everything on offer.

Rebecca had reached the passage leading to the throne room, but she didn't walk to the end. She was sure Robin would look for her there, so she needed to wait until he had done so and gone away again.

She tried the first door in the passage, between tapestries showing a dispute involving a savage dog and a bitten child (*open and shut, that one*) and one apparently concerning the lopping of branches from a tree, in which the man holding the axe was receiving poisonous glares from all directions.

The door was unlocked: thank goodness – she had been banking on that.

The room behind the door was the size of a small church hall and opulently furnished in deep, kingfisher green. There were high-backed chairs that looked grand but uncomfortable, and tall mirrors in carved and gilded frames. Were supplicants encouraged to look into their souls while they waited for their cases to be heard? Rebecca glimpsed her own, pale reflection of white skin and silvery gown, her hair a black rope of plait down her back. Her expression was steady and unafraid, and even a little grim.

Good.

Robin was bound to search these rooms, though: what she needed was a wardrobe.

There was a door at the back which opened into a narrow vestibule with another door opposite. When Rebecca tried that, she found herself in the second antechamber, almost identical to the one behind her but this time decorated in claret and burgundy. She wondered whether the colours were significant.

The vestibule was an office of sorts, plain and functional and fitted with shelves, and at the end, where the outside passage must lie, was yet another door. And that, Rebecca was pleased to see, revealed a deep cupboard – deep enough to swallow her and Beauty both.

The difficulty was going to be knowing when Robin arrived and when he left again.

Rebecca retraced her steps through the antechamber and listened at the door to the passage.

Silence.

She opened the door an inch and put her eye to the crack. The passage was empty. So now she had to wait.

While she waited, Rebecca thought.

The goblin that only she could see was not the only puzzle facing her.

Open Michael's box. Remember Jack's tallixer. Use Uriel's knife. Wear Emily's necklace. Find the Jack of Hearts.

Five commands that had led her to commit herself to entering this strange world.

But suppose that was not all? Suppose the commands had another function still to perform which she had yet to discover? What if they were still *live?*

She had opened Michael's box, one he had made rather than one he merely possessed, and found his coded message. She had remembered Jack's tame tallixer, Gira, and not run screaming from Beauty, which might well have saved her life.

She had used Uriel Passenger's knife to gain access to the secret compartment in this box of Michael's just as she had with the carved box from Ashendon Cottage, although in this case other knives equally slender would have done the job just as well. Perhaps the meaningful use of Uriel's knife had yet to come.

And she was definitely wearing Emily's necklace, that was for sure; she would not take it off even to sleep tonight, just in case it held some protective power against goblins.

All that remained was the fifth command: *Find the Jack of Hearts.* But Robin did not need to be found; he was here, available, already.

Which meant that if the commands held relevance, there was

really only one possible conclusion to be drawn.

Footsteps on rush mats are muffled but not silent. Rebecca heard somebody coming before anyone appeared round the corner at the end of the corridor, and she was able to reduce the gap to a mere sliver, which was shortly filled by a tall figure dressed in rich royal blue.

Rebecca closed the door softly and scampered across the room. She whisked into the dividing office, careful not to close the door on Beauty's tail, and then shooed the great beast into the cupboard and followed her, holding the door ajar.

Nothing.

Rebecca waited, breathing silently, concentrating.

Still nothing. He must have gone straight to the throne room. So would I, Rebecca thought, it's the obvious thing to do. But when I found that it was empty…

A door latch rattled and footsteps entered the room nearest the throne room: the burgundy room. Rebecca froze and superstitiously crossed her fingers.

The footsteps retreated and a door closed.

Okay, he now had the second antechamber to search and the office. Would he check the office? I would, thought Rebecca. But would he also check the cupboard?

The sound of the second door unlatching reached her straining ears, and footsteps crossed the floor of the kingfisher room. Rebecca drew the cupboard door tight against the door jamb, and in the blackness there was only the heat of the tallixer, muscular against her thigh, and the hard wood of the door panel where she leaned her forehead.

Please, please don't come in.

What would happen if he did? She was the Queen of Clover, didn't that give her political immunity? But if he was not, after all, the Knave of Vines…

Beauty can get him. I'll launch her at him.

Rebecca imagined herself releasing the tallixer: *Beauty – kill!* She pictured the long wolf-like jaws seizing Robin's throat…Or was this the moment to use Uriel's knife?

It wasn't going to happen. So far as she knew, Robin wasn't a murderer; he just wasn't who he claimed to be, who he was supposed to be, and once again, only she seemed able to see it.

Did he even know it himself? Was he deliberately masquerading as the Knave of Vines or was he the dupe of this wretched goblin? And to what end?

Her nerves leapt at a sound horribly close: Robin was checking the office, as she had expected.

Please, please...

And then the door closed again. He hadn't entered, just thrown a quick glance inside. It was likely, then, that he did not yet suspect her of deliberately hiding from him, only of having gone absent without leave.

Rebecca breathed again, listening to his footsteps as they retreated across the antechamber. The outer door closed. She opened the cupboard to admit some light, and waited for him to get well away.

Where would he search next? She had no idea, but there was a lot of castle; he wouldn't be back for hours, and she shouldn't need that long.

Rebecca sat on the throne.

The room was chilly, but although her arms were a little cold the thick bodice kept her body warm. The air was stone-scented, inorganic, neutral, and there was no sound. It was as if, Rebecca thought, the space about her were waiting.

The tallixer stretched, relaxed, at the foot of the dais. It was comforting to have the great beast for company even if she couldn't bring herself to use her as a weapon.

Rebecca was thinking, and the thoughts, still like birds, were beginning to resolve into coherent groups now, gathering restlessly as if in readiness to migrate.

Sitting on this throne, her hands resting on the gilded arms, her back straight, Rebecca felt authoritative and self-possessed. *No more hiding in the stationery cupboard,* she thought. *If I'm challenged about this now, I'll explain exactly what I'm doing. I'll bring everything out into the open; no more skulduggery.*

The box and the tallixer were dealt with; the knife and the necklace could wait for events to arise. But on the subject of the Jack of Hearts she needed to get pro-active.

I have to 'find' him, not create him.

He wasn't just some guy who would do the job better, waiting for her to recognise his potential and promote him. He was out there, somewhere, already in existence, and she had to search for him and reinstate him.

But where? And how could it be managed in twenty-four hours, which was all she had left?

Perhaps Michael's letter would help.

She had cracked the code easily, if you could use that word for a device so simple. It was a straightforward static letter substitution, and the number Michael had chosen was seven: magic number seven. So basic a cipher would not hinder anyone with half a brain, but it was enough, Rebecca supposed, to stop someone reading or memorising it at a glance. She had the first two lines in moments; she would transcribe the rest when she returned to her room after dinner, which would be her last dinner here.

Tomorrow was her final day. In less than twenty-four hours she would be heading down through the wood to the wall and the clearing and the anomalous stone hut, with a basket of picnic food and warm clothing, because she had no idea how long she would have to wait before the light from Ashendon Cottage fell through and opened the way home.

The great, prowling shadow that accompanied her everywhere now would have to be left outside the stone wall. It was a pity, but unarguably necessary.

In twenty-four hours, or twenty-five, or maybe thirty but surely no more, she would be back in reality, where her old life waited for her to take it up again. There would be her Mini to carry her vast distances by burning fossil fuel, radios and televisions to tell her what was happening on the other side of the world, convenience food in metal cans to save her the trouble of cooking. Her stepfather would be extracting milk from his herd in what amounted to a factory; Connor would be writing some essay and, she hoped, wondering what was happening to her; and Will, presumably, would be waiting for her return. She hoped he had a bloody good apology ready for having betrayed her so ruthlessly.

Although she thought she had guessed his reason.

I'd like an apology even so!

The room held her as a casket might hold a single pearl; there was so much empty space, but anything smaller would feel cramped. She felt calm here and relaxed, as if she had been meditating.

Perhaps I have.

Yes, perhaps.

Tomorrow morning this room would be populated, the floor taken up with supplicants and secretaries and VIPs and the public audience, all anxious to see how she would fare and hear what she said. That would be the right time to deal with everything, her own matters as well as the specific case they presented to her. The witnesses would be required to do double duty.

Rebecca's thoughts converged into a flock at last and took flight, a coherent force that knew now where its destination lay and how to reach it.

She found she was smiling.

Tomorrow was going to be good.

Chapter Thirty-Nine

The last day: only hours left

'The blue gown,' Lorian said, and Rebecca thought, I know that, I don't need to be told.

The blue gown was the one her mirror-self had worn in her little house on Skye. Now, putting it on, she found it fitted her perfectly, the neckline and plunging waist and long sleeves close about her wrists.

Well, of course.

For the first time the golden vine leaf on its golden chain lying over her collar bone was in full view, and the vine leaves she had found in Michael's box were entwined in her hair, where the filament that linked them was lost in the dark and only the leaves winked and sparkled like stars.

Inspecting the result in the mirror, Rebecca acknowledged to herself that it was a fabulous look. It was a pity she had to take it into the risky environment of the kitchens.

'What!' Lorian looked aghast. '*Why?*'

'I need a few things. Don't worry, I'll be careful.'

The people in the kitchen were aghast too, but Rebecca moved carefully among the cupboards and tables, making sure her skirts did not come into contact with anything, while she gathered what she wanted. She did not explain and the staff did not challenge her, although they stared at her, some of them with their mouths dopily open. She put everything into a basket and left them all to speculate.

Lorian did not question her either, and even Robin, self-styled Knave of Vines, began but then thought better of it and shut his mouth leaving the words unspoken. He appeared to be fixated by her neckline, and Rebecca guessed it was the necklace rather than her décolletage, although one never knew for sure…

Everyone was very subdued as she led the way to the throne room, Beauty at her side. In the passage people parted, making way for her as she processed towards the twin columns of mosaic and the wide doorway between them, standing open now and inviting her to enter.

Beyond waited her throne, like a friend with open arms, and she could just see, behind it, the twitching motion of the smoke-blue curtain and the bulge she had known would be there.

People fell away as she entered the hall and she walked the final yards alone but for her tallixer. She climbed the steps of the dais, set the basket down, and turned to face her audience in a silence broken only by the quiet scratching from behind the curtain.

Rebecca sat.

I am not nervous at all, Rebecca thought, faintly surprised. But she was focused. Everything since New Year's Day had led to this, and she was damned if she was going to fall short of the mark.

She was the Queen and she was going to be Queenly.

The air carried the sulphurous odour she had noticed last week – no, four – no, damn it, *three* – days ago; her sense of time was completely up the creek. The smell helped to keep part of Rebecca's attention fixed on the shuffling behind the curtain, which no-one else seemed to have noticed, not even Beauty.

Fine cat you are, Rebecca thought at the tallixer sprawling languidly at the foot of the dais. How peculiar that magic worked even on animals and yet never on her.

She hoped her basket of tricks was going to work. She was horribly conscious of the looming requirement to use Uriel's knife.

Oh Michael, why couldn't you be more specific?

She had transcribed the remainder of the letter before she went to bed and had learned it by heart. It wasn't long.

Dear Rebecca,

So you are here despite everything, and the one of us who least wished to see into the World Invisible has penetrated its heart. I expect it has been a shock, but a good shock I hope. You were preparing for this for some time, I know – or did you not notice that you were growing your hair even as Connor was shortening his?

(No, she hadn't noticed that; and she noted Michael hadn't

pointed it out to her at the time either.)

Don't worry about the trials – you will do well. If ever there were a Queen of Clover in waiting, it is you. So remember everything you have been told; remember what you have drawn; and remember me. And then trust your own judgement – you usually do!

(Was that a jibe?)

We all love you, we always have and always will. Be yourself, be strong, and come visit me in the mountains as soon as you can.

Michael

She thought of the purple and grey mountains she could see from her window. She couldn't wait. It would be so lovely to see him again, and explore the climbing with him – he would be climbing, surely?

But I can't!

The truth struck her like a physical blow: there was no time, because today was her last day. She had forgotten…again.

Remember everything you have been told; remember what you have drawn; and remember me.

Rebecca watched the supplicants approach.

'…will abide by your judgement.'

Both men bowed and withdrew.

So I should jolly well think. Otherwise why was she here?

It was about wood; or rather it was about trees, but the evidence, if that was the right word, was about wood. Rebecca held the box, which was nothing like as nice as Michael's, and examined it, buying herself time. She was acutely aware of all the eyes trained on her, and breathed with careful deliberation. She wasn't nervous, and there was no way she was going to allow herself to start being. But it might take some effort and planning to avoid.

Accuser A (she wasn't allowed to know names) was a paunchy man whose wild red hair corkscrewed around his broad face and joined up with an equally wild red beard. He waved his hands a lot, and stabbed the air with splayed, stubby fingers while he claimed that Defendant B had made the box out of wood from a tree so ancient and mysterious and so steeped in legend that using even fallen branches was forbidden.

Rebecca checked that he meant a type of tree, not an individual specimen, and learned that it was, indeed, the entire species that was protected. It was now extremely rare and hard to find, but the Defendant had located one and done the dirty deed.

Defendant B protested innocence, denied any hand in an act so heinous, and said he had made the box from a tree that grew on his own land. He said he didn't know what species of tree it was, but that he had used branches pruned from it in the past for all sorts of items and no-one had ever accused him of sacrilege before.

He was another portly chap, taller and heavier than his accuser and clean shaven, but he lacked the energy of outrage and instead looked affronted. He spoke quietly and delivered his speech in injured tones, avoiding everyone's eye including Rebecca's.

So it all hinged on identifying the wood of this box. How on earth was she supposed to do that?

Rebecca stroked the lid. It had been rough-finished, not sanded and waxed like Michael's work, and the grain was coarse against her thumb. It looked old. Rebecca rubbed and then lifted the box and blew sharply across the top, clearing the grooves of the dust that had gathered there.

Cleaned of dust, the grain pattern was clearly defined: long, snaking, almost-parallel lines like contour lines on a map of steep hills and valleys, with isolated flecks and dashes in between. Rebecca narrowed her eyes and thought.

The grain of each species of tree is unique and identifiable, she knew that. It was like fingerprints. Michael had books full of photographs intended to help one identify wood; but those were in a different world.

Remember me.

Michael.

Remember everything you have been told.

But by whom, and when? Everything she had been told *ever*? Or did he mean the five commands Will had set her? But what had they to do with wood grain?

People were waiting. The smell of rotten eggs was turning her stomach.

Remember what you have drawn.

What had she drawn? Animals and birds and mountains and, yes, trees and...

...and wood grain.

I drew wood grain.

And she had never, so far as she could recall, drawn wood grain before. It had to be significant, but how could it help her identify this box?

Oh Michael...

His letter was not enough. Indeed it seemed scarcely necessary to have wrapped it up in a cipher at all, so innocent were its contents. Yet he had encoded it and tucked it away in a cunning compartment she had needed the slim point of a knife to access.

Her knife. Uriel's knife.

Use Uriel's knife.

Yes, she had, although any knife would have done.

The connection burst before her like a firework, and Rebecca closed her eyes.

A knife was more than just a blade; it was a blade and a handle.

Uriel's knife had been made here; the handle was made of wood from this world; and she was sure, certain, that she remembered his journal mentioning the tree from which that wood had come. *A powerful tree,* the spidery brown script said, forming itself again before her mind's eye, *now very rare.*

What were the odds? Worth a gamble, surely?

Rebecca drew from her pocket the knife and laid it on the lid of the box.

Together, one on top of the other, they confirmed her guess. The two grains aligned perfectly, revealing the truth clear and indisputable.

The wood was the same. She had done it. All she needed to do now was announce it.

Rebecca opened her mouth and took breath, and in that instant all hell broke loose.

Chapter Forty

When Rebecca was fifteen a spider ran over her lap.

She had been curled, feet tucked beneath her, on the sagging sofa in the back parlour of the Suffolk farmhouse, and the spider – heavy and the colour of charcoal, and at least four inches from front to back – ran straight across Rebecca's thighs *and wrist* before disappearing over the cushion.

Rebecca remembered the two seconds it took with great clarity, and she also remembered standing on the far side of the room a moment later with every muscle hurting. She had erupted from her position in pure reflex, her aim simply to escape. Her sketchbook – she had been drawing, naturally – landed upside down, creasing several pages, and her pencil soared across the room to hit the tiled hearth and break its lead all the way up so that later she had to discard it.

And that was only a spider.

The goblin shifted every bit as quick and it was way, way bigger. It landed on Rebecca's lap with the weight of a medium-sized dog, something like a spaniel, but leathery instead of furry, and stinking. A second later Rebecca found herself with the wall behind her shoulders, facing the empty throne, her heart thudding and her entire body aching.

At least she hadn't squealed; she might have yelped, though.

And still they couldn't see it! Everyone was looking at her, clearly astonished and bewildered.

Okay then, now or never.

Rebecca breathed out slowly, clearing the panic, readying herself for action. She would have to be quick, and she would have to be prepared to stand her ground no matter how the goblin reacted.

The basket was still beside the throne, upright and intact, unlike the box she had been holding, which had been hurled across the floor. The knife was gone too, so thankfully that option was withdrawn.

Rebecca darted to the dais and scrabbled at the cloth sack. It would have been easier if her hands had not been shaking, but it opened well enough and she scooped out the flour with the saucepan she had chosen for being just small enough to fit into the bag.

Now where had it got to?

Rebecca pivoted, saucepan poised, conscious of the eyes watching her, including those of her tallixer. How was it possible Beauty had not smelled the disgusting thing?

Magic. Rebecca hated the stuff.

She hated herself, too, because she jumped and let out a squawk as something hot and hairy brushed her ankles. A dirty, matted shape lolloped on hands and feet towards the front row of the audience where it would strike them at knee height and bowl them over like skittles if they couldn't see it coming.

Rebecca aimed and threw. There was a communal gasp as white flour fell in a cloud, and the front ranks retreated, sneezing and coughing.

And then there was a second gasp, which turned into a shriek, as Rebecca's plan paid off.

To her, the homunculus with the snout and tail of an animal and the arms and hands of a man had turned from dingy brown to speckled white; to her audience, it had become visible for the first time, and they recoiled in panic.

This was disappointing. Rebecca realised she had not looked further than convincing everyone the goblin was real and present. She had somehow thought that once that was achieved then other people would take over and actually deal with it. Surely Robin...?

But the less-and-less-convincing Knave of Vines was over by the window waving his hands weakly and wearing an expression of paralysed indecision.

Yet she was not entirely without help. Even as Rebecca sighed with exasperation, there was a fresh collective exclamation followed by a nauseating crunch, and Rebecca turned to see her tallixer crouching, lion-like, with shoulder blades high above her back and her head twisted sideways as her molars got to work.

Okay. Good. Phew...But she shouldn't eat it.

People fell back as Rebecca crossed the hall and seized the thick fur of the tallixer's neck. She took care not to look at what was on the floor.

'Leave it. Beauty, come on, leave the horrible thing. I'll find you something else instead.'

Anything must taste better than this. Rebecca looked round at her audience.

'Can someone please go and fetch me a goat?'

Two hours later the morning sunshine had turned to afternoon clouds, and the kingfisher chamber was chilly. Rebecca opened the door and greeted the man standing in the passage with a chilly gaze to match.

'Come in,' she said, with no smile at all. 'Sit down, please.'

How things could change in the space of a day. Less than twenty hours ago she had cowered in a cupboard to avoid being caught here by this man. Now she held ownership of the room and it was obvious that Robin knew it.

She held ownership of the cupboard too if she wanted it, and she probably did because those ledgers looked very interesting...

Except that I won't be here to read them.

Oh yes.

Rebecca walked to the window beyond which the distant mountains glinted in the afternoon sunlight. Somewhere in their folds Michael was living, and making beautiful objects out of wood, and maybe thinking about her sometimes.

She turned back to the room and leaned lightly against the narrow windowsill, her arms folded. She preferred to be on her feet for this, her final task.

Already the events of the morning seemed distant and closed.

The goat when it arrived was, regrettably, a bonny little thing still very much alive, which had to be led back out and swiftly slaughtered to ease Rebecca's conscience before being used to distract Beauty. Then someone with a strong stomach and little imagination got rid of the sticky mess of skin and guts on the floor of the throne room (a carefully considered reward was due there) and the spilled flour was swept into a heap by the wall.

Rebecca retrieved Uriel's knife and the box from the bottom of the steps and returned to her throne, where she made use of the time while the audience shuffled into formation again to clear her throat and marshal her thoughts. She hoped nobody was remembering her yelp.

'*That,*' she said sternly, 'was at the root all the trouble recently. Souring the milk and causing accidents. It is *very important* that we all remember and look out for anything like it in the future. Be on guard.'

Her audience gave the impression they were paying attention. Some looked thoughtful. Robin, in the corner by the door, was a bit pale.

'Now,' she continued. 'This box has definitely been made using wood from the protected tree. But the tree might indeed be growing on the defendant's land as he claims, and he might not have realised what it is. So somebody competent must inspect his tree and identify it. Robert, you can arrange that.'

That would protect his status for the time being, just in case anyone else was beginning to doubt too.

She had then announced the penalties, which had formed in her mind even as she was scampering about throwing flour into the air, which was quite impressive really.

If they found a tree and it was of the protected species, then the guy would have the benefit of the doubt and be bound over to behave himself in future. If there was no tree on his land then he could be assumed to be dishonest and would have all his tools confiscated. If her reading of the character of these people was correct, that ought to do it.

So far as she could gauge, it had all gone down very well; the business with the goblin had definitely impressed.

That just left Robin, whom she was going to deal with now.

She watched him sit down on the high-backed chair she had dragged into the middle of the floor, and wondered whether he guessed what was coming.

'Robin,' she said, 'where is the Knave of Vines?'

The shadows lengthened across the floor as he talked, and the light falling through the windows slowly dimmed to grey. Eventually Rebecca moved from the window and took the chair opposite him, leaning forward as she listened to what he had to say.

It was Will's fault, really: Will's magnetism and whatever there was in Robin's character that left him susceptible to it; and it had begun a long time ago.

Rebecca had not yet got to grips with how time passed here, or with the relative ages of people. She knew Uriel had been incredibly long-lived, and also Connor's three Dons, who were of mixed parentage. She had no idea at all what Will, for instance, numbered in years, or even whether years in this World Invisible were roughly equivalent to those in her own world, although judging from Connor's experience they clearly passed under the bridge at a different rate.

She could not tell the age difference between Will, a true Knave of Vines, and Robin, a false one, but Robin was clearly younger because he told Rebecca about meeting Will once, briefly, when he was not much more than a boy and Will had been organising flood relief for a corner of the land that had suffered torrential rainfall.

Bad weather happened here, too, and crops had been washed away, livestock drowned. Will had arrived in the village like a meteor, lit fires under everyone, and departed like a tornado, leaving the population slightly dazed and young Robin star-struck: such dynamism, he had thought, such unchallenged authority, such *style*.

From that day his course was set. He yearned to become Will, or someone like him, but it sounded to Rebecca like Knaves were born rather than made and Robin just didn't have it. He was bright, earnest, hard-working and ambitious, but not charismatic. He became a good strategist and a capable manager, but he lacked the spark that ignited the people he met and made them drop everything and jump. He was an administrator, not a leader – a lieutenant, not a captain. And for Robin, that wasn't enough.

So when Will vanished into another world, Robin presented himself as his successor, and because he had a good level of Skill, he was able to make the castle accept him. Basically, he had bamboozled them.

'And what do you imagine you'll do when Will comes back?' Rebecca asked. 'Or did you think you'd cross that bridge when you came to it?'

Robin looked puzzled. 'But he won't be coming back.'

He was delusional. Rebecca said, 'Of course he will. Tomorrow, probably.' *Just as soon as I get home and report all this to him.*

But Robin shook his head. 'No, he can't. He's crossed too many times. He can't come back any more.'

Rebecca felt the hairs on her arms rise. 'What do you mean he's crossed too many times? What has that to do with it?'

'You can't go to and fro. No-one can. Passing through *does* something to you. You can get away with it a few times, so long as you take different routes, but eventually you're...used up.' Robin shrugged, but sympathetically. 'That's just how it is. He can't go through any more. He can't come back.'

You can't go to and fro.

Was that what happened to Uriel Passenger? Was that why he stayed on, an ancient recluse in his museum of antiquities, hiding from the world so that nobody would guess the number of his birthdays? Rebecca was silent, following a trail of thoughts that brought in Connor and the Dons and Michael, and the pirate who had swept past her on that cold January day and changed the course of her life.

He must have known even then that he could never go home. His betrayal of her had not been simple pragmatism on his part: pushing her off the edge so that she would realise how well she could swim. It had been inevitable, his only option. It was all he could do, then and forever.

He was at Ashendon now, preparing to move the prisms out of alignment so that the light beams would mingle and she could step through. He would look through the sparkling brilliance into the bright air of his own world, his own country, all the while knowing he would never again be able to breathe it.

Rebecca thought of the purple mountains and the forest, and the little white unicorn in the hunting tapestry, and became aware of the water gathering in her eyes.

She blinked, and blinked again with determination. This was not queenly.

Robin sat watching her. She swallowed and said, 'So how do I find another Knave of Vines? Because I have to replace you.'

It was harsh, but it was true. He had been acting fraudulently for weeks, if not months. In any case, she was under orders to find the Jack of Hearts, which made sense now in the light of what she had learned. She had to find Will's successor, although how she could possibly do that in the space of a couple of hours was beyond imagining. If he was shut up in a room somewhere under the eaves, fine, but if he had allowed that to happen then he could hardly be a Knave of Vines as she understood it.

Robin shrugged again, opening his hands. He looked helpless. 'He'll be out there somewhere. There's always an interval, a little while without him, but then he turns up. Always. I knew that.'

Rebecca looked at him, twisting her mouth as she considered. She thought he was telling the truth now. It sounded plausible, and explained why Robin himself had been so readily accepted by the castle when he arrived out of nowhere.

In that case she did not need to seek out Will's successor; the right man would turn up sometime soon by himself. The point of the final instruction, perhaps, had been simply to alert her to Robin's hoax.

And what was she to do about that, exactly?

The interloper met her eyes with an expression of resignation. He would accept whatever she decreed, she felt sure.

So, life imprisonment, or a smack round the head? Rebecca nodded, a small movement, and made up her mind.

'Right,' she said. 'This is what I'm going to do.'

Chapter Forty-One

Nobody wanted her to go. Lorian cried.

'You'll be fine,' Rebecca told them. 'The Knave of Vines will turn up soon, and he'll set you right.'

He would, she was sure of that, and in the meantime Robin would do a good job as interim manager. He had been disarmingly humble and so grateful not to be ejected from the castle outright.

And anyway, it really was none of her business.

None of her business at all.

They packed her a basket, because she did not know how long she would be waiting in the stone hut before the way opened for her. She had a good, woollen cloak with a hood, and had tucked a few folded sheets of thick paper into the basket as well, so she would be able to draw.

She must be able to draw.

At the last moment she left them all standing in the passage and pelted up the stairs to fetch Michael's box from the Queen's studio. Her heart thumped at the thought of how close she had come to forgetting it.

It was too big to fit in the basket, so she walked down between the trees hugging it against her ribs with her free arm. It was awkward, but it wasn't too far.

As always, walking downhill was easy to begin with and then became a strain on her calves and thighs, but her walking boots did their job and kept her ankles firm and her grip secure. In time she left the wood behind and crossed the open meadow towards the high stone wall and the tops of the trees enclosed within it, and then she had slipped through the open door and was winding her way between more trees, twigs cracking underfoot, trying to keep to a straightish course.

And there, at last, was the clearing, the hut with the door hanging ajar, and inside, her passage home.

Rebecca stepped over the threshold.

There had been something here, something she had done…

Yes – the thesaurus. It was gone. The floor of the hut was empty.

Suddenly tired, Rebecca chose a flat spot and sat down. She

wasn't hungry, and for the moment she didn't feel like drawing either. For now, she wanted just to sit with her eyes closed and breathe in and out, in and out, with only the distant rustle of the forest in her ears and the scent of grass and stone…

The colours woke her, swirling and dazzling and only lasting a few moments.

Rebecca grabbed her box, scrabbled to her feet, and plunged into the light.

THROUGH THE LOOKING GLASS

Chapter Forty-Two

The floor was stone. Rebecca's knee and the heel of her hand came down hard, and the corner of the box dug into her ribs.

'Ow!'

She flexed her wrist to check for damage, and got to her feet just as the light vanished and she found herself standing in pitch dark.

'Damn!'

Where was the door? Where was the box, as well, because she was probably about to stub her foot on it.

Rebecca stooped and groped for the box, and found it exactly where her first step would have taken her. She pushed it aside for the moment and moved cautiously towards where she thought the door ought to be, sliding her feet along the floor and holding both arms in front of her, one outstretched, reaching, and one in front of her face just in case someone had left something hanging from the ceiling to catch her out. It didn't seem likely but she felt vulnerable.

Her fingers made contact with the wall, but not the door. She felt her way along the rough stones.

Come on, come on...

The room was stuffy and smelled dead – not *dead* as in something rotting, but lifeless, inorganic, stale – and the dark was oppressive. Rebecca couldn't wait to get out.

There: a door frame followed by a vertical crevice. Rebecca was fumbling for the handle when the door swung into her. There was a flood of light and her eyes, just beginning to adapt to the dark, recoiled, squinting. It was like being attacked. Rebecca staggered backwards, her heels jammed up against the wretched box she had abandoned on the floor, and she nearly, oh so nearly went down for the second time.

Will stood silhouetted in the doorway. He laughed.

'So you're back,' he said. 'I'll make you a cup of tea.'

Rebecca sat curled into the corner of the sofa, nursing her

scraped hand. She had lost some skin from the heel of her palm and it had begun to sting. She pulled up a fold of her skirt and wrapped it round the mug to protect the graze from the heat. It seemed ironic that after five days in Faerie dodging goblins and wild animals it was coming back home that had injured her.

'I want coffee,' she had said, but Will had made tea despite her.

'Tea is best when you've had a shock.'

'What do you know about tea? Tea is from my world, not yours.' Rebecca was aware she sounded petulant.

The fairy man shrugged. 'Mine now.'

Yes.

Subdued, Rebecca accepted the mug he handed her and wrinkled her nose at the not-coffee smell. At least she had shed her boots and didn't look like an idiot any more. She had caught sight of her reflection in the many mirrors lining the wall of the parlour, an angry-eyed woman in skirts and heavy walking boots, hair escaping from its braid. There were stains clotted on one side of her gown which puzzled her for a moment before she recognised them as a rich mixture of goblin blood and flour. *Tch!* Lorian might have warned her.

Small wonder Will had laughed.

Embarrassed at being caught reeling about like a drunk, Rebecca had retaliated by attacking him: 'Why weren't you here to meet me? I think you might have stayed up.'

But he had stayed up, evidently, or he wouldn't be dressed. Being awake wasn't the problem; watching the door open which was forever denied to him was. Excluded from his home for the remainder of his lifetime, he chose instead to wait until the way was closed and safely invisible before finding out whether she had arrived.

It seemed every line of conversation left her chastened.

Rebecca sipped the tea, wishing it was coffee, trying not to think about the goo on her clothes.

'I want a bath,' she said, regretting yet again that there was no shower in the cottage. 'Haven't you opened any windows this week? This room smells awful.'

'Yes, it will do.'

What did that mean? She felt unpleasantly grumpy and hoped a hot soak would sort her out. Her eyes fell on the thesaurus lying on the table.

'You got my note!'

'Yes.'

Rebecca frowned. 'Wait a minute. How? If you couldn't–'

Will said, 'Connor fetched it.'

'*Connor?*'

Ah. The webcam.

'So you left the prism out of place all week?'

'Of course. You could have come back any time you chose.'

Rebecca thought about the doorway, open and passable for a minute every twenty-four hours when the light from two worlds collided in chaos, and Connor in his room in Oxford with an image on his laptop screen showing a hut that existed in another plane. He would have noticed the thesaurus had been picked up, closed and set back down tidily, and perhaps even glimpsed the white paper peeping out from the top.

One minute would be long enough to dart through, snatch it up and leap back.

'Is he–?'

'No, he went home.'

'But did he…did you…'

'Rebecca, we did not fight over you.'

Rebecca flushed. 'No, I know, of course not! I just…'

What? Found it difficult to picture the two of them here, together, discussing her? Had Connor been angry at Will for sending her through, alone? Did Will realise who Connor was, what they had been to each other, and still were, at least in part?

And now she had attempted to voice thoughts which should have remained private, and laid herself open to complete misinterpretation.

Partial misinterpretation.

'And Rebecca?'

'What?'

'Give yourself a little time. To adapt.'

Rebecca stared. 'Pardon?'

'Pardon?'

'I didn't catch what you said. You said something.'

Will looked at her steadily. He said slowly, *'Give - yourself - time.'*

The consonants and vowels seeped through. Electric synapses in Rebecca's brain sparked and connected and woke up forgotten pathways, and meaning arrived in her head along with disorientation and a sense of shock.

'Oh! Yes. Right.' The words felt peculiar to her lips and tongue. Rebecca huffed a sigh of irritation and relapsed into the language she was still thinking in. 'I definitely need a bath. Thanks for the tea but there's no need to wait up.'

The bath took a while to run, the plumbing system being what it was, but the water was hot and Rebecca sank into it thankfully, not caring that her hair went under as well or that her knee and her hand stung. She would stay in here until the water cooled and she was feeling calm and able to face the world.

But she wondered what her tallixer was doing without her.

Chapter Forty-Three

'Your keys,' Will said.

'What? Oh yes. Keys.'

Rebecca took them from his hand and wondered how she had managed to get this far without thinking of them.

They stood next to her Mini in the corner of the hotel car park, which was still the closest a car could be brought to the cottage. Rebecca unlocked the door and then lifted the tail gate to sling her bag into the boot. There would have been room on the passenger seat because Will was not coming, but she kept forgetting that. It seemed wrong that he was staying behind.

'I'm not your Knave,' Will had said.

'I know that!'

She was living in a constant state of mild irritation, which in itself was irritating.

For heaven's sake, stop harking back, she told herself. *I'm here now; it's over.* But the air, even in the morning in the gardens, smelled stale, and she kept looking for lucifers – no, *matches* – instead of light switches.

She presumed she hadn't forgotten how to drive.

Will was staying on at Ashendon. She had introduced him to Bridget Dixon wondering whether he would be recognised as Guillermo Garcia, the dubious Spanish hiker up to no good back in January, but saw no trace of it in the woman's eyes as she shook hands with the same man two months later.

Really just two months?

Rebecca wondered whether he was still bothering to exercise Skill or whether Bridget would return to her office bemused and temporarily unable to concentrate, dazzled by the wild beauty of the new cottage tenant.

She herself could now look at Will dispassionately, she found, able to assess his appearance without risk of dissolving or turning tail to flee. The electricity had gone.

Was that also because he was not her Knave?

The implication was that somewhere, somehow, there was somebody else who was.

She thought of asking: 'What is he doing, this Knave of

Vines?' but she was afraid of the answer.

Looking for you.

'I've done my five days and I'm not going back,' she had said, and Will replied, 'Of course you have,' neatly leaving the second part of her statement hanging.

Rebecca settled herself behind the wheel, and then remembered about the ignition and fished for the key. The motor purred into life; at least her car hadn't forgotten how to behave.

'Bye, then.'

Will raised his hand in reply, and Rebecca drove, carefully, out of the car park.

She did remember how to do it. Nevertheless she stalled twice, at a roundabout and at traffic lights, before she reached Scotland.

Her house was still there; it looked...compact.

Rebecca moved through the rooms, those few there were, picking things up and putting them down again, staring out of the windows, reminding herself of what it felt like to live here. Everything was on a small scale and it confused her.

From time to time she looked down, but nothing was there.

I could get a dog.

But she didn't want a dog.

She had stopped in Portree to buy food. Queuing in the supermarket had been bizarre. But she was getting the hang of things again, and remembered that she had to turn the hob off after cooking. She even remembered to lock up before she went to bed.

Although if a burglar wants to break in he's welcome.

Where had that thought come from?

Rebecca opened her eyes in the dark, lying on her back. Was that really how she felt? What about her beautiful studio, with its great angled window facing the sea?

Not as beautiful as the Queen's studio, facing the mountains.

But her studio was everything; it was almost the whole point of being on Skye.

Rebecca thought some more, wide-awake and lonely in the still room with only the rain on the window for company. Finally, having come to no conclusions at all about anything, she turned onto her side and curled her legs up, and tried to empty her mind so that she could sleep.

But it didn't work.

The monolith squatted between the tumbledown walls, coarse grass and chickweed sprouting round its base. Rebecca laid her palm against it, the rough surface cold against her skin. It was immovable. Well, of course it was, that was the point of it.

Immovable by her own efforts, that was. It could be moved with the help of a machine.

Rebecca herself had set it down here three years earlier using a tractor with forks on the front. She saw no reason why Douglas Cameron should not lend her the tractor again if she asked. It would be a longish job, Douglas living on the other side of the island and the roads going round rather than over the top of the mountains in between, but it could be done.

There would be no-one to replace the stone afterwards though, and that was a serious problem.

Rebecca walked on up the track to the hillside. The sun was out now and surprisingly warm on her face, but it had rained earlier and the grass was wet. When she reached her favourite spot she sat down anyway, not inclined to care about a damp seat, and gazed over the moor.

It was a stupid idea anyway.

Sheep edged into view beyond the crag, the ewes looking bulky under their fleeces. They'd be lambing soon.

I hope they're feeding Beauty.

Although the tallixer had probably shoved off by now.

No, the thing to do would be to use Ashendon. That was the only properly managed route, after all.

There remained the issue of whether she could use the same way again, but it would only be for the second time, and Will had never mentioned a problem. Perhaps it didn't apply if you were a Queen.

Will would know.

Suddenly the view was of no interest. Rebecca stood up and

brushed off the dirt. She couldn't get going immediately, she needed tomorrow to settle business, but she'd rise early the day after that and leave before dawn.

Her mind was made up.

Chapter Forty-Four

The route down to London passed well to the west of Matlock. Rebecca had no intention of stopping off on the way.

In this direction the tricky, twisty roads were behind her after the first few hours and then it was motorways all the way. Rebecca pulled into services for an early lunch, and then again in the late afternoon when she knew she needed half an hour's sleep, and hit the outskirts of London after the main close-of-day rush.

Even so the final stretch, along narrow, congested streets made worse by vans unloading into shops, was tiresome and tiring. When she finally turned into Manorfield Road Rebecca was hungry again and longing to stretch her legs.

There was a space big enough for the Mini three doors up from Aunty Edie's. Rebecca nabbed it and climbed out onto the pavement, groaning. Over twelve hours of sitting in a car is not good. She felt clumsy and stiff as she let herself through the front door, as was her habit of old.

'Aunty Edie? It's me, Rebecca.'

Strains of Gustav Holst strayed from the front parlour. Rebecca followed the sounds and found her aunt comfortable in front of the gas fire watching a television screen where great spheres of coloured light moved about one another in a slow dance.

'Rebecca! How wonderful! Would you like a cup of tea? Mince pie?'

Surely not? Rebecca stood in the doorway. 'Don't stop watching. I'll make the tea.'

But her aunt had already switched the set off. 'It's only the solar system. It's recorded. I'll watch it later.

'Now, tell me all your wonderful news.'

It was colder than New Year's Day but also brighter, and Rebecca sat outside the café she and Steph had used, with her chair turned to face the river. There were very few street performers, although a wistful-looking guy in a battered top hat was rolling a rubber chicken along the pavement on the end of a stick as if he were taking it for a walk.

Rebecca was staying at Aunty Edie's, sleeping in the bedroom above the kitchen one last time. She had needed a day in London to...wrap things up.

The V&A first. If it had been possible she would have packed up this ridiculous, glorious, intricate confection of galleries and corners and stairs and taken it with her. How wonderful would that be? She'd want all the contents too, of course, including the objects in storage.

Her casket, she noticed, had gone from the Small Sculpture Gallery, its roundels of vine leaves removed for cleaning perhaps, or perhaps on loan to another collection.

The museum was in a state of perpetual flux anyway, ever changing, renewing itself, presenting fresh images for hungry eyes. The Devonshire Hunting Tapestries had been rehung in a wider, better lit gallery, very different from the gloomy corridor where Michael had paced, his thumbs hooked in his back pockets, gently introducing her to the notion that maybe there was more to existence than she had thought.

Rebecca stood back, enjoying the scenes of lords and ladies in costumes better suited to court life than to rambling about in the countryside, already planning designs of her own.

Something caught her attention and she stepped closer. A woman was making notes in a spiral-bound book, and Rebecca touched her elbow.

'Excuse me?'

The woman looked up.

Rebecca pointed at the tapestry. 'What do you think that is?'

The woman peered and shrugged. 'Fox?'

'An animal, then?' Rebecca asked. 'Not just a pile of leaves?'

'Definitely an animal. Look, can't you see the eyes, and ears?'

'Yes.' Rebecca nodded. 'Yes, I can. Thanks.'

From the V&A Rebecca had walked to the flat on Trentham Road that she still thought of as Michael's. It took her the best part of an hour, but the exercise was a relief after the driving of the day before, and she was confident of a cup of coffee when she got there.

Roly Pidgeon and his wife Alice, the tenants of the ground

floor flat, had been good friends to both Michael and, later, herself, and she knew they had looked on her a little as, well, if not a granddaughter then perhaps a great-niece. She continued to get Christmas and birthday cards from them, always with some news tucked inside written in Alice's round hand, and she needed to know she had given them a proper farewell.

They sat in the back room, where a French window looked out over the orderly vegetable garden, and Rebecca said, 'A very long way away.'

'Australia?' Roly asked, interested. 'Had a chum went there, back in the sixties.'

'Maybe,' Rebecca said, hedging. How do you talk about distances greater than dreams? The Pidgeons would never visit Australia, but the miles were at least something one could imagine.

Aunty Edie's documentary on the solar system tried to get you to imagine distances too, but light years were beyond Rebecca's grasp. At that point it all became fiction, didn't it? The stuff of legends, way beyond reality.

She said, 'I'm going to visit Michael,' and the conversation moved on.

Now, outside the café, Rebecca smiled. She had been happy to see the Pidgeons again. When she left, she had avoided being weighed down with fresh produce by telling them she was on foot and had more errands to run, but in truth the errands were finished. There was only this, the wide pathway along the south bank of the Thames, where the final trail had begun, incredibly only seven weeks ago. And in truth there was no real reason to be here either, other than a sense of…completeness.

I had that dream again last night, she had said to Steph that day.

She wouldn't dream it again. She knew what was behind the curtain now.

Heading for the bridge to Waterloo Station, Rebecca passed a movie pirate lookalike. He had a red and white tea towel round his waist and wellies for boots.

Hopeless.

* * *

She hit the Oxford Ring Road just before midday and shortly after was parking in the Westgate.

She had sent Connor a text, of course. By the University's own eccentric method of reckoning dates, it was the middle of Fifth Week in Hilary and Connor would be in the thick of work, but he'd said he'd collect her from the Porter's Lodge and she could have lunch in the buttery as his guest.

They ate minestrone soup and fish pie at a refectory table beneath heavy portraits of famous alumni, and afterwards climbed the spiralling stone staircase to Connor's room. The soles of Rebecca's feet found the gentle dip in each step where the stone had been worn away by centuries of undergraduates.

'It's not unlike this,' she said, 'the castle there. But lighter. Lots of windows.'

And without the modern adjustments, she thought: lavatories squeezed into corners and notice boards on the landings. And without that institutional feel, too.

How strange, that all of Connor's experiences of living should be so different from hers, from his deeply unpleasant family home through his long tally of temporary quarters to this close community of students. None of them bore any resemblance to her childhood on her stepfather's farm or her bedsit at Aunty Edie's, or her small house on Skye.

She hadn't always thought of it as small.

They were like opposite poles, she and Connor. Yet as if to prove her wrong, Connor closed the door behind them and said, 'When are you going?'

'You guessed!'

Connor shook his head. 'Not a guess. I've suspected for weeks. But this was all the confirmation I needed.'

He drew a small folded paper from his hip pocket and handed it to Rebecca. She opened it and recognised her own handwriting.

I'm alright. Don't worry. But now I'm here I'm going to take a look.

I'll decide what to do when I've seen what it's like.

She had meant that she'd decide whether to stay the agreed five days, but she saw now that the wording was ambiguous.

Rebecca looked up and found Connor's eyes meeting hers.

'It was obvious,' he said. 'After all, you are the Queen of Clover.'

Everyone seemed to have known except her.

'I'm going into another world, Aunty Edie,' she told her aunt gently, never imagining the old lady would believe her. 'A world where there is magic. Fairyland.'

And her aunt said, 'I thought it was something like that. About time, Rebecca. Make sure you look after that necklace!'

So little left to do now, and that little left her impatient and over-wrought. It was becoming hard to breathe.

'Don't worry,' Connor told her, still her rock as he had always been. 'Everything's safe here. The monolith will keep Skye closed, and Will can go up there from time to time.'

Will was going to stay on at Ashendon.

'Another fairy recluse,' Rebecca said. 'The Hermit of Ashendon Cottage. And I suppose Skill will stop anyone questioning the decades.'

'I don't think he'll become a recluse just yet,' Connor said.

'No.'

Beware, fair maidens.

'There's still Geoffrey Foster,' Rebecca added. 'He's a menace.'

But Connor laughed. 'I don't think he is, actually. He called me last week. Wanted to pick my brains about colleges. He's applied to do a DPhil.'

'You're kidding!' Rebecca snorted. 'Surely he hasn't got a hope?'

'I wouldn't say that. He got a First, apparently. He's always kept abreast, generally, just out of interest, and don't forget he's spent the last three years researching pretty much full-time. And on top of that, he's independently financed. I'd say he's got a very good hope!'

Just before she left, Connor placed a small, slim pamphlet in her hand.

'Just some poems. I had them run off by a local printer. No ISBN or anything.'

'Connor–'

'Don't read them until you get there.'

And he kissed her cheek.

Chapter Forty-Five

Dusk, and the lamps were lit behind the curtains.

Rebecca's hand hovered over the door knocker, but then she drew out her key and unlocked the door for herself. In the parlour, Will sat in the wing chair under the pool of yellow light, one ankle crossed over the other knee, a book open on his lap. He looked up.

'Hallo.'

'Hi.' Rebecca shut the door and set down her bag. She realised she didn't know what to do with the car keys in her hand.

Will put his book on the table and stood up. He took the keys gently from her. 'I'll deal with it.'

'Yes.'

She felt insubstantial, scarcely aware of the pressure of her feet on the ground. It seemed to her that there was a deep need to tread carefully, quietly, as if a baby were asleep somewhere close by, or an invalid. She moved slowly and smoothly, with minimal fuss.

Will was speaking quietly too. 'When?'

'Oh, tonight.'

Rebecca watched him pick up her bag and carry it out of the room. There was no electric spark from him at all, and she wondered, for an instant, whether she had imagined it before and there was nothing special about him after all...in which case Robin...

But then he came back and she looked into his dark eyes and saw that he was suppressing it. He was being considerate of her fragile state. He was taking care of her.

She said, unaware of the idea until it was voiced, 'Connor would make a good Knave of Vines.'

She surprised herself but not, it seemed, Will.

'Yes, he would. But he doesn't want it. You have to want it.' Then he said, 'Don't worry. He'll be coming.'

He'll be coming. He meant the Knave of Vines, the new one, the real one, the one meant for her. Predestination. Rebecca pictured a man striding through the cornfields on his way to meet her, the wind in his hair and electricity in his veins, elements of Connor and Will, and Michael too. His face was not revealed to her yet, but she knew him from her dream, for it was this man who had stood, silhouetted in the night, and turned to face her, not Will after all.

Rebecca shivered.

Will cooked for her – soup and an omelette – and they talked, but Rebecca found she no longer wanted to work systematically through her great store of questions. Instead she asked only those that floated to the surface, a frivolous and inconsequential selection.

'So is Professor Peregrine correct? Is that where William Shakespeare spent his lost years?' Connor had shared the dominant points of the lecture with her.

'Of course. Where else would a boy with his background have garnered those ideas? And his vocabulary, of course. You are aware that he introduced hundreds of words into English? Did you think he made them up?'

'And the Dark Lady?'

Will smiled, one side of his face lifting. 'Who do you think?'

Later, Rebecca asked, 'Will I grow old before everyone else?'

'No. It doesn't work like that.'

'But I'll be living my life quicker there than here. Time happens faster.'

'Time is slippery,' Will said. 'You can't write rules for it. For every Rip van Winkle there's a child who meets his playmates as old men.'

'I'm twenty-five,' Rebecca said, as if to anchor herself for the last time, and was surprised when Will said, 'Yes, of course.'

'Of course?'

'One quarter of a century. The silver birthday. Your coming-of-age.'

Rebecca narrowed her eyes. 'This is relevant?'

'Naturally. I've been waiting for you.'

Predestination. Rebecca sighed. 'Will, am I doing the right thing? The right thing for me?'

The fairy in the wing chair opened his hands. 'Only you can decide that.'

Yes. And in truth, how much does one ever know about the rightness of one's decisions? Once you've chosen a course, your life has been altered. It is all a lottery, Rebecca thought, and you must simply throw your dice and cross your fingers.

She had already thrown her dice and had no desire to scoop them up and throw again. Gooseflesh and the butterflies dancing in her stomach were irrelevant. All she really wanted now was for two twenty-five to come.

'I won't be able to sleep,' she said.

But surprisingly she did, for a couple of hours at least. When Will woke her it was already two o'clock, and he had made her tea.

'For shock,' he said.

'I'm not in shock.'

'But you will be.'

Rebecca threw him a sharp glance and he grinned wildly. The electricity was back, and seemed to be catching. Rebecca grinned too, and accepted the mug of tea.

Then they stood side by side in the stone room, where in a few minutes Rebecca would see grass growing beyond an open door.

She had not asked what Will was going to do after she had gone. But perhaps it was better not to. She was excited now, and selfishly did not want to spoil the moment.

I didn't email Steph.

Connor would tell her. Not that she would believe him.

The neighbours would look after Aunty Edie, as they always had.

'My stepfather!'

'I'll sort that,' Will said.

Skill, she supposed. Well, sadly there was no real love lost there, and a little magical tweaking would allow him to believe she had emigrated to Australia or something.

Two twenty now, and Rebecca's ears were picking up a faint thrumming.

'It's coming.'

'Yes, it is.'

There had been three diving boards at the public swimming pool in Ipswich – a springboard on the side, a platform at five metres, and another ten metres high used for competitions only. Rebecca had ducked under the cord once and climbed up there, stood on the edge with her toes curled over as the Olympic divers do, and held her arms out. She wanted to experience what it felt like up there in the realms of the gods, although she had believed then that to leap off would always be beyond her.

The thrumming had grown and was filling her body. Lights were playing beyond her closed eyelids, and distantly she heard Will's voice, although the words were unclear.

Magic – Stuff and Nonsense!

Rebecca laughed, and walked forward.

Epilogue

The pencil lightly held between index finger and thumb, resting on the curled middle finger; the hand relaxed, the wrist stable, only the arm in motion as the pencil point slides over the paper and the graphite trail is laid…

A single curving line, slow and sure, winding across the white field of the page and looping back upon itself twice, ending in a delicate curl…And where before there was only paper and graphite there is now the tendril of a vine, two-dimensional but unmistakable, a true representation of a living plant saved on the page for anyone to see.

How immensely satisfying to identify the correct place for each element and then to put it there.

What magic there is in drawing.

A World *Invisible*

by

Joanna O'Neill

"You're telling me the Victoria and Albert Museum only exists because seven Victorians needed to hide a handful of objects for a hundred years?"

Finding she can draw nothing but vines, Rebecca reluctantly puts her ambitions as an illustrator on hold when she is drawn into the machinations of a Victorian secret society founded to make safe an interface between parallel worlds.

But first she has to grow up.

Dragged into helping a cause in which she barely believes, Rebecca finds herself playing Hunt-the-Thimble amongst England's oldest institutions. Over one summer she will break a code, discover her astonishing ancestry, and half fall in love – twice.

But what begins as a game will shake her to the core.

A World Invisible begins the trilogy completed by *A World Possessed*.

Available from booksellers: ISBN 978-09564432-0-5

A World *Denied*

by

Joanna O'Neill

'Stand on the island of glass and look toward the great circle.'

Somebody had known something once. Why would people not keep records?

Three years ago Rebecca was drawn into hunting for a doorway to another world, and cannot forget the terrible consequences of finding it.

And it seems she is still involved.

When the heating in her flat breaks down, Rebecca pays a visit to her friend in Oxford – good company, a change of scene, and warmth; what could be better? But by Sunday the university boathouse has burned down, there are reports of a strange animal loose on the streets, and three old Oxford professors are showing far too much interest in her.

What is being built amid the ashes on the riverbank? Who is the mysterious tramp in outlandish clothes? And what is the significance of the Queen of Clubs?

Soon Rebecca has embarked on a quest for another rift between the worlds, and this time she fears she is alone. But the World Invisible stretches wide, and there is a stranger in Vermont who is trying to reach England…

A World Denied continues the trilogy completed by *A World Possessed.*

Available from booksellers: ISBN 978-09564432-1-2

ABOUT THE AUTHOR

Joanna O'Neill is a textile artist and horse whisperer, and the author of many articles for both textile and equestrian magazines.

A World Possessed is the final book in the trilogy, which began with A World Invisible.

For more information, visit www.joanna-oneill.co.uk.

Lightning Source UK Ltd.
Milton Keynes UK
UKOW051009021211

183023UK00001B/2/P

9 780956 443229